DEATH IN THE CITY THAT CARE FORGOT

CHARLES CRUTHIRDS

BARBARA CRUTHIRDS

About the Author

Charles Cruthirds

Charlie, a lifelong resident of Metairie, Louisiana, is the author of the first two J.C. Net mysteries, The Road to Darkness and UNRECOGNIZABLE! He worked in the insurance industry for almost 40 years prior to retiring. He is a graduate of the University of New Orleans with a BS degree in management. This is his first collaboration with wife, Barbara, in writing the third installment in this series because of her legal knowledge and theatrical experience.

Barbara Cruthirds

Barbara, is a lifelong resident of New Orleans, Louisiana and the surrounding area. She worked as a paralegal for attorneys for over 40 years. Barbara has a history of participating in the musical theater in New Orleans. She is a gourmet cook, winning several awards for preparing local dishes.

Dedication

This book is dedicated to our children who are actually no longer children. We are proud of the grownups they have become.

Christopher

Lauren

Lindsay

Special thanks to Lauren who contributed some psychological information in the text of the book and for having to listen to Mom and Dad argue back and forth for months in writing of this book.

Author's Note

The following story is fictional and does not depict any actual person, place, entity or event.

Table of Contents

CHAPTER 1
Laissez Les Bon Temps Rouler

The Crescent City – a popular nickname for the city of New Orleans. The name comes from a sharp bend in the Mississippi River located across from the Vieux Carré also called the French Quarter, resembling a crescent moon.

J.C. Net and Rhonda Bordelon were returning to Boston from their trip to New Orleans. The Boston wind was blowing hard, and snow was starting to accumulate on the ground when their plane touched down at Logan International Airport. He was returning from a three-week vacation in New Orleans with his fiancé and FBI partner, Rhonda Bordelon. Net and Rhonda were scouting New Orleans for their possible honeymoon destination. Since Net was from Louisiana, they had made plans for their trip to coincide with Mardi Gras. He was engaged to a Yankee girl who had never been south of the Mason/Dixon line and had never experienced the food and culture of New Orleans. She was leery about going, but after the first week, she was wearing Mardi Gras beads around her neck and he swore he detected a slight southern drawl. The food was amazing and reminded Net of all the things he had left behind when he moved to Boston. Besides soaking up the culture, food, and night life, Net ran into an old friend, Rodney Park, aka "Pants".

When Net worked for the State Police in Keister, La. on a murder case, Pants was the deputy sheriff of the small town. Pants was now Deputy Police Chief of New Orleans, a promotion he received shortly after marrying the mayor's daughter. Nepotism has always been a thing in the south.

Rhonda and Net departed the plane, hailed a cab, and headed back to Rhonda's house in the suburbs of Boston. The cold February air was biting their cheeks as the snow and wind whipped through their thin jackets, which is all they needed in New Orleans. Practicing for the honeymoon, Net carried Rhonda over the threshold and placed her gently on the couch. Net suggested a glass of cabernet to warm them up and they decided the unpacking could wait until morning. The wine was welcome after the long flight, as they cuddled on the couch and reminisced about the prior three weeks.

They had stayed at a riverfront hotel, with a view of the Mississippi River and a short walk to the French Quarter. If they were anywhere else Net would have been content to stay in their beautiful suite and make love for days, but this was New Orleans. After a bottle of champagne, a fast rumble between the sheets, they showered and went off to explore the French Quarter. After dinner, they walked down Bourbon Street to a jazz club. Rhonda was amazed that she could walk down the middle of the street carrying a large alcoholic drink and no one gave her a second look. After a long night of drinking and walking, they took a cab back to their hotel. After making a half ass attempt to make love to his fiancé, they both fell asleep. Rhonda was also glad to postpone lovemaking until morning since she was not used to staying out all night and consuming more alcohol in one night than she would in a month in Boston. Day two started off with beignets.

While waiting for the waiter to deliver the powdered sugary donuts, Net caught a glimpse of a familiar face, Rodney Park, aka Pants. Net gave Pants a big hug and introduced him to Rhonda.

Pants was a local character from Keister, Louisiana, currently working in New Orleans. Net and Pants had worked a murder case together in Keister and became good friends after vying for the same love interest. He got the name "Pants" from an incident in Keister where he tried getting out of his police car wearing a police belt with attachments that weighed more than he did. Needless to say, his pants ended up around his ankles in front of a large crowd of spectators. After the laughter subsided, the nickname stuck. Pants was no longer the country hick from Keister. He had met his wife, Charlotte Hebert at an LSU football game 6 years ago and moved to the big city of New Orleans. She was the daughter of Mayor Clyde Hebert and a former debutante. Pants was now a member of New Orleans society by marriage and had access to all the Mardi Gras events.

Net and Rhonda were content to spend some alone time in the city, but agreed to meet the following Saturday to take in a Mardi Gras parade and to be Pants' guest at a Mardi Gras extravaganza. Net and Rhonda strolled through the quarter taking in all the sights and sounds of Mardi Gras in the Big Easy. Locals were throwing beads from balconies to tourists in the street and a local entrepreneur approached Net and told him he could tell him where he got his shoes. But Net, being from Louisiana, knew the answer was "on his feet" and didn't fall for the scam. They came upon children dancing to boombox music as people threw money into a box they'd set up on the sidewalk.

A little further down Bourbon Street they got to witness the yearly "greasing of the poles" contest in front of a local hotel. Apparently, drunk revelers were known to try to shimmy up the poles in front of the hotel to get to the balconies above, many of which had half-naked people exposing themselves to the crowd below. The greasy poles not only prevented drunks from climbing, but in some cases stopped them from severely injuring themselves or others. The contest participants were scantily clad women and a few men or gays, vying for first prize. They were each handed a large jar of petroleum jelly and seductively slathered the poles as the crowds cheered. The judges voted on the most original and crudest contestant, who was awarded a magnum of cheap champagne. Rhonda's eyes were wide with amazement at the sights that would have been unheard of and probably illegal in Boston. They finally hit Canal Street and headed back to the hotel to prepare for a shopping spree on St. Charles Avenue in search of formal attire for the Mardi Gras extravaganza . Net on the other hand, was not as excited at the thought of renting a "monkey suit".

Pants, Charlotte, Rhonda, and Net headed to St. Charles Avenue for Rhonda's first parade and it certainly was an eye-opener. Rhonda had been to a few Thanksgiving parades up north, but nothing prepared her for what she experienced in New Orleans. They made a quick stop at a street vendor for Bloody Marys, in a "go cup". After downing the parade day equivalent of breakfast, Pants ran into a convenience store to purchase a suitcase of cold beer to take to the parade route.

Rhonda was doing a great job of containing herself, until the third beer kicked in and she heard the sound of one of New Orleans finest high school bands coming down the street. Rhonda pushed several children and old ladies aside to make it to the front of the crowd. It wasn't long before she was rolling on the ground for beads and trinkets. Some college girls next to Rhonda lifted their shirts, exposing their bare breasts, which got them flooded with long beads. Net saw what was happening and quickly ushered Rhonda back to their original spot. It was at this point that

Rhonda was introduced to another New Orleans tradition, the porta-potty outhouse. Her breakfast cocktail, along with two hot dogs purchased from a street vendor were quickly deposited in the portable toilet, where others had made deposits before her.

Pants' wife, Charlotte, remained very quiet during the parade. She was a member of New Orleans society and frowned upon such behavior. She kept giving Pants a side glance, indicating she wasn't exactly pleased with his choice of friends. Charlotte's dad, Clyde was the mayor and had believed marrying Rodney, aka Pants wasn't a good idea. The group decided to cut the parade short and Rhonda and Net headed back to the hotel. It was obvious to Net that Rhonda's day would come to an early end. After a quick shower to remove any traces of portable toilet remnants, Rhonda downed an antacid and fell into a deep sleep, lying perpendicular across the entire bed. Net knew no love making would take place, so he grabbed a pillow and blanket and headed to the couch.

Sunday morning Net awoke to find Rhonda quietly sitting up in bed with a cold towel on her forehead. Net wasn't sure what Rhonda felt worse about, her excessive drinking, or showing Net and his friends a side of her which she wasn't proud and had no clue existed. After a small breakfast ordered from room service, Net and Rhonda made up for lost honeymoon time. They decided to make it a quiet day by taking a walk along the riverfront and taking in the sights from their balcony suite.

The following day they took a streetcar ride up St. Charles Avenue and enjoyed chargrilled oysters in the hotel's restaurant. Net finally got the alone time he was looking forward to and for the next two days they barely left the hotel room.

The day of the dinner party started off with room service breakfast and a couples' massage at the spa. Rhonda then had her hair and makeup done while Net picked up his tux. The dinner party spectacular was even more than Net and Rhonda expected. Rhonda looked every bit the beauty pageant winner she once was in her blue one-shoulder gown which split up to her long thighs and Net was quite handsome in his black tux with a blue cummerbund that matched Rhonda's dress. Pants wore a plain black tux and his wife, Charlotte wore a pink high-necked gown which looked more appropriate for a sweet sixteen dance. Charlotte was quiet all through dinner and appeared to look upset. Just when the music started and the dancing began, Charlotte announced she had a headache and needed to go home immediately, Pants agreed to take her home and return to his guest.

Pants returned within the hour and apologized for his wife's behavior. He explained that Charlotte suffers from social anxiety, which makes it awkward for her in large social situations. Pants explained that Charlotte's mom, Reba, had mental problems, which had kept her in and out of private hospitals since Charlotte was a young child. Apparently some of the incidents involved violence, but Pants was never told the entire story. Because of the amount of wealth in the Hebert family, the press was never aware of any of these events. Reba was now living a mostly secluded life in a private hospital under an assumed name to avoid publicity, with around-the-clock nurses. Pants was keeping Charlotte under a physician's care and had hired a caregiver to be sure she took whatever medication her doctor prescribed.

It was going on 2 a.m. when Pants' phone rang. His face turned as pale as his shirt. He explained he had to leave immediately. There was a murder in a French Quarter hotel and one of New Orleans' well-known politicians was the victim. Pants stated how great it was to see Net again and they should make plans to meet again in the near future. Net and Rhonda decided to call it a night and head back to the hotel. Their plane to Boston left at 10:00 a.m., and they still had a lot of packing to do, including at least a gross of Mardi Gras beads.

***

It had started to rain in the French Quarter and the weather had turned cold. Pants was the last to arrive at the Chez Hotel, which was already swarming with police and the coroner's assistant. He was still wearing his tuxedo, having just left the Mardi Gras spectacular. The police captain at the scene joked that he was just slightly overdressed for this area. After reviewing the scene Pants immediately stationed an officer outside to prevent any reporters from entering.

The hotel room was covered with blood and it appeared the victim, lying face down on the bed, put up a valiant fight. The hotel was off the beaten path in the quarter and frequented by ladies of the evening and prominent people wishing to enjoy themselves without being caught. The victim in this case was one of the latter, a well-known former senator, Nathaniel Lawrence, known as Buck Lawrence. He was currently a preacher at a local church.

From the looks of the room he may not have secured his place in heaven. Drug paraphernalia was found on the floor and empty liquor bottles were on the nightstand. The sheets were soaked in blood and a condom was in the trash can.

After the crime lab had taken dozens of photographs, the coroner turned the body over. Pants gasped at the sight, even though he had investigated many gruesome crime scenes. The man's penis was gone! It appeared to have been removed using a serrated knife. His underwear had been shoved in his mouth, which muffled his screams.

A search of the room found the victim's wallet, but no cellphone. Judging from the wad of cash and credit cards in his wallet it appeared robbery wasn't the motive.

It would have been days before the victim was found, but the room had been rented for two hours and their time was up. The manager banging on the unlocked door had made the discovery. Pants interviewed the manager and learned that this establishment didn't have surveillance tape, but he remembered the couple well. The victim and a female rented the room. The female wore a long dark coat, possibly covering a long gown. Her hair appeared to be blonde, but it was tucked beneath a floppy hat. The female was wearing sunglasses. Normally the sunglasses at night would be suspect, but given the clientele that frequented this place it wasn't out of the norm. Most of the hookers in the area had pimps who worked them hard and it was not unusual for them to sport a shiner or two. The victim, on the other hand was no stranger to the establishment. The manager knew he was someone important, but was paid to look the other way.

The police taped off the area and the coroner loaded the body in the van and drove off. They searched all around the area but could not find the missing penis. Crime lab continued to comb though the hotel room, but no fingerprints were found, not even on the drinking glasses. A fluorescent light indicated lots of sexual activity had taken place in that room. Given the amount of bodily fluids throughout the room it would probably be impossible to pull off some DNA related to the victim. It appeared the sheets and towels weren't frequently changed. The condom was bagged along with the victim's wallet and clothes; these would be sent to the lab for further evaluation.

Pants headed to the hotel lobby, anxious to get out of this area. Standing by the exit door Pants recognized Tabares Jaimez aka T.J., a noted pimp, and police informant. T.J. pretended he hadn't noticed Pants and tried to make his escape through the front door but two officers were standing in his way. "Not so fast T.J. You're not in any trouble. I just want to ask you a few questions." Pants asked him if he knew anything about the girl or victim.

"No, senor." T.J. stated that the girl couldn't be one of his, but he would keep his eyes and ears open. T.J. didn't want any part of murdering any Johns since he wanted return business. He did know the victim, who would sometimes use his services. Pants handed T.J. his card in case he remembered anything. Pants was anxious to get back to his cozy uptown home on St. Charles Avenue, get out of his tux and wash the stench of blood and despair off his body. He assumed Charlotte would be sound asleep after leaving the Mardi Gras party early and taking her medication.

***

Pants quietly entered the bedroom, trying not to disturb his wife. He could hear her muffled sobs so he turned on the light. Charlotte was sitting on the edge of the bed in her bathrobe. Her hair was soaking wet as if she'd just exited the shower. He questioned Charlotte as to why she had decided to shower in the middle of the night, but her words slurred. Pants was concerned that Charlotte was mixing alcohol with her medication again. There had been a previous incident about a year earlier when Charlotte had disappeared for over twelve hours after consuming a combination of drugs and scotch. The police found her in the French Quarter, wearing a mini skirt, tee shirt and no bra. She had been dancing in bars on Bourbon Street and had a group of men buying her additional drinks. They weren't sure what kind of trouble she'd gotten into before they found her. Thank God they recognized Charlotte from the society pages and photographs of her with her father. They quietly placed her in their patrol car and brought her home. Pants had taken her to her doctor the following day and the doctor had had a stern talk to her about mixing medication and alcohol. Pants thought she had the problem under control, but it was impossible to watch her 24 hours a day. He was afraid she'd end up like her mother, having to be under the care of nurses the rest of her life.

Pants placed a call to Charlotte's dad, Clyde Hebert, Mayor of New Orleans, who wasn't thrilled about being awakened at 4:00 a.m. Pants explained the situation and asked if they could meet later in the day. The mayor did not want to wait and rushed to his daughter's home, driving in his personal car so he didn't call attention to himself by using the city vehicle and chauffer.

"What the hell is going on Rodney?" The mayor refused to call his son-in-law Pants.

"I don't know, sir. We attended the Mardi Gras ball with some friends but she complained of not feeling well and left early. I found her like this." Rodney pointed to Charlotte who remained on the bed in tears and not responding to either of the men's questions.

"Charlotte!" Clyde tried to get her attention in his deep and loud tone. Clyde was a man of rather large stature. About 6'4 and 290 pounds he could intimidate most people he encountered. "Hand me that phone, Rodney," he demanded. "Jeff, I need you to come to my daughter's home immediately. She's having an episode." There was a pause in the conversation. "Yes, damn it. I know what time it is. Just get over here."

Dr. Jeff Howser was Charlotte's psychiatrist. He'd always felt that Charlotte needed professional care that she couldn't receive at home. Pants did his best, but his job wouldn't allow him the time to provide the proper care. The mayor preferred Dr. Howser because he provided for her at her home in lieu of her being seen by the public entering his office. Waiting on the doctor to arrive, Pants made Charlotte as comfortable on the bed as he possibly could.

"Clyde, there's something else I need to tell you."

"Oh, dear God, don't tell me she did something else?"

"No. No. Senator Lawrence was found dead this morning."

"I told that old man he needed to take better care of himself. What happened? One too many cigars?" asked Clyde.

"No sir. He was murdered. Found him naked in a French Quarter hotel with his penis sliced off."

"For Christ's sake. Who in the fuck would do something like that?" This made Clyde very uneasy as he adjusted his package as though he felt the pain. "Was this another one of these prostitute murders?" asked Clyde.

"We believe so. This is number three Clyde, and each one is getting more violent."

"What are your plans to take this culprit off the street?" inquired the mayor."

"Well, first off, we need to keep this out of the press as long as possible, given his position in this community. Buck's wife, Edith, is head of the school board, so it will not reflect well on her standing. We've got every available detective on this case pursuing what few leads that we have." Pants paused for a moment and then proceeded. "There is something I've been thinking about," offered Pants.

"Anything that would quickly solve this case, I would be all for." Clyde always seemed more concerned about his political reputation than the victims of crime in this city. The media was constantly on his case with regard to the crime rate which he knew would be used against him in the next election.

"I have a friend," Pants began, "who is the head of a new unit within the FBI that specializes in the capture of serial killers. And this being at least the third murder, apparently by the same person, qualifies this as a serial murderer."

"Will this cost the city any money?" Clyde's only concern was the criticism he may face from the public.

"I don't think so, Clyde," responded Pants shaking his head with disbelief at this question.

Dr. Howser's black car pulled into the driveway and under the enclosed carport, hidden from street view. He was grossly overweight and always chewed on an unlit cigar. He hurried into the house and went straight to Charlotte's bedroom, where Clyde and Pants were anxiously awaiting his diagnosis.

"Dr. Howser at last," Clyde ushered him to Charlotte's bed. Pants told Dr. Howser that he found her crying in her bed, but it was obvious she had taken a shower.

"Hello Charlotte," said Dr. Howser. "How are you feeling?" Charlotte stared into space and didn't acknowledge his presence. He felt her pulse and inquired if she had taken her medication as he prescribed. Pants told the doctor that they had gone to a Mardi Gras ball earlier in the evening, but Charlotte became ill and asked to go home. He verified that she hadn't had any alcohol that he knew of, but he had gone back to the ball shortly after taking her home. Dr. Howser checked her pill bottles and determined she was not abusing her drugs. He asked that Clyde call Mildred. her caregiver into the room. Mildred confirmed Charlotte's arrival time, but went to sleep shortly after, so she couldn't enlighten the doctor as to what Charlotte did after coming home. Dr. Howser gave Charlotte an injection to help her sleep and told Pants to call him when she woke up.

He exited the house by the side door, jokingly telling Clyde that his bill for the house call would be doubled for the late hour.

CHAPTER 2

Second Time is No Picnic!

Pants sat in his office at the police station. He was waiting on Detective Mark Rodriguez to accompany him to the Lawrence house and break the news to Edith Lawrence. He wanted to express his condolences and assure her that the murderer would be brought to justice. Suddenly the door flew open and two deputies, Colin Kennedy and Mike Smith came rushing to his side.

"Chief, we have another one," said Smith, short of breath from running down the hall. "This one, a white male, approximately 25 years old. He was not found in a quarter hotel, but on the levee across from Jackson Square."

The body had sustained several stab wounds and his wallet, phone and watch were missing. Pants asked Mike the obvious question, "Was his penis missing?" Mike had to laugh at the question, but responded that the victim was stabbed several times, but his manhood was still attached. It was a known fact that prostitutes used the area when they didn't have hotel connections. This area was also known for drug dealing since the levee provided shade for the illegal transactions. Pants grabbed his gun and keys and headed to the area.

The levee was roped off with yellow police tape, but tourists were hanging over the tape trying to catch the show. Pants looked over the scene as the police photographer snapped pictures. It was obvious from the stench of alcohol coming from his body and clothes that the victim had been drinking.

It wasn't unusual for a young guy who'd come to New Orleans during Mardi Gras looking for a cheap drink and to get laid. The forensic group took over after the photographer wrapped up and proceeded to check the area for clues. His first thought after seeing the body was he'd pissed off a street walker, probably a dispute over fees for services and paid the ultimate price. Pants and his deputies questioned some of the people in the area, but no one had seen or heard anything.

The coroner, Dr. Josh Hancock arrived and formally declared the victim deceased. Evidence was still being gathered by the forensic team when Pants told Josh he could proceed to wrap up the body and he wanted to be present during the autopsy. Pants had no love for the coroner. During several autopsies that Pants had viewed, Hancock had made him uncomfortable with his crude remarks and how he handled the bodies, especially those of young women. Hancock was a young doctor, not much past 30, with long hair that he kept in a ponytail or man bun. Not much was known of his personal life and some even suspected he was gay. The way Josh was able to turn everything into something sexual, Pants wondered if he could find a partner of any persuasion. He also wondered how this shady character had been elected to such a prominent position, but given the fact that Clyde knew his father, the reason was evident.

***

Pants headed to the city morgue directly from the crime scene. Dr. Hancock was suited up and ready to begin the autopsy. Usually it would take several days or weeks to get an autopsy done, but Clyde had dropped a dime to Josh that this one was to take priority.

"Hello chief," said Josh. "You just made it in time for the show".

Pants suited up and took his place behind the glass screen, where he could still view and hear the entire autopsy.

"Josh, please do the senator first and take your time. I'm interested in any forensic evidence on this body".

"Do you think old dick-less picked the wrong whore this time," laughed Hancock.

"Enough of your wise cracks, Hancock, he was somebody's husband and father,"

Josh proceeded to scrape Lawrence's skin and under his fingernails and put the findings into glass vials. He then turned on his microphone and grabbed his scalpel. Blood samples had been taken previously and they were still awaiting the tox screen. With skilled precision, Josh proceed to cut Senator Lawrence from his chest to his navel, removing and weighing vital organs. He also took additional photographs of Lawrence's genital area.

"I know it's too soon to be positive, but is there any way you can tell if his penis was removed before or after he was killed?" asked Pants, "and the cause and time of death?"

"No clue," replied Josh, "but if it was done before, he was sure in for a world of pain. We'll know more when the tox screen returns, but given the temperature of the body and rigor mortis, my guess is sometime after midnight last night. It appears that the weapon was some sort of serrated blade. As far as cause of death, I don't see any wounds except to his genital area. He was obviously a heavy drinker, judging from the condition of his liver, but again, this is all speculation."

Pants told Dr. Hancock to let him know immediately when his report was available and that this had to remain private information, available only to him and Mayor Hebert. On his way from the morgue, Pants began dialing his phone hoping to reach his friend J.C. Net.

Net and his fiancé and FBI partner, Rhonda Bordelon, answered on speaker phone knowing that Rodney Park was calling. "What's up, Bud?" answered Net. "Be careful. You are on speaker phone and my bride to be is sitting next to me."

"Hey, Pants," Rhonda declared.

"Hi, guys. Guess you all are getting back into the swing of things there in Boston."

"Oh yes, never a dull moment," responded Rhonda. "A local case getting a lot of press up here that we've been asked to assist with."

"Pants, you didn't call to find out what we are doing after we just left your amazing city," J.C. commented. "What's going on?"

"We could sure use your help. There have been 4 murders here, with 3 definitely being tied to the same killer. We're pretty sure it's a serial killer, which is right up your alley. The perp is getting more and more violent and we're assuming it may be tied into the local prostitution trade."

"Sounds interesting Pants, but you will have to send the request to my boss, Sam Huddleston. I'm pretty sure he'll approve our coming down, but will need to reassign our current case. In the meantime, can you arrange a place for us to stay? We enjoyed our riverfront room, but anything available in the business district will do."

"I'll work on that J.C., and will be sending the request to Huddleston as soon as we hang up. I'm looking forward to working with you again, even under these circumstances. Will talk later, bye."

***

Net walked into Sam Huddleston's office, chief of the FBI Boston office. "Hi chief, can I have a word with you," asked Net?

16

Sam Huddleston was a handsome guy, barely 40 years of age. He had become head of this office just a few years after graduating from the FBI academy. He was very good at his job, but some questioned the nepotism since his father was a US congressman.

"What can I do for you?" said Sam.

"You will be getting a request any minute for our help with a serial killer case in New Orleans. I just got off the telephone with a guy I worked with years ago in another case in Louisiana. Apparently this killer is targeting prostitutes or Johns and they believe we can be of assistance."

"Since you are now head of the serial killer unit in this office I think we can spare you for a while. We can assign Agent Sloan to your current case."

"Thanks Chief, I'd like to take Tatiana Sokolov with us and, of course, Rhonda."

Tatiana was a Russian defector who was highly skilled in computers. She was a few years older than Net, with shoulder-length brown hair and a pale face. The FBI had been suspect of hiring her because she was so advanced in computers. Net had worked with her on several cases and trusted her explicitly. He had no doubts about her loyalty to our country or the Boston office. The fact that she spoke fluent Russian was also an asset.

Rhonda walked into Tatiana's office, which she called the dungeon. "Hey Tatty. You can thank me later for taking you away from this cold weather. You need to pack a bag and be ready to leave in the morning. We're being assigned to a serial killer case in New Orleans. We are planning to leave at 8:00 a.m., so you will need to hurry and tell your sons you'll be away for a while." Tatiana's two sons were in their mid-twenties, but they checked on their mom daily.

"*Khorosho*," said Tatiana, which was Russian for good. "I'm happy to get away from this frozen tundra. I'll be packed and ready to go in the morning."

The morning couldn't come sooner for Rhonda Bordelon. She loved the time she'd spent in the Big Easy. Besides, the weather was much more to her liking this time of year.

J.C. and Rhonda arrived at the airport first thing in the morning to catch their flight. Tatiana had asked to take a later flight so she could make arrangements for room and board for her two Golden Retrievers, Toby and Tyson. Net's flight was a connection from Minnesota, which had been delayed approximately one hour but was non-stop from Boston to New Orleans. Once arrived, the plane was loaded with tourists travelling to enjoy the numerous St. Patrick's Day celebrations and parades that New Orleans was noted for. Net and Rhonda were lucky enough to get first-class seats, which made Rhonda feel like she was on vacation again. That is, until they landed.

***

Tatiana caught a noon plane, which was scheduled to stop in Atlanta. She boarded the plane and took a seat in the rear, which was her favorite place to sit. The flight attendant made her rounds and was just starting her pre-takeoff speech, when two foreign looking men took the seats in front of Tatiana. She caught a few words that they were saying, and quickly realized they were speaking Russian, her native language. Not wanting to appear rude, she tried to ignore their conversation until she heard their reference to the KGB. Tatiana leaned a little forward to try to hear more of their conversation. They were barely whispering, so she only was able to recognize a discussion about a planned meeting in New Orleans. Not sure what to do, she tried to text J.C. Net, who had already arrived at Louis

Armstrong Airport. Her text read, "Net, this is Tatty. I'm aboard Flight 407 in route to New Orleans, but we will be stopping over in Atlanta. I've been listening to a conversation in front of me in Russian. I haven't been able to hear all of it, but I did hear some words that frightened me, such as KGB and New Orleans. Please advise how I should proceed. We are only about a half hour out of Atlanta and I'm not sure if they will disembark."

Net replied, "Be careful Tatty. Don't put yourself in danger. We don't want to tip these guys off. I will contact the airline and have them send you a copy of the manifest to your laptop. Hopefully you can run the names and get back to me."

Tatiana nervously stood up to reach for her laptop in the overhead bin, which was directly over the men's seats. As she reached up she realized that her FBI badge was visible under her sweater when she raised her arms. She wasn't sure if the men saw it, but their conversation ceased from that point forward. Tatiana quickly opened her laptop and started searching the names. The names of the two passengers were American names and not Russian. Before Tatiana could even get back to Net, they were landing in Atlanta. Much to her surprise, the men departed from the plane. Tatiana hurriedly contacted Net by phone, notifying him of their departure. "Damn. My fault they left. I think they saw my badge. Can't find anything on their names but they are obviously aliases."

"You did your best. No worries. According to the flight manifest, they were scheduled to continue on same flight to New Orleans. I'll notify the Atlanta FBI office of their names and their description. Let them handle it from here. When you arrive in New Orleans, we have rooms reserved at the Port Orleans Hotel on the riverfront. Contact me when you arrive."

***

The standard black SUV used by the FBI was awaiting the two agents, except Rodney Park was also there. "Guys, over here," Pants yelled as he met them in the baggage claim area. "Thought I would catch you before you headed to your hotel. There's been another murder."

"When? Where? Same circumstances?" asked Net.

"Just found the body. Forensics are on their way. Thought you might want to take a quick look at the scene."

"You thought right," answered Net with Rhonda nodding her head in agreement. "Here come our bags. Text me the address and we'll use the car's GPS to get there."

J.C. and Rhonda arrived just at the same time as Pants at a small hotel located on the end of the French Quarter. The Bywater Hotel was frequented by gays as well as straight prostitutes. There was an inordinate number of policemen at the scene while any observers, including media, were kept a far distance down the street. The body of an older man lay in the bed surrounded by a considerable amount of blood, as the forensic team worked the room. The blood stemmed from his throat area where it appeared it had been sliced from side to side.

"What have you found?" asked Pants of the forensics team.

"Obviously this is what killed him," the attendant answered pointing to the wound on his neck. "But whomever did this seemed determined to decapitate his head. The cut is extremely deep and I suspect the only reason that they weren't successful was they weren't strong enough. Coroner will have to tell you what was used to cause this kind of cut."

Dusting for fingerprints around the nightstand next to the bed, an investigator was bent over discovering an item on the floor. Using a pen, he picked up what appeared to be a necklace resting almost under the bed. The necklace had several strands of blonde hair attached, as if it had been yanked off of someone's neck. Carefully, he placed it in a plastic evidence bag calling Pants' attention to what was found.

"Can I see that?" asked Net. Holding the bag up to the light, plenty of sparkling gemstones could be seen. "I don't know if these are real or not, but if they are this is worth a lot of money."

Rhonda snatched the bag from J.C.'s hand to examine the necklace herself. "I'd say these are very real and this necklace could be worth thousands of dollars. I think this would look perfect on me," Rhonda joked.

"So, what do we have here? An expensive present from a John to his mistress or is she just a wealthy killer?" pondered Net.

"Anybody identify the body?" asked Rhonda.

"Wallet and phone are not anywhere to be found," said the detective. "Maybe robbery was the motive, but not many perps wear that kind of jewelry."

Net introduced himself to the assistant coroner, Jennifer Davison, and asked that he be notified before he started the autopsy. After instructing the investigators as to additional photographs he'd like them to take, Net and Rhonda headed to their hotel.

"Give us an hour or two to settle in our hotel and we'll meet you at police headquarters," said Net. "We have another member of our team en route and would like her to also be present. Her name is Tatiana Sokolov and she is the smartest person on a computer I've ever seen."

Pants agreed to meet them at police headquarters and said they would have a conference room and computers available. "I will have the files on the other three murders waiting for you to review." Pants instructed the forensic team and assistant coroner to give Net and his team their upmost cooperation and left to return to headquarters.

***

Tatiana arrived at the Port Orleans by taxi. She headed to the lobby where Net and Rhonda were anxiously awaiting.

"Tatty, there was another murder this morning and we just came from the scene. This time the victim had his throat cut, but we are awaiting toxicology and forensic reports to confirm the exact cause of death," said Net.

Tatiana was still apologizing for losing the men on the plane. "I could kick myself in the *zadnitsa*," muttered Tatty in Russian! "I know better than to wear my FBI badge in public view. I was too lazy to pack it and thought I needed it handy. Please forgive me, *medovyy*."

"The FBI in Atlanta were notified, so this matter is out of our hands. We have bigger fish to fry here," said Net. "This morning's murder was number four and judging from the violence and blood, the killer has no plans on stopping. I took the liberty of checking into the hotel for you. We are all on the fourteenth floor, with rooms across the hall from each other. Please go unpack and meet us back here as soon as possible. We are scheduled to meet at police headquarters to review the files."

***

When they arrived at police headquarters Pants was waiting in the lobby. He ushered them to a conference room on the fourth floor, which had file folders lined up on the table in order of their occurrence. Tatty found a small corner of the desk and quickly set up her laptop. Glancing at the photographs Net was glad he'd decided to wait until after the meeting to eat.

The first victim was found at the Brooks House, a small, inexpensive hotel a few blocks from the quarter. He was identified as Max Cooper, a 57-year-old white male who was a computer software salesman who had been in town from Evansville, Indiana for a convention. The coroner had listed the cause of death as multiple stabbings, one of which pierced his heart. Toxicology reports indicated he had consumed alcohol and had a paralytic drug in his system. The drug had rendered him unable to move, but very aware of what was happening and cognizant of the pain. A credit card receipt from the Kitty Club was discovered in his pants pocket. It was obvious to Net that the murderer wanted the victim to feel every cut. Net's first thought was, *how could a lay person acquire such a drug?* This type of drug, a neuromuscular blocking agent, was often used during anesthesia to prevent movement during surgery. They are administered together with general anesthesia, so the patient will not be aware of the procedure. *Could the perpetrator have a medical background?* Net wondered.

A review of the report from the Evansville police department indicated that he was happily married for over 30 years to Mary Cooper and had two grown sons. He worked for the same computer company for over 10 years. That's as far as the report delved into his personal life. Net made a note for Tatiana to do a thorough background check to determine more information.

Net picked up the second folder. Victim number 2 was a forty-five-year-old local man. Jimmy Schwartz, who actually lived in the French Quarter. It appears his body had been discovered by his housekeeper on March 8th, who had a key to his apartment. According to the coroner's report, he had been dead at least 24 hours before he had been discovered and cause of death was multiple stab wounds to the genital area, with blunt force trauma to the head. He was a lawyer and active member of the gay community and was well-known to star in local theatre productions. Net turned to Rhonda, "This puts a hole in our hooker-killer theory, doesn't it?"

Rhonda looked over the file. "Maybe, maybe not." Rhonda reminded Net that during her college days she had been part of the local theatre company and had many gay friends. "From my experience Net, theatre companies are comprised of mostly gay guys and straight girls. They would party together after rehearsals and shows, and even had a name back in my college days for the straight women who hung out with gays," laughed Rhonda. "We called them 'fag hags'."

Net laughed at Rhonda. "You lived an entirely different life before we met. Aren't you glad I saved you from your evil ways?"

It was at that moment that Pants entered the room with an excited expression across his face. "I was just sent a text from a girl by the name of Lorena Gonzalez stating she has information about the Buck Lawrence case and wants to meet with me."

"How do you know this Lorena?" asked Net.

"I don't really. I know she dances in one of the French Quarter establishments."

"So, she's a stripper?" questioned Rhonda.

"Yes, among other things, I suppose." Pants smiled. "Anyway she wants to meet me later today in front of St. Louis Cathedral."

"Why don't I go with you to meet this Lorena and Rhonda stay here and continue to review these files?" suggested Net.

"Oh, I'm sure you would love to go meet this lady of the evening. Why don't I go and you stay?" Rhonda countered.

After much back and forth, it was decided that Net accompany Pants to the meeting. It didn't take long before they encountered Lorena. As she approached them from a distance, it was apparent that she had been beaten about the face and arms. As she drew closer, she motioned the two men to follow her into the cathedral.

"Before I say anything I need your promise of protection. I believe I saw the killer."

CHAPTER 3

The City has no Angels

Net and Pants sat behind Lorena in a pew located in the rear of the church. She wore sunglasses inside to try and hide a black eye on her left side. Her pink hair attracted attention from tourists visiting this historic New Orleans landmark. Judging from her attire, it was obvious she was more than a stripper. The slit in her skirt and her see-through blouse wasn't appropriate dress for this location.

"I was at the Chez Royal Hotel the night that senator dude got cut," whispered Lorena not turning around to face the men. "Dude came in with a bitch on his arm when I was bouncing out. At least I think it was a bitch. Hard to tell these days. Had sunglasses on and blonde hair tucked under a hat. Looked like some cheap wig. That old fat fuck was drunk and almost fell on me. I knew his face because he tapped dis ass a few times before," Lorena boasted. "I don't think I could identify the bitch in a line up, but she got a good look at me. This is my working turf and I'm not shitting you, it scares the fuck outta me."

"Tell me more about where and how you know Buck Lawrence," asked Net.

"Old fat fuck Buck is or was a regular at the Kitty Club on Bourbon Street. He was always there trying to find a bitch to service him, but he'd seen the last of my ass. Our preacher was trying to fuck his way to heaven, on the back of any bitch that would ride him. He paid well, but last time I did him he was getting too kinky for my ass. He liked to tie me up and take me from the rear. I'm usually ok with anal for a price, but this 300 lb. fuck wanted to choke me while he came. I get enough rough stuff from my man, without fat fuck preacher man roughing me up."

"Can you give me any description of the woman with him, like race, height, weight, eye color?" asked Pants. "I'd also like to interview the person you were with at the hotel. I'd like you to sit down with a sketch artist and see what you may remember. In the meantime, I can have one of our deputies drive by your house hourly as protection. Just give me your address."

"As far as the guy I was with, you shit outta luck. He was just some fucking kid that was in town for a party. He finished and left before me, so no telling where he is now. I think his name was Chad, but we don't ask for ID in my line of work. I'm staying in a green double in the eighth block of Burgundy Street. Here is my address and phone number."

Pants took her information and arranged for her to come down to headquarters the following day.

Net and Pants returned to headquarters, where Rhonda and Tatiana were entering information into Tatiana's laptop. "Have you found anything, Rhonda"?

"I suggest we contact the director and cast of Schwartz's theatre group. Maybe he had an angry lover or female friend that was out to get him," suggested Rhonda. "Since he was also a prominent lawyer, we should pay a visit to his office and look at his client list. Tatiana did a background check on Schwartz and many of his clients were accused of heinous crimes, including local drug dealers. She has started to comprise a list of those we need to interview, and it's a long list."

"I hate to leave you like this, but it's almost 8:00 p.m. and I really need to get home. Charlotte is still not feeling well and I want to be home for her," Pants said.

"I fully understand. We can take the remaining files with us and review them over dinner," Net replied. "You are more than welcome to join us."

"Thanks, but I'll take a raincheck. We can meet here tomorrow morning at 8:00 a.m. to review your findings," said Pants. "I'll plan on meeting you back here at 8:00 a.m. I will also have Deputy Mike Smith pick up Lorena and bring her down to review some photographs."

Net decided to order food delivered to their room, so they could spent some time reviewing the next file, Nathaniel "Buck" Lawrence. His background check indicated he was a senator from 1994-98. He lost the reelection to an unknown, primarily because of rumors of shady dealings and kickbacks. He had been divorced from Shelly for over ten years and had at least 5 children, but none were by Shelly. After marrying his second wife, Edith, he had opened a non-denomination church on Decatur Street around 2000. His congregation consisted of mostly strippers, gays and quarter rats. He had the reputation of being a heavy drinker and shirt chaser. Tatiana ran a deeper check on Lawrence and found he was under investigation by the Louisiana Attorney General for tax evasion. Net looked at Rhonda and frowned, "It appears the list of suspects in Mr. Lawrence's murder will be a long one." A review of Lawrence's credit card records indicated that beside French Quarter businesses, he was a frequent visitor to the Kitty Club on Bourbon Street, where Lorena worked. "I think this is a good place to start," said Net. "Tatiana, why don't you settle in for the evening? Rhonda, change into something sexy and join me for a visit to the Kitty Club."

***

Standing outside of the club's front door was a very large and scary looking man checking IDs as people entered. There was no reason for him to check the age of Net and Rhonda but he refused to allow Rhonda access until he had inspected her ID. She became very uncomfortable as he stared her down, not even glimpsing at her driver's license. Net grabbed her arm and pulled her inside the establishment while this bouncer watched her from behind. The music inside was blaring as naked girls danced on the stage. Sitting at the end of the bar was a familiar face, Lorena. Net knew better than to walk up to her, since she had a large, tattooed man buying her drinks. Rhonda and Net got seats at the other end of the bar and they watched as men came and went, many leaving with dancers.

Net asked, "Are the girls available for private parties?" The bartender looked over Rhonda and assumed they were into swinging. "Any chance I can speak to some of the girls in private?" Net slipped the bartender a C-note and he smiled showing his rotten teeth. "Go sit at the table by the dressing room door and I'll have someone meet you. Don't worry about the little lady, I'll keep her warm for you."

Net moved to the table while Rhonda started talking to the bartender. "I've heard there has been some trouble in the quarter lately," said Rhonda. "We're looking for a good time, but don't want to fucking leave in body bags. What's the word on the street, are they close to catching him?" Before the bartender could answer, a drunk slid on the seat next to Rhonda. "I love the way that dress looks on you and bet it would look just as good off you," slurred the drunk. Rhonda smiled, but turned her back to the drunk.

Net was talking to a girl named Butterfly, who had a butterfly tattoo on her left butt cheek, visible with the G-string and bra she was wearing. "I'm interested in having a private party at my hotel," whispered Net, "but heard a few Johns have turned up dead in the quarter. I want to make sure I'm not putting myself or my girlfriend in danger".

"It's been wild lately," advised Butterfly. "A girl can't be too careful these days. I've been around some of the hotels where the murders took place, but no one knows whose doing the killing. One of the girls saw the trick who was killed at the Chez Royal, but didn't recognize the bitch he was with. A lot of girls come and go from this place. Some are straight and just trying to make a buck, but some of these bitches are fucking crazy. Just a few weeks ago they had to fire the broad named Sin-D, because she pulled a knife on a customer who was a little feely stuffing a fin in her G-string."

Just then, a loud noise came from the end of the bar. Net looked over and saw Rhonda had sucker punched a guy, who was flat on his back. Net gave Butterfly a fifty for her time and told her he would contact her shortly for a date. He walked over to Rhonda and asked, "What happened?"

Rhonda leaned close to Net and said, "I hate drunks with six hands."

As the man began to pick himself up from the floor, Net felt it imperative that he and Rhonda vacate the place before any retaliation occurred. Any further activity might expose their FBI identities. With a quick glimpse to the other end of the bar, Net could no longer see Lorena nor the tattooed man. "Tomorrow, we will hit that theatre Jimmy Schwartz belonged to. What was its name?"

"I don't know if we got that far," responded Rhonda. "I'll text Tatiana for a name." As the two agents strolled back to their hotel, The Port Orleans, they decided to walk down Bourbon St. in the heart of the French Quarter or as the French would say the Vieux Carré. Even though there was no particular celebration in the city, the street was crowded with pedestrians enjoying alcoholic beverages as they peeked through doorways of strip clubs and music venues. A jazz band caught Rhonda's ear as they walked past one of the many clubs. "Let's go in here," she suggested.

Net was exhausted but Rhonda had already begun her entrance into this establishment. The beat from the band had both of them tapping their toes, until Net recognized a familiar face across the room. Lorena's tattooed man was leaning against the far end of the bar drinking a beer while he observed every female in the place.

"Stay here for a minute. I'll be right back," Net suggested. As he approached this stranger, their eyes met and this man became very uneasy. "Hey man, how do you know Lorena? Where is Lorena?" As soon as the mention of Lorena was made, the man pushed two patrons in Net's path and he ran towards the back of the bar.

Obviously familiar with the premises, he knew there was a rear exit. Net drew closer as he continued to push and overturn any object that would block Net from reaching him. After an exhausting chase, the stranger's knowledge of the area was too much for Net to overcome and he lost him in the general vicinity. Rhonda met Net on the street but was too late to offer any assistance. Exhausted, they decided to head back to their hotel.

***

The next morning Net sent Pants a text that he was going to interview people at Le Bon Theatre and that Rhonda and Tatiana would head to police headquarters to interview Lorena.

Net took a cab to Esplanade Avenue and walked into the back patio of the theatre. He flashed his badge and asked to speak to the director, Zack White. The director was a young, effeminate man of about 30ish. He approached Net and looked him up and down appreciatively. "I guess you're here 'bout poor Jimmy's death. I still can't believe anyone would want to hurt him, but in his line of work I'm not surprised."

"Do you know of anyone in particular who might have a grudge with Jimmy? How about fellow actors here at the theatre?"

"Jimmy was loved by everyone in the theatre, both figuratively and literally," chuckled Zack. "The gay community is pretty free-loving and Jimmy was very popular in the local scene. His favorite bar was a speakeasy on Bourbon Street called Joker's Wild. You may want to talk to them. I know those queens can be real bitches when rejected. Now if you don't have any other questions, I'm conducting auditions for a new play and I'm having a hard time finding real women to play the female roles. I don't want this to turn into a drag performance, since we attract a mostly straight audience."

Net thanked him for his time and asked if he could talk to some of the cast members, but Zack declined, suddenly annoyed with these questions. "Say don't you need a warrant or something!?" stated White. Before Net was able to retreat through the front door, he was approached by a female, or so he thought, who slipped a note in the palm of his right hand. Unfolding the paper, the note read: "Meet me across the street in five minutes."

As it turned out, this female was not a female at all. Honey Moon was a popular drag queen who performed in various clubs throughout the Quarter including performances at this theatre. "Everything Zack White told you was a lie. He hated Jimmy Schwartz. Not many people liked Jimmy. But Zack had a particular dislike for him. Zack ran the theatre but Jimmy made the rules and all decisions. He had the money and everyone resented him. You didn't get a part in any play unless you slept with Jimmy first, man or woman."

"So, does that include you?" Net asked.

31

"Not a chance, doll." Just as Honey uttered that statement, several actors exited the theatre. Honey shoved a business card into Net's pocket and suddenly rushed away so that she would not be seen talking with the detective.

Net then walked to the Joker's Wild bar since it was only three blocks away. He walked in and sat at the bar, ordering a beer, even though it was only 9:00 a.m. The bartender gave him a wink and a smile, acknowledging his handsomeness.

"Well, what's a hot guy like you doing alone in here? If you're looking for company, I get off at 11:00." Net smiled and told the bartender he was spoken for, but didn't clarify that his partner was female.

"I heard that one of the regulars was murdered," said Net. "Any word on who would have done such a thing?"

"You talking about Jimmy? Sweetie, those jealous bitches who hang in here loved Jimmy. He had many lovers who came and went and he helped a lot of queens out with their legal problems."

"Anyone in particular that was angry with Jimmy? What about his legal clients?" asked Net.

"Sweetie, my lips are sealed about matters of the heart, unless you want to unseal them for me?" The bartender winked.

Net said he might take a raincheck and before he headed out the bar, he handed the bartender one of his cards. "If you think of anything, please give me a call."

"Oh, FBI. How awesome! Don't you want my name and number?" he yelled as Net left the bar. "Well it's Biff Holder." His name fell on deaf ears as Net had already closed the door behind him.

***

Net was anxious to get back to headquarters and find out about Lorena's interview. Rhonda and Tatiana were waiting for Net when he arrived. There had been no sign of Lorena at that point. Net walked into Pants' office to inquire about her whereabouts. "Pants, has your detective picked up Lorena yet?"

"J.C., something I've been meaning to ask you. No one around here knows me by the name of Pants including my father-in-law, the mayor. He already thinks his daughter married lower on the social scale then she could have." Pants was carefully choosing his words out of embarrassment.

"I get it. You want me to call you Rodney. No problem. I'll let Rhonda know as well."

Rodney looked relieved as this had been on his mind since J.C. and Rhonda arrived in New Orleans. "Okay. Let's get Mike Smith on the phone and find out what the delay is. Hey Mike. Have you made contact with Lorena?"

"I'm sitting in front of her house right now Chief. She hasn't been answering her phone so I just came over here. I'm about to reach her front door. I'll call you back." Smith took a quick glimpse into the front window of Lorena's side of the double house. Noting nothing unusual he began to knock on the front door, off and on three times with no response. Becoming impatient, the detective approached a gate on her side of the home. Smith was always hesitant to enter a backyard as he was once attacked by a vicious dog, and he needed rabies shots over several weeks. He slowly opened the gate calling out to determine if any animal would come forward. After a moment he felt comfortable enough to approach a window on the side of the house.

As he peered inside he could see that the room had been ransacked with overturned furniture and broken glass throughout. He had seen enough to allow him to break inside. There were blood stains on the carpet and a trail of blood that led Smith into the back room of the house where he discovered the badly beaten and partially dismembered body of Lorena. Her tongue had been severed and placed on the floor along with every finger from both hands. The fingers were placed in a circular display with the tongue in the middle. Her hair was soaked with her own blood and her throat had been slit. It appeared there had been an attempt to also remove her toes. This scene was probably as gruesome as Mike Smith had ever seen. Smith removed his phone from his pocket. "Chief, I have some bad news."

CHAPTER 4

Birds of a Feather

Charlotte Park had spent this morning preparing her home for her every-other-Wednesday tea party. They just called it a tea party but it really wasn't. It was more of a gossiping gathering than anything else. They consumed anything from tea to tequila shots depending on the mood of the group. Her get-together included three of her very close friends, all of whom had graduated from college together. Her best friend, Eve Harrison, was the first to arrive. Eve always came prepared bringing pastries from her cousin's bakery. "How are you feeling, my friend?" inquired Eve.

"Oh, you know. Same old feeling." Charlotte embraced Eve tightly with both arms. Charlotte had actually made tea for this occasion as Dr. Howser's lecture about mixing alcohol and her drugs remained on her mind. Her intention was to never drink any alcohol again but she was so weak. She hoped that making tea would set the tone for this get-together. "It is always so good to see you. I feel so much better when you're around."

"Is that husband taking care of you? Are you taking your meds?"

"Sure. He treats me like a princess but he's always working. Mildred was hired to help." Charlotte observed Eve was a little withdrawn this time. She was normally always so bubbly and energetic. Charlotte glimpsed at the date on her phone. "Oh my God. Honey I just realized what the date is." Eve had lost her husband on this very date two years ago.

"I'm okay Charlotte, time heals all wounds. My husband, Chad wasn't the man I married ten years ago. It was only after he was killed that I learned he had me totally fooled. I knew he had an eye for a pretty face, but apparently he did more than look. When the police knocked at my door, telling me he had been shot, I was in disbelief. They seized his laptop and they discovered his hidden life. Several women, including some from the country club were on his computer. I felt so betrayed. If he wasn't discovered in the bedroom by a jealous husband, I might have continued thinking I had the perfect marriage. You are so lucky to have a faithful husband like Rodney."

Before Eve could continue the final two members of the afternoon tea had arrived. "We're here," announced one of the ladies entering the premises on their own. Leah Bishop and June Hollins always came together since they lived in the same neighborhood. Leah was a beautiful African-American woman who had recently served as queen of the Zulu parade. Her father had been chosen king and because her mother was deceased, she was selected to reign with her father. June was a high-society white woman from an old-money New Orleans family. Her husband was a well-known and ruthless criminal defense attorney representing politicians and elite businesspeople who have run afoul of the law. Her father had also been a well-noted attorney who now occupied a seat on the Louisiana Supreme Court. The two ladies immediately noticed the gloomy mood in the room.

"Oh no! Let's get this party started," declared June as she lifted a bottle of bourbon from a brown paper bag. She poured each lady a shot into their cup of Earl Grey which definitely changed the atmosphere in the room.

"I shouldn't be drinking this with the meds I'm on," giggled Charlotte, as she poured bourbon into her cup, without tea.

Eve agreed and tried to remove her cup from her possession. Charlotte would have none of it as she forcefully pushed Eve away, landing her on the sofa. The three ladies were shocked by Charlotte's outburst.

"Well," said Eve. "Charlotte you know you shouldn't be drinking with your medication. Come on. Let us make you some coffee."

"I'm so sorry. I didn't know," apologized June. "Maybe we should go," she continued looking at Leah.

"All of you can get the fuck out of here," Charlotte screamed just as her cell phone rang. "What?" she yelled into the phone. "Not a good time." By now she had begun to slur her words. "I'll meet you there," she answered abruptly hanging up the phone.

"Eve, maybe you should stay with her for the time being," June suggested.

"I want all of you to get the fuck out of here!" Charlotte picked up a small vase sitting on the coffee table in front of her and hurled it over their heads across the room, smashing it into the wall. She began to charge in their direction as they hurriedly got out of the front door and away from the house.

Charlotte suddenly felt relieved to be alone. She began to clean up the area while humming a song that seemed stuck in her mind. She smiled as she traveled up the stairs to her bedroom and didn't come down until she had changed into a slinky, revealing dress. Her appearance was notably different from her normal look. Besides the dress, she had painted her face with makeup, including eye liner, shadow and dark red lipstick. But the one thing that stood out the most was the blonde wig she was adjusting to fit her head as she slowly moved down the staircase.

***

Net and Rhonda arrived at the scene of Lorena's murder while Tatiana traveled to the New Orleans office of the FBI in order to utilize their more advanced computers. Numerous policemen and forensic personnel walked in and out of Lorena's home. A female sat on the porch by the second door of this double, holding tissues to her eyes while cats lay on each leg of her lap. "Ma'am, did you know the victim?" asked Net as he approached this lady.

"I live here," replied the sobbing female pointing to her front door.

"Oh. Very sorry for your loss."

Rhonda stepped in front of her partner to comfort her. "It's best if I take it from here," Rhonda told Net. She figured the lady would be more comfortable talking to another female. "May I ask your name? I'm Rhonda Bordelon but I don't know what to call you."

"Aurora, yes, Aurora."

"Why don't you give me your real name, sweetie." Assuming she was of the same profession as Lorena, Rhonda spoke softly so not to upset this neighbor of the victim. "Did you work with Lorena?"

"Susie Rubenstein. Yea, what a name, huh!" she chuckled sarcastically before continuing to cry. "What a name for a Bourbon Street stripper!"

"Those beautiful cats," Rhonda suggested as she stroked the head of both. "Did you work with Lorena at the Kitty Club?"

"Yep. We worked the same hours so we could come and go together. You know, for safety reasons. After performing, we liked to hang out at the Joker's Wild. Biff, the bartender would look out for us. We could relax without being bothered. It was a gay bar so nobody was interested in us."

"Are those your pretty cats?"

"No. They both belonged to Lorena. This pretty, fluffy, white one is Sugar and this one is Merry. Merry is quite a character. One would almost think she can speak to you. Unfortunately, I'm not able to keep them because of my allergies. I hate to see them go to the pound."

Rhonda fell for them immediately upon seeing them but she wondered what Net would say if she decided to take them.

Net entered the area of the home where Lorena's body was discovered. The coroner's team was in the process of placing the victim in a black body bag. Her fingers and tongue were stored in a separate container. There was so much blood on the walls and floor, it was difficult to maneuver about without stepping in the way of evidence. It appeared to Net that the victim had put up quite a fight before meeting her fate. A bloody handprint was found on a table which was the only piece of furniture remaining upright. Forensics was in the process of photographing the stain as Net approached. "That's a perfect print of a hand," Net commented to the forensic photographer."

"Yes sir. We also discovered fingerprints all around this area as well as all over the room. I don't know how much entertaining Miss Lorena did, but there are fingerprints all over this room."

"Well, I can't say for sure, but I would be surprised if a lady in her business would want her Johns to know where she lived," offered Net. Net looked about the room before he joined Rhonda on the porch.

"Susie, this is my partner, J.C. Net." Rhonda introduced her fiancé as her FBI partner.

"Susie, again so sorry for the loss of your friend," Net began. "Did you hear or see anything last night or this morning? Were you home all night until now?"

There was a hesitation before Susie's response which was a simple "no". She stated that she did not come home with Lorena last night as usual but heard her door open and close sometime during the night.

"Do you know what time that was?" asked Net.

"Not really. I was tired and went to bed early. We worked early evening but she wanted to go to the Joker's Wild but I came home. I was sleeping but I don't think it was too late." Susie shrugged her shoulders. "I really don't know."

"Are you a sound sleeper?" asked Net. "Because it looks like there was quite a fight over there and there is only a single wall between you and her room. There had to have been quite a bit of noise."

"I really didn't," she countered as she became more defensive. Without notice, she rose and entered her half of the double slamming the door.

Net and Rhonda walked away from this home allowing the police and forensics to do their job. "I don't think she's telling us the whole story," Net stated. "Oh, hey guys. Can you canvass the neighborhood and determine if any neighbors heard or saw anything?" he instructed the police.

"Give her a break, J. She just lost her best friend to a violent death. I'm sure she's scared and shaken by it.

"Maybe so but you didn't see what that room looked like. There was no way anybody didn't hear want went on in that room."

***

Tatiana arrived at the New Orleans FBI office. They were unaware of the Boston team being called into the case and gave her a cool reception. She offered to share her information, which endeared her to the IT staff. They were impressed on how quickly Tatiana was able to search names and profiles with limited information. Tatiana put in a call to Net for his assistance in warming up the agents. He agreed to join them after lunch.

Net and Rhonda were enjoying a bowl of gumbo at an outdoor café on Canal Street. The weather was warm for a March day and they enjoyed the sunshine and people watching. Suddenly, Net's face turned pale as a woman passed across the street that triggered an unpleasant memory. As he got to his feet to get a closer look, the woman disappeared into a nearby hotel. Rhonda noticed Net's expression and asked what was wrong. "Oh nothing. Just thought I saw someone I knew."

Net's face still offered a sense of concern but Rhonda decided to let it go. In his mind, he wasn't certain what he had seen. His memory brought him back to a time when he was working for the Louisiana State Police as a homicide detective investigating a series of murders in Keister, La.

It was a tiny town where there had been a string of murders involving former members of the KKK. Net had thought he had met the love of his life in one, Susan Griffin, during that investigation. She was thought to be an investigative reporter covering these crimes. They had a very passionate relationship until Net discovered her true identity, Sabrina Keister, which tied her directly to the murders. Net was convinced who he had seen couldn't be her yet he couldn't get it out of his mind. It was part of his life that he had never discussed with Rhonda and didn't feel this would be the appropriate time to do so now. Nothing should sidetrack them from finding this New Orleans serial killer. Net did the best to clear his head and once lunch was finished, they were to head to the local FBI office.

Tatiana introduced Net and Rhonda to Agent-in-Charge, Saul Bernstein of the New Orleans FBI office. Both Net and Rhonda put on their charm act, having been forewarned that his feathers were ruffled by their taking lead on the serial case.

"I'm sure glad you're available to assist us Agent Bernstein. We're unfamiliar with our surroundings and could use your expertise. We just came from the murder scene of our potential witness, Lorena Gonzalez. She was tortured and had her fingers and tongue removed. We spoke with her next-door neighbor, Susie Rubenstein, aka Aurora who claims she didn't hear anything. Judging from the crime scene and the violence, I believe she's hiding something or is afraid of someone. We could really use your help interviewing Susie and other neighbors in the area. If you could send your crew to handle that, we could meet at Rodney Park's office tomorrow around 3:00 p.m. to discuss our findings."

Tatiana walked into the room and gave Net a knowing smile.

"I did a thorough background check on Lorena Gonzalez and Susie Rubenstein. Both ladies were arrested numerous times for prostitution and lewd acts in public. Apparently for a generous tip, the pasties and G-string are optional. I crossed reference both women and found that the common denominator was named Tabares Jaimez, aka T.J. He made bail for both ladies on numerous occasions and was arrested for assaulting Lorena Gonzalez. The charges were dropped because she refused to identify him as her assailant."

Net was aware that Tabares Jaimez was present at the hotel on the night of Buck Lawrence's murder, but he wasn't ready to share this information with Bernstein. He planned on calling Rodney and seeing if he knew where they could find Tabares, since he was Rodney's confidential informant.

CHAPTER 5
Deja Vu

Josh Hancock contacted Rodney Park and advised the coroner's report was ready on the John Doe found by the levee. Rodney immediately called Net and asked him to meet at the coroner's office.

The body was identified as Joseph Carson, a recent college dropout from Alabama. He was identified from a missing person's report and his fingerprints were on file. Apparently, he had had a few run-ins with the law in Alabama, mostly drug related. He also had an assault charge pending in Tuscaloosa, Alabama from a bar fight.

"Do you think Carson's murder is connected to the other homicides?"

"I would be surprised," said Hancock. "The MO is totally different. He was not sexually assaulted and the cause of death was a stab wound that severed the carotid artery. He probably bled out in less than 3 minutes. He had track marks on this arm and between his toes. It seems Mr. Carson was living his life on the streets and my guess, he was in town to score some drugs."

"I'll have my office notify his next of kin and they can make arrangements to pick up the body. Send your report to my office," Rodney advised. "My men are still searching the area for evidence. It will be crucial to find the weapon. Unless we get lucky with a tip, that weapon might be our only link to the killer."

"It was probably tossed into the river. With that current, we will never find it," suggested Net.

Just at that moment Hancock was handed a piece of paper by a clerk in his office. "Well, looks like you're in luck. Just received notice from your office, a knife with a 7-inch serrated blade was found but not close to the scene, hidden in a patch of bushes. Wasn't very well hidden as a child found it while playing with her dad. Appears to be covered in blood." Hancock showed a picture of the knife to the two detectives. "As soon as I receive it, I'll compare it to the wounds on the body and run it for DNA and prints."

"Sounds like the killer planned a return to the area to retrieve it at a later date," suggested Net. "Did the child or dad handle it?"

"Hope not," Hancock snapped.

The two detectives left the coroner's office and proceeded in the direction of the police station. "Hey, you got time for a cup of coffee?" asked Net.

Park and Net walked across the street to a small coffee shop. Net was the first to take a sip of coffee from his cup. He had forgotten what it was like to taste the strong flavor of chicory.

"Okay Net, what's up? I can tell from the look on your face that something has you bothered."

"Rodney, I may be losing my mind, but yesterday when Rhonda and I were having lunch, I swore I saw Susan Griffin across the street."

"Our Susan Griffin from Keister?"

"Yes, one and the same. I still remember both of us acting like school kids, vying for her affection. I thought I found the love of my life… that is until we discovered she was killing people in Keister. Ha!"

"You don't still have feelings for Susan, do you? I moved on from that crazy lady long ago."

"Well, the fact that she picked me may have had something to do with it," Net laughed. "No, I have no feelings for Susan Griffin. I found my soul mate with Rhonda and never want to be with another woman. The fact that she was never brought to justice for her crimes has me wondering why she is in New Orleans and what her plans are. Can you put one of your detectives on this? If she is here, we need to finally bring her to justice."

"I'll have one of our men check the local hotels and see if, by chance, she's registered. Does Rhonda know about Susan?"

"I've never told her. Just haven't found the right moment to do so."

This discussion brought back bittersweet memories for Net. He couldn't accept what she had done but at the same time, it was difficult for one to say they wouldn't have done the same. Her brother had been murdered by local members of the KKK simply because he was in an interracial marriage. Revenge was her sole motive. It wasn't until she disappeared that authorities connected her to the crimes.

"Well, that's in the past. We need to find this T.J. guy, and bring him in for questioning."

"Let me handle that," suggested Rodney. "I think he will be more comfortable if I make direct contact.

Net and Rodney went their separate ways. Rodney travelled to his office at the police station while Net returned to the FBI office to reconnect with Tatiana and Rhonda. There was quite a commotion at police headquarters when Rodney arrived.

"What's going on?" questioned Deputy Chief Park.

"We identified the killer in the Joseph Carson killing," exclaimed Detective Colin Kennedy. "The coroner matched the knife found as the murder weapon and his fingerprints were all over it. The blood on the knife matched the victim. Mike Smith arrested him near the area where the knife was found. They're on their way here."

"Find me when they arrive," requested Rodney. I want to be involved in the interrogation. We haven't ruled him out of the other murders."

When Net arrived at the FBI office both Rhonda and Tatiana were curious as to what he learned from the coroner but before he could say anything, his phone rang. He reached into his pocket to retrieve his cell when he discovered the card that Honey Moon had given him. Rhonda seemed puzzled when Net handed her a business card for Sal Siegel, Proprietor, The shop was located on Decatur St. Before he could explain, he answered the call recognizing Rodney's number. "What's up?"

"Just letting you know we've arrested a suspect in the Joseph Carson murder. I don't believe that he is involved with the others but we need to eliminate him as a suspect. I expect the coroner to let us know soon whether that knife was also used in the other deaths."

"What in the world is this?" Rhonda asked referring to the card she held in her hand. "Are you trying to put a spell on me?"

"Nah. These places are all over the Quarter. They're for the tourists. Most people go to these places to buy a voodoo doll, or a get-rich-quick pill, or even a witch's brew to put a spell on their ex. People buy these things as a joke or a prank. Although…there are some people that really believe." Net smiled as though he wasn't telling her the truth.

"Well, what in the hell am I supposed to do with this? Do you want something from this shop?"

"No, it's part of this case. Honey Moon gave me that card in case…" Net was interrupted by Rhonda before he could finish.

"Who?! Since when do you know someone named Honey Moon? And who is this Sal Siegel?"

"I think Sal Siegel and Honey Moon are one in the same. I met Honey, who is a drag queen at the theatre where Jimmy Schwartz performed. She seemed to know more about Schwartz than others. I think we need to speak to him again. We were interrupted the first time."

"I guess you want me to go talk to him…her."

"Yes. I need to meet Rodney, who is bringing in a suspect in the murder on the levee. Meet me back at the hotel when you're finished."

***

Rhonda made her way to the voodoo shop on Decatur Street. When she walked through the door she got a deep whiff of pot mixed with incense. A tall man was at the register, dressed in flowing scarfs and a long red wig.

"What's your pleasure doll? I can see from your beautiful face and rocking bod that you're not in need of a love potion."

Rhonda handed him the card he gave Net and identified herself as his partner.

Sal told her to wait a minute and put the closed sign on the front door. He ushered her into a back room, filled with colored bottles, voodoo dolls and candles in various colors.

"Like I told your partner, Jimmy Schwartz was loved and hated by most people in the quarter. He was a heavy drinker and when not fucking anything that moved at the theatre, you'd find him at Joker's Wild. He wasn't too particular if he was being serviced by male or female. He was never faithful to either sex, and I don't believe anyone that will shed a tear at his funeral".

"What about his law practice? Do you have any information of any clients that wanted to see him dead?"

"Most of his clientele were fags, drug dealers and hoes, so I guess I'd say all of the above. I did overhear a pretty loud argument a few weeks ago at Jokers between Jimmy and some pimp named T.J. Jimmy had been representing some of T.J.'s hoes. Apparently T.J. has both males and females in his stable and Jimmy was willing to trade blow jobs for retainers. From what I overheard, T.J. sent over some blonde to take care of Jimmy, but when Jimmy asked for a rim job, the bitch got violent and pulled a knife on him. Jimmy threw a beer on T.J., who took a swing at Jimmy. Biff ended up throwing T.J. out the bar, but he threatened to kill Jimmy as he was leaving. Biff wouldn't dare throw out Jimmy, since he spent a great deal of money at the bar and when no one else was available and Jimmy was horny, Biff would be his lay of last resort."

"And what about you? Did you also have a sexual relationship with Jimmy?"

"Honey, you'd be hard pressed to find a man or woman around the quarter that didn't fuck him at least once, but once was enough for this queen. I like my men to decide if they are the needle or the thread and stick with it".

Rhonda chuckled and thanked him for his help.

"Can I call you if I have any more questions?"

"Sure doll, but don't let any of those jealous bitches at the theatre know I've been talking to you. Some of those cats have sharp claws."

Rhonda started asking questions about the various potions and toys in the shop.

"Voodoo is serious business in this city. A lot of the stuff in my shop is basically to get tourist money, but I do have a large followers that practice voodoo as a religion. If you ever visit St. Louis Cemetery you'll find the grave of Marie Laveau, the voodoo queen of New Orleans. You'll find candles, dolls and notes left at her grave by her worshipers. Some believe that she will grant wishes, even if the wish is for revenge."

Rhonda couldn't help but purchase a few lucky candles, a fertility doll and some candy that was guaranteed to keep you youthful for life. She even picked up a voodoo doll for Tatiana, complete with pins. Rhonda departed from the voodoo shop feeling very silly about her purchases, but knew she must visit St. Louis Cemetery before she returned to Boston. There was no rush to meet Net back at their hotel as he was to meet Park at police headquarters first. She was concerned about the well-being of Charlotte Park and decided to ride a streetcar down historic St. Charles Ave. to the beautiful garden district of New Orleans.

***

She arrived at the Park household, which was an elegant white mansion over one-hundred years old. The white colonial-style columns spanned from the ground to the second floor and the place was considered one of the most must-see destinations on tours of this New Orleans neighborhood. Rhonda rang the doorbell and was surprised by a young lady answering the door.

"May I help you?" asked the very soft-spoken female with an unfamiliar accent.

"Is this the home of Rodney and Charlotte Park?" Rhonda inquired.

"Why, yes ma'am. I am the Park's caregiver, Mildred Monroe." The more she talked, one could hear a very distinctive southern accent.

"Hello Mildred. My name is Rhonda Net...er...Bordelon." Rhonda was trying to see how her soon-to-be new name would sound but it was misleading. "Is Mrs. Park in?"

"Yes, she is. Let me see if she is available." Mildred escorted Rhonda into the foyer area of the home. Like the outside, the interior was very elegant. A mammoth staircase captivated a visitor's attention as it was perfectly centered in the entranceway of the home. Many old paintings, including portraits, lined the walls throughout the area. The depictions were of people who were probably descendants of the Hebert family, as Rodney had no such background. Mildred returned moments later and announced that Charlotte would be with her shortly.

Charlotte slowly made her way down the stairs as Rhonda greeted her nearby. She seemed to have trouble getting her balance as Rhonda took her arm and led her to a chair in the living area. Her swollen eyes were lined with rings below and her hair didn't look like it had been combed in days.

"Did we wake you up?" asked Rhonda concerned about Charlotte's well-being.

It seemed like minutes for Charlotte's mind to start working and even then she seemed dazed. "I'm just tired," mumbled Charlotte. "Haven't slept well lately."

"Is there anything I can do for you? Mildred can you get Mrs. Park some coffee or tea?"

"I think she prefers tea, ma'am." Mildred's answer sounded resentful of Rhonda's demand.

"Well, then please get her tea!"

Mildred, who was probably in her early twenties, headed towards the kitchen mumbling all the way and continued while placing the tea kettle on the stove. She deliberately took her time before Rhonda joined her in the kitchen.

"How's that tea coming?" Rhonda asked.

"It's coming fine," Mildred stated in her stern southern accent.

"Look, I don't mean to offend you," offered Rhonda. "I'm just very concerned about Mrs. Park. I don't think she can take care of herself."

Rhonda was trying to make amends for her perceived intrusion into this household. "I'm so glad Charlotte has you by her side. I don't know what she would do without you." Her compliments seemed to soften Mildred's initial opinion of Rhonda.

"Thank you ma'am. Would you like me to make you a cup of tea also?"

"No thank you. I must be on my way. Take good care of this lady. I know you will."

Mildred escorted Rhonda towards the front door. As they passed the living room, Charlotte had curled up on the sofa and was sound asleep. "I guess that tea will have to keep for later. Miss Rhonda, I'm just as worried about Ms. Charlotte as you. I couldn't sleep last night and Mr. Rodney was working. I heard Ms. Charlotte come home in the middle of the night. I peeked out of my door and she stumbled all the way up to her room. Even her outfit looked a little befuddled."

Rhonda handed Mildred her card and said to call her at any time. Texting Net she discovered he was still at police headquarters.

CHAPTER 6

Body Count

Net met Deputy Chief Park in the interrogation room to begin questioning the alleged killer of Joseph Carson. Adonnis Jackson was a local drug dealer, well known by the police. He had affiliated with several gangs over the years and had been arrested on numerous occasions for distribution and possession of various drugs. Based on his criminal history, he should have still been in jail, but the DA's office had a new "catch and release" program which was making life difficult for the police department.

Rodney was already seated in the interrogation room with Jackson when Net entered.

"I ain't answering you nothing," blurted Jackson.

"Adonnis, we haven't asked anything yet. As a matter of fact we'd like to tell you a story," Rodney began.

Jackson raised his nose as though he was sniffing something in the room. "It stinks in here. I smell me a Fed."

Net placed his hand on his friend's shoulder as if to stop him from answering. "That's a good observation, Mr. Jackson," Net responded laughing. "We already have you with the murder of Joseph Carson. Now it's just a matter of time before we connect you to the other murders."

Net knew that Jackson was probably not the culprit in the others but wanted to get him talking.

"What you talking about, Pig!" Jackson shouted excitedly. "This Carson dude wanted to buy some drugs and tried to rip me off. I got to answer to my boy, so I can't let any punk not pay me. I was defending myself."

"How was that self-defense, Adonnis?" asked Rodney. "Carson had no weapon. Let me tell you what we think really happened. You saw the wad of c-notes Carson had on him and you decided that would look good in your pocket and still have your drugs."

"No, that ain't what went down. He jumped me and tried to steal my stash. It was his knife and I took it from him and defended myself."

"Then how come the knife only had your fingerprints on it? Tell us who your boss is Adonnis and maybe we'll put in a good word for you with the DA."

"Does this face look like a rat? I don't know any names. If I tell you anything I'm a dead man on the street or in prison. I ain't saying another fucking word! I want my lawyer."

Net looked at Rodney and they both knew this interview was over. Rodney called in Deputy Mark Rodrigues. "Okay Mark, book him and place him in a holding cell. Notify the public defender's office that we have a live one for them."

Net told Rodney he'd call him later and was going back to the hotel to meet up with Rhonda and Tatiana, who had been cross referencing all of the victims and the MOs. Net again offered to buy Rodney dinner at the hotel and this time he agreed to meet them at 8:00 p.m.

***

Sal Siegel, (Honey Moon) was in the rear of the voodoo shop, working on inventory. Mardi Gras was only a month ago and tourists flocked to his shop to buy trinkets and potions that they could never find in their mid-west states. He was glad for the business and needed the extra money. He pulled out his supply of various sized bottles and commenced making potions using tap water and food coloring. He was at his computer, making labels for the various bottles, when he heard a noise from the front of the store. He got up from his desk, thinking that another rat had made its way into the store. Being so close to the river, rats were a constant problem. The store had long been closed and he was sure he had locked the front door. He turned on the light in the shop, grabbed a broom and started looking for the unwelcome visitor. After a few minutes he gave up and went back to his computer. His label maker was spitting out colorful labels, some decorated with skulls and crossbones. The lights flickered twice and then went out, together with his computer.

"What the fuck?" He searched around for a flashlight, but couldn't find one. In desperation he fumbled for one of the lucky candles he kept in a cabinet. As he stood at the cabinet he felt the breath of someone behind him. Before he could turn to look, a knife was thrust into his back. Stumbling forward he tried to hold on to the cabinet, knocking all of the candles on the floor. He lay on the floor feeling the warm blood around him and the life draining from his body.

***

Rodney arrived at the Port Orleans Hotel precisely at 8 o'clock. Net, Rhonda and Tatiana had already secured a table by a window in the restaurant. The hotel was not exactly brimming with guests this time of year and the attendance in the restaurant reflected the same. The wait staff had no other tables to service at this time as they continuously checked with the patrons to provide exceptional service. Rodney had brought a folder with him which contained the latest coroner's report.

"The coroner ruled that the knife used by Adonnis Jackson to kill Joseph Carson was not the same as the one used in the other killings," read Rodney from the report. This was not a surprise to them and they knew that their work was still in front of them to capture this serial killer.

"I heard you visited my wife today," Rodney mentioned to Rhonda.

"I did. I was concerned about her and I had some time, so I went to check on her. I met her caregiver Mildred as well." Rhonda's statement was short and to the point leaving it open for interpretation.

"Mildred has been a godsend to us. She makes sure Charlotte takes her medication on time and eats properly. Matter of fact I called home before I came here and Charlotte was out roaming the streets. She must be feeling okay."

The bluntness of Rhonda's comment about Mildred went unnoticed by Rodney but she didn't want to make an issue over it. After all, it was her first meeting with Mildred and even though Rhonda was always a good judge of character, maybe she had got the wrong impression.

"Can I see the coroner's report?" asked Rhonda. As the waiter brought a first bottle of wine to their table, they remained quiet while Rhonda read over the report.

Rodney requested to be the one to sample the first taste of the wine and upon his approval he insisted that the wine sit and be allowed to breathe before pouring. Net chuckled at the pomp and circumstance of Rodney approving the wine.

"You've come a long way from the Rodney I knew in Keister who thought a box of wine was the epitome of class. If we can rule out the connection between Carson and the other victims, let's put this murder to bed and start reviewing the remaining information. Tatiana, please hand Rodney the findings you comprised on the other victims."

Tatiana opened the folder marked victim 4.

"The coroner finally identified victim number 4 found in the Bywater Hotel. His name was Sidney O'Conner, 62 years old and recently retired from the post office. He was never married and had no next of kin who reported him missing. His wallet and cell phone were missing, but he was able to be identified from a laundry tag in his jacket. The cause of death was a severed carotid artery. The wound was inflicted with a serrated knife, approximately the same size as the one used on all other victims. The toxicology report indicated he had alcohol, Viagra and the same paralytic drug found in not only Buck Lawrence's system but the others as well. The necklace found at the scene was examined for DNA and the hair found on the necklace was from a cheap blonde wig."

"I reviewed the coroner's report," stated Rhonda. "I thought it would be helpful to have the local FBI office visit O'Conner's apartment. "I think they are feeling left out, so maybe this will appease them. They found the apartment in disarray. Not sure if robbery was the motive, but even the mattresses were slit open. O'Conner's apartment was in the lower Garden District in a fairly expensive apartment building. One wonders how someone on a postal workers salary could afford such accommodations. The local FBI is currently canvassing local jewelry stores to see if anyone can identify the necklace found in the hotel."

"Rodney, I'd like to go to the O'Conner apartment first thing in the morning and see if the FBI missed anything," suggested Net. "Tatiana please continue to comprise any similarities between the victims."

"We already know about the other three," she began. "All had been drugged in the same manner and a serrated knife was used to kill them, although the wounds were not identical. All three had ties to either Le Bon

Theatre, The Kitty Club or Joker's Wild. I haven't found any connections to each other but I'm still working on that."

Rhonda, raised her hand and asked if they could do without her for the next day. "I'd like to go back and visit with Sal Siegel again. Honestly, I'd like to buy a few more souvenirs." Net looked surprised by her statement. "Okay, Okay. I want to get some things to take back to the ladies in the Boston office. I think they'd get a kick out of this. I'll meet you at your office at the end of the day, Rodney, if that meets your liking."

"That's fine Rhonda, I really need to head home now to check on Charlotte. Thank you again for checking on her. I'm sorry she isn't well enough at this time to entertain. Hopefully with the proper rest and medication she will make a complete recovery."

Rodney shook Net's hand and gave both Tatiana and Rhonda a kiss on the cheek, which took both ladies by surprise.

"Don't take offense at the kiss on the cheek, I meant no disrespect, it's just a southern thing," Rodney said.

***

He arrived home only to find an empty house. Neither Charlotte nor Mildred where anywhere to be found, so he assumed they must have gone somewhere together. Rodney poured himself a glass of scotch and reclined in his chair anticipating to watch any sport that would be on TV. He had hardly taken one sip of his drink when he was surprised by someone entering through the back door. Startled he jumped up reaching for his gun, but he immediately recognized Mildred hiding behind several grocery bags. Rodney rushed to help, peeking through the door, expecting Charlotte to be close behind. "Where's Mrs. Charlotte?" he asked as there was no sign of her.

"I don't know, Mr. Rodney. I was in the laundry room washing clothes when I went to check on her and she was gone. I assumed she went to a neighbor or to see her father. Since she wasn't here, I took the opportunity to go to the grocery store."

As they continued their conversation, a noise by the front door caught their attention. Charlotte appeared bewildered as she entered into her home. Rodney immediately noticed the stale smell of cigarettes and alcohol exuding from her person.

"Where have you been?" He didn't wait for her answer before another question. "What are you wearing?" he asked referring to the leather mini skirt and purple low-cut blouse leaving very little to the imagination. Again he asked, "Where have you been?"

Charlotte slowly climbed the stairs to their bedroom without a word. Finally, as she reached the side of her bed, "I don't know. I don't know," she replied as tears formed in the corner of her eyes.

Despite the alcohol odor, she didn't appear drunk to Rodney but her statement of not knowing where she had been, was very concerning. He helped her lie on the bed and no sooner did her head hit the pillow, she was asleep. Rodney returned to the kitchen where Mildred was still putting the groceries away. "Has Mrs. Charlotte been taking her medication on a timely basis?"

"Oh, yes sir. I give it to her myself. She is totally up to date."

"I'd like to see her pill bottle, Mildred," requested Rodney.

Mildred reluctantly handed him the medicine, feeling that he wasn't trusting her. The bottle was kept in a cabinet in the kitchen where it was handy for Mildred to retrieve it. The medicine was prescribed with a thirty-day supply and Rodney wanted to check to see how many pills remained. He counted each pill until he reached twenty-three and noted that the medication had been refilled seven days ago. Satisfied with this outcome, he gave the bottle back to Mildred so she could return it its storage place.

CHAPTER 7

The Honeymoon's Over!

Rhonda was awake bright and early the next morning. It was a beautiful day in the city so she decided to have breakfast in the courtyard of the hotel. J.C. had already set out to meet Tatiana at the New Orleans FBI office. Rhonda was seated in the patio where she had a clear view to the street. She obtained the local newspaper from the lobby, reading while she awaited her food. She was still not able to find the correct recipe of cream and sugar to offset the bitterness of chicory in the hot coffee that New Orleans was known for. Instead, she seemed to settle comfortably with her glass of orange juice just as her breakfast, consisting of grits, eggs and bacon were delivered.

"This is my first time trying grits," she laughed with the server. She poked it around her plate before she finally had the courage to taste it. "Hmmm, not bad," she murmured to herself.

She wondered if she said that loud enough for others to hear. There weren't many people in her general area but as she looked through the courtyard, she could see someone appearing to stare at her. The person was close enough for Rhonda to see this was a female but was far enough away to be able to get a really good look at her as a hoodie partially covered her face and hair. The strange female continued to focus on Rhonda.

"Can I get my check please?" Rhonda requested as her server approached.

"Oh, you're not going to finish your grits, honey?" asked the waitress.

"They were delicious. I just don't have as big an appetite as I thought."

"Do you want to take that with you?"

"No thanks but I'll charge it to my room." Rhonda wanted to hurry and get a good look at this stranger, but by the time she signed the receipt, she was gone. Rhonda rushed onto the street but there was no sign of this outsider. "Maybe this was just my imagination," she wondered. "Probably a tourist but that was strange."

Three young ladies walking past thought Rhonda was talking to them. "Oh, I'm sorry," Rhonda said smiling. "You caught me talking to myself." The ladies continued on, giggling to themselves, as Rhonda stood there embarrassed.

The weather was so nice that Rhonda thought this was a perfect time to walk down to the voodoo shop and visit Sal Siegel once again. On the way, she couldn't resist stopping in some antique shops and a few boutiques. Nothing was cheap but Rhonda was determined to buy one particular dress she spotted in the window of one of the clothing establishments. Needless to say, she was elated when she tried it on and the fit was perfect. Looking at the price tag, she knew she would have to do something special for J.C. The sales lady neatly folded her purchase and placed it in a handy carry bag. Rhonda continued on her journey and finally reached the cross street where the voodoo shop was located. By now it was after ten o'clock in the morning and the closed sign still hung in the doorway.

Rhonda jiggled the door handle and found the door unlocked. "Mr. Siegel, Mr. Siegel. Sal," she yelled. "It's Rhonda Bordelon. Anybody here?" Rhonda slowly opened the door wider and noticed all the lights were turned off, but nothing in the store looked out of place, including the cash register.

She called out again and walked towards the back of the store. She pulled open the office door and let out a gasp. On the floor was Sal Siegel, covered in blood. He was lying face down and she could see from the wound in his back that he had been stabbed at least once. Not wanting to disturb the scene, she called Net on her cellphone.

"J.C., we have a problem at the voodoo shop. Sal has been murdered. I discovered the body in his office, but haven't touched anything in the office other than the door handle. Can you send a forensic team and notify Rodney. I will stay here until they arrive".

The local FBI forensic team arrived within 20 minutes. They took photographs all around the shop and waited for the coroner to handle the body. Broken glass covered the floor from the candles that fell out of the cabinet when Siegel had tried to brace himself. Forensics took photographs of other items in the office. In the rear of the office was a velvet sofa with numerous throw pillows. Next to the sofa was a small wastebasket that contained a few empty mini liquor bottles. As they moved the bottles around, using a pen, they discovered a used condom in the bottom of the trash basket. They carefully bagged the condom and the bottles and packed them to be sent to the lab.

Josh Hancock and the coroner's van pulled up to the shop. "Well, what queen met her demise now?" asked Josh.

"A little respect Dr. Hancock, Sal Siegel was a nice guy and a possible witness in our investigation," said Rhonda.

"Sorry, I just have little use for the quarter trash or their lifestyle. I've seen firsthand what a vicious bitch they can become when someone fucks their trick."

"Regardless, he is a victim here and deserves to be treated with dignity. We don't need your homophobic comments."

"Ok doll, we can agree to disagree. I'll have my men bag the body and take it back to the lab."

Rhonda called Net and told him that the FBI had found a used condom in Siegel's trash can. "Do you want to meet at FBI headquarters, or head to the coroner's office?"

Net knew Rhonda wasn't very fond of Hancock. "Why don't you go to the FBI office and I will observe the autopsy that Hancock will perform on Siegel?"

***

Net arrived at the coroner's office shortly after noon. Hancock had stepped out to get a bite to eat, so Net was greeted by his assistant, Dr. Jennifer Davison. They had already prepared Siegel's body and were waiting for Hancock to return to start the autopsy. Jennifer was an attractive blonde, approximately 35 years old. She was instantly attracted to Net and wasn't very subtle in flirting with him. Jennifer informed Net that the condom found at the murder scene contained semen and had been sent to the lab. The knife wound in the victim's back was approximately two inches below the shoulder blade and made in a upward trajectory. From the angle of the cut, the perpetrator was shorter than the victim and left-handed. Jennifer motioned Net to come closer to see the cut, as she purposively lean forward, exposing her cleavage under her white lab coat. Net chuckled to himself, but did take a quick glance at her ample breasts.

Josh Hancock came into the office just as Jennifer was adjusting her lab coat.

"I hope I'm not interrupting a party here," chuckled Hancock, as he threw the wrapper from his chicken sandwich in the garbage. "I've already completed my initial report regarding the wound and outward findings.

Jen and I were just getting ready to slice and dice this queen if you want to stay for the show."

Jennifer gave Hancock a fuck-you look and insisted that Net stay for the autopsy. Jennifer had little use for Hancock and had witnessed the way he treated corpses when he thought no one was watching. She thought about blowing the whistle on him, but knew he had friends in high places. She was secretly wishing karma would catch up with him soon.

Just as Hancock hit record on the tape, the computer started printing out a report from the lab.

"Well, it looks like Ms. Siegel should have paid more attention to who she/him was doing. It appears he has HIV and so did the person whose semen was in the condom. J C, you may want to send this to the FBI and see if you can identify the donor. I know if someone gave me HIV I might want to knife them in the back."

"Thanks Josh. I'm headed to the FBI office now to meet my fiancé, Rhonda."

Jennifer sent a disappointed glance his way, but still told him if he needed anything to give her a call.

Net called Rodney Park and told him he would pick him up on his way so the two men could make a quick commute to the FBI office.

***

Rhonda and Tatiana were sitting together behind a computer screen trying to find any connections between the victims and/or suspects, although suspects were few and far between. "Anything?" asked Net.

"We have nothing," responded Rhonda. "Victims all tie into the Joker's Wild bar or the Le Bon Theatre. I guess any patron or employee of either place could be a suspect."

65

"Let's run the names of anyone affiliated with both places and any known connections to them. Tatiana, can you hack into video cameras in the area of the voodoo shop and see if there was anything that could help? I understand the camera in the shop itself was inoperable. Just for show. Rodney can you have your detectives canvass the areas around this shop and also Lorena's residence and see if anybody saw anything."

"Will do," affirmed Rodney. Just at that moment he heard several loud voices coming from the rear of the office. "What's going on?" he asked.

"Oh, FBI Agent Caden Caruso is questioning, as I understand it, a 'usual' suspect, one Bernard Lampino."

"What!?" exclaimed Rodney as he scurried towards the back room where this Lampino was being questioned.

Lampino was thought to be the head of a small group of Italian mafia operating in the French Quarter. "Anytime someone litters the quarter, you guys think I did it," Lampino suggested.

Those words had hardly left his mouth when Deputy Chief Park burst through the closed door leaping at the Italian. "You mother fucker, I've been waiting for this for a long time." Rodney's first punch landed directly across the mouth of Lampino. Just as he was about to strike him again, Net intervened, grabbing Park from behind and holding his arms in a locked position.

"What in the hell is wrong with you?" screamed Net. Rodney shook off the grasp Net had on his arms and began to walk away. He turned, as if to attack again but as Net showed he was ready to stop him, Rodney permanently walked away. Agent Caruso joined Net outside the room to provide assistance. Park was no longer in sight.

"Do you know what that was all about?" asked Net.

"I think you need to ask Deputy Chief Park about that?" responded Caruso.

Net searched for his friend and it didn't take him long to find him already sitting behind a glass of whiskey at a bar across the street. Net pulled up a chair next to him without saying a word and ordered the same drink.

"I guess you want to know what that was all about," offered Park.

Net shrugged his shoulders. "Whenever you want to talk, I'll listen."

"That bastard. He screwed Charlotte. He raped her." He had Net's undivided attention. "I know he did it. Charlotte was off her meds and drank too much. Ended up at the Joker's Wild. He took advantage of her. Claims she came on to him and he didn't know who she was." Tears began to form in Rodney's eyes. "Took her back to his French Quarter apartment and raped her. She has no recollection of it but I know he did it. DA wouldn't charge him because of lack of evidence. So help me, one of these days I will get him."

"I'm very sorry my friend. I don't know what I would do if someone did that to Rhonda. What do you know about this Lampino?"

"Nothing happens in the Quarter without his knowledge. Problem is, he has ready-made alibis set up for every incident that might happen. His hands never get dirty but he has men who carry out his orders. I believe one of his corporations owns the Joker's Wild but we have never been able to tie it back to him. If you go in there late at night you'll find his ass sitting in a dark back corner of the bar with girls on both sides of him. He has a regular harem who stay by his side for his pleasure. I guess they weren't available that night," Rodney spoke of the night with Charlotte.

"Promise me you won't take this any further," demanded Net.

"Yeah, yeah. He'll get what's coming to him sooner or later. I won't have to do it."

Net was disturbed by his friend's statements but he had done all he could at this time. They finished their drinks and walked back across the street to the FBI office. The two men watched as Agent Caruso escorted Lampino out of the FBI office.

"You're releasing him?" asked Net.

"We have nothing to hold him on. Not a shred of evidence pointing to him having any involvement in any of this."

"I told you," added Park as he spoke to his friend Net. "There never is. His henchmen do all the dirty work."

"If he's guilty, we'll get him. I promise you that." It was at that moment Saul Bernstein and Tatiana walked up and handed Net a piece of paper which contained the DNA results from the condom found at the Siegel murder.

CHAPTER 8
Undercover Ladies

Biff Holder had been the bartender at the Joker's Wild for quite some time, despite having a long criminal record dating back to his juvenile days. The bar owners either didn't do background checks or didn't care. Many of his charges had been dismissed for lack of evidence but he did accept a plea deal which included his name being listed as a sex offender. Disturbingly, his name was mentioned in various child molestation cases but the district attorney was never able to prosecute. Now it seemed he may be involved in the murder of Honey Moon (Sal Siegel) as his DNA was identified from the condom.

"Please have Biff Holder picked up," Net requested of Agent Bernstein.

"Net, I think we should go undercover to the theatre and Joker's Wild and see what we can find, since most of the victims have ties to either place," offered Rhonda.

"I can visit the theatre tonight. I read in the Quarter Voice that they are holding auditions from 7-10 tonight for a new play."

"Not really wild about you going undercover in this place. I know you've done this before but…"

"Don't be ridiculous! This is my job. I know you don't like it but it's something that comes with this work."

"I guess but keep in touch." Net seemed uncomfortable with this but he knew Rhonda was right. This was part of the job.

"Tatiana, how do you feel about doing some undercover work?" asked Rhonda,

"I'd love it. You want me at the theatre too?"

"No, not there. Please put something provocative on and head over to Joker's Wild. If you can get any of the ladies to talk about the recent murders and who they suspect could be involved. I know you are not required to work undercover Tatty, but we can have some of the local FBI agents there to protect you."

"I don't mind helping, *milyy*. I actually enjoy getting out in the field. I just hope I can find something suitable to wear."

***

It was just past 8:00 p.m. when Tatiana walked into Joker's Wild. She took a seat at the bar and ordered a vodka on the rocks. She chuckled to herself, "You can take the *zhenshchina* out of Russia, but can't take the vodka out of the *zhenshchina*." Glancing around the bar she noticed two men seated at the last table by the bathrooms. She recognized them immediately from earlier in the day at FBI headquarters. This eased the butterflies in her stomach as she sipped her drink. A woman of about thirty years old climbed up on the barstool next to her. Looking at her smeared makeup and short, tight skirt, it was obvious she wasn't coming from the cathedral.

"Rough day doll?" asked Tatiana in her best fake southern accent. "My name is Tanya." She decided that it wasn't wise to use her real name.

"Hi, my name is Peg, but I'm known on the street as Sunshine. Yes, every day is rough in this city. It's bad enough you have to worry about some John getting violent, but now the word is that we have a serial killer in the city."

"I'm new in town, but I did hear about a few murders lately. It seems as though the victims are mostly Johns and a few queens."

"Welcome to the Big Easy, or Big Sleezy as we call it on the street. Do you have a man for protection? Working solo can be dangerous in the quarter. Two of the local talent were recently murdered. Both worked at the Kitty Club, but moonlighted as escorts."

"Do you know of anyone who might want to hurt them? I thought most of the recent murders were men, this seems a little off-course."

"Honey Moon could be classified as either. The only connection between the two are the strip club and of course here. Most of the locals hang out here. The bartenders look out for us and when we're a little short they'll let us drink on the house. That is unless the old fat fart, Lampino is here. He either owns or runs this bar. Word on the street is that he's connected to the local mafia. I'm not sure if that's true, but don't want to end up swimming with the fishes," chuckled Peg.

"Thanks for the warning. I noticed quite a few gays hanging out here. Don't guess they throw much business your way?"

"You'd be surprised how many of those bitches swing both ways, but we have learned not to steal each other's tricks. I just learned of Sal Siegel's murder. He was a nice guy, but the way he fucked everyone in here I can see why someone wacked him. I know he was doing Biff, the bartender, here, as well as that lawyer guy that was killed, Schwartz. I wonder where Biff is today? He usually works the 7-3 shift."

Just then a man walked into the bar and came directly up to Peg.

"Unless the pretty lady next to you is paying for your time, shouldn't you be moving along?"

"Tanya, this is my boyfriend, T.J. T.J., this is Tanya, who's new in town. I was just telling her that she needs to find a man for protection if she's going to work these streets."

T.J. broke out in a wide smile as he put his arm around Tatiana's shoulder.

"My pleasure baby. I hope Sunshine had nice things to say about me. If you need a place to stay, or someone to introduce you to the proprietors of the local hotels, I'm your man. It's not safe for someone as pretty as you to be alone in this big city."

T.J. put his hand on Tatiana's knee and was just starting to slide it upward when Bernard Lampino came through the front door with his entourage. Bernard looked around to see what local talent was in the club, which was T.J.'s cue to get out. He took out a piece of paper with his telephone number and carefully placed it in Tatiana's cleavage, spending a little extra time removing his hand.

"Call me tomorrow and I'll make it worth your while."

T.J. exited the bar, followed by Sunshine. He tried not to make eye contact with Bernard.

Tatiana sent a text to Net saying she met T.J. and one of his girls but they had just left. She told him Bernard Lampino was at the bar and asked if she should make contact. Net told her to get out of there and head back to the hotel. One of the agents from the back table walked up to Tatiana and asked for a date. They left the bar together, as Lampino was eyeing her up from the rear.

Lampino began to wonder who the fresh meat was that had been with T.J. He lit a cigarette and took one long drag. No one was about to tell Bernard Lampino that there was no smoking in this bar. Picking up his cell phone, his curiosity soon got the best of him. "Hey T.J., who was that bitch your hand was all over here in the bar."

"Boss, that was my squeeze, Sunshine. You know her," answered T.J.

"No, I mean the other one with the tight ass."

"Never seen her before. Sunshine says her name is Tanya. Seemed to be looking for some action. I gave her my phone number. Asked plenty of questions about crime in the city. Specifically these murders. You interested, Boss?"

"Maybe, just maybe," Lampino thought. "Let me know if she calls you." Lampino seemed intrigued about Tanya but was it a physical attraction or curiosity as to who she might be? He continued to take long drags on his cigarette until he realized that no one had served him a drink. "Hey, what the fuck does it take to get a drink around here," he yelled. "Where's Biff? Shouldn't he be here?"

Biff Holder sat alone in an interrogation room located in the FBI office. Net and Bernstein watched his movements for several minutes through a two-way mirror. He sat and paced back and forth an equal amount of time and at one point even tried the door handle which was locked. The longer they watched him the more agitated he seemed to be. Once they felt they had peaked his stress level, both agents entered the room.

"Mr. Holder, I'm Agent Bernstein and this is Agent J.C. Net. Do you know why you are here?"

"I already know Agent Net," he said with a wink. "And no I don't know why I'm here." His nervousness returned instantly.

"Do you know this man?" Bernstein place a picture of Sal Siegel in front of Holder.

"He looks familiar but I'm a bartender so I see plenty of faces."

"Well, Mr. Siegel was found dead, murdered, at his voodoo shop. A used condom with your DNA was found at the scene on the same night as the murder. Come on Biff, we know you were there."

Biff was either a good actor or was legitimately upset by this news. "Okay. Okay. I had sex with him in the shop after closing but I didn't kill him. I was in love with him."

"Can you tell us exactly what time you were with Sal in his shop? How long have you and Siegel been an item?" asked Net.

"I was there about an hour and a half after he closed at 10 o'clock. We have been together for a few months but we didn't want anyone to know about our relationship. I get better tips if customers think I'm single."

"How did he feel about you?" asked Bernstein.

"I hope the same. Oh my God! Are you sure he's dead? I mean how did it happen?"

"Stabbed in the back. Was there anyone who might have had a problem with this relationship? Any exes of yours or his?" asked Net.

"I haven't been in a relationship for some time before now, at least nothing other than a one-night stand. I don't know about Sal. He really didn't like talking about past relationships."

"Mr. Holder, we appreciate your cooperation and we will probably have more questions in the future. Please do not leave town," demanded Net.

"You mean I'm free to go?" asked Biff. As soon as both agents nodded affirmatively, he wasted no time rushing from the FBI office.

"Unfortunately, there was not enough evidence to hold him. No motive, no murder weapon and the used condom was just not enough," offered Net. "Let's see if we can get Hancock to be more exact with the time of death."

***

Rhonda arrived at the Le Bon Theatre at the time of the auditions. Unfortunately, there were over one hundred people already in line waiting for their chance to become a star. Parts for both male and female actors were available but there were only ten parts to be cast. Rhonda had experience in the theatre but with so many people auditioning it would be hard to get noticed. She felt her best bet was to try and get a preliminary copy of the script and study one particular part that she could perfect. She waited patiently in line until she reached the registration desk. Rhonda completed her paperwork under the name of Beth Randle and as she returned it to the desk, she clumsily tripped and knocked several papers from the desk. As she apologetically retrieved every paper, she returned each one to the desk except a partial copy of the script for the play which she managed to hide under her blouse. She took the paper away from the site, studying the part until she was called to try out. With all the candidates in front of her, it was some time before her cell phone notified her she was next in line. The play director met her at the door and escorted her to the stage for her reading. She was handed a copy of the play and was asked to read for the character Mary, who was an elderly woman who dies in the first scene.

"Oh my, I thought I would be perfect for the part of Brenda. You know I've had plenty of acting experience."

The director was not happy being told what he should do. "Thank you for coming, Ms. Randle. Please call the next candidate please," the director yelled out to a stagehand.

"You mean that's it. You are dismissing me because I made a suggestion?"

"The role of Brenda has already been cast. Next candidate please!" he yelled again.

"That's it? You're not going to give me a chance?" Rhonda blurted.

"Please escort Ms. Randle from the premises." The director motioned to security.

Rhonda exited the theatre to the street, where at least a dozen people were waiting to be called to audition. She started a conversation with a pretty blonde about the same age as Rhonda.

"If you're here to audition for Brenda, don't waste your time. It appears the role was precast."

"Thanks for the heads up, but I'm only auditioning for the chorus. My name is Estelle, but my friends call me Stella. I don't think I've seen you here before. I hope you didn't think you could walk in as a newcomer and land a leading role?"

"I was hoping for at least an audition. I have lots of theatre experience."

"Things might be different where you're from, but in NOLA, Zack White usually has his leading roles selected before he selects the play. Believe me, casting is done on the couch in his office, not on the stage. At least Zack is an equal opportunity creep and will accept service from all genders."

"Then why are you here? You don't look like the type that needs to trade favors for anything."

"I have lots of friends in the theatre and live just two blocks away, in a slave quarter apartment on Decatur Street. I enjoy doing the chorus work, but don't have the ambition for a speaking role. I don't have much of a social life and the men in this town leave a lot to be desired."

"You must live close to the voodoo shop. I'm sure you heard about Sal Siegel being killed three days ago?"

"Sal was a friend of mine. I'm heartbroken about what happened. I was in his shop the day before he was killed. He was all excited about his new love interest. He didn't mention his name, but I assume it was either someone from the theatre or the bar he practically lived at. Sal worked as a female impersonator on weekends at a club on Bourbon. It was a lunch/dinner club that attracted both straight and gay people. Sal, or Honey Moon, did a fantastic impersonation of Barbra Streisand."

"Wow, you seem to be very dialed in with what goes on in the French Quarter," suggested Rhonda.

"Well, not really. I enjoy the theatre as a hobby and I usually land a small part either in the chorus or as an extra. They all know me so I'm an easy choice because they know what I'm capable of doing. Outside of the theatre I don't run in their circles. I'm not gay. I tell you what. I've done these plays so many times if they really need me they will call. I'm hungry. How about we grab something to eat? I'm sorry but I don't even know your name."

Rhonda paused before she answered. "Umm. Beth, Beth Randle."

"Well okay Beth, let's try this place over here. I haven't eaten here before but I heard it's very good." The ladies glimpsed at the sign that read, "The Sandwich Bag".

There was a good crowd inside as the overflow from the theatre tryout was significant. No seats were immediately available so there would be a several minute wait.

"I heard they make a great shrimp po-boy here, or if you're not into seafood I'd recommend the roast beef debris sandwich, which is what I'm having," suggested Stella. "Why don't you grab us a table and I'll get us the food?"

"Sounds great. Just order me whatever you're having," said Rhonda.

After they were seated and started lunch, Rhonda began to delve into Stella's background.

"How long have you been in the city? I don't detect much of a New Orleans accent."

"I was born in the south, but lived in several states. My dad was in the service so we never stayed in one place long enough to pick up the dialect. What about you? I don't hear a drop of southern in your voice?"

"I was born in the Boston area and haven't ventured very far away from home until now. My fiancé has some business here so we plan to be in New Orleans for a while so I was looking for something to occupy my time. Some people say that New Orleanians speak with a northeast accent, but with a southern drawl. I have had roast beef sandwiches before, but never like this!"

"It's the bread," stated Stella. I've been told it has something to do with the water in the city that makes the French bread so good. I've also learned to order it 'dressed', which means fully loaded with lettuce and tomatoes."

"Well, you've made a believer out of me. Now tell me what are your thoughts on all the murders going on in this area? Living on Decatur Street doesn't make you a little nervous to venture out alone at night?"

"All of the victims have been Johns, hookers, and a few gays. I really don't fit into that profile. I have a few suspicions of who could be doing this, but snitches get stitches, or a lot worse."

"Well, just between us girls, I'm interested in your theory."

"You ask a lot of questions," frowned Stella.

"I guess I'm just a curious person. It fascinates me. My boyfriend has always told me that I have the mind of a detective." Rhonda began to laugh. "He also tells me curiosity killed the cat." The laughing continued.

"Say, I have an idea. There's a little clothing shop in the Garden District of New Orleans I've wanted to go to. How about it?"

Rhonda wanted to question Stella more but felt she may become suspicious so she decided to go along with the idea. "That sounds like fun." The two ladies hadn't quite finished their lunch. "Stella, what do you do? What type of work are you in?"

"I work mostly temporary jobs. Mostly clerical. My parents are both deceased and I inherited a fair amount of life insurance money from each of them."

"Besides part-time detective, what do you do Beth?"

Rhonda was uncomfortable with the question but she was quick on her feet to think of answer. "My boyfriend is really the bread winner. He makes enough that I haven't needed to work. He's in the financial banking business but don't ask me any questions about that because I wouldn't have a clue," Rhonda laughed nervously.

The two boarded a streetcar at the intersection of St. Charles Ave. and Canal St. heading in the direction of uptown New Orleans. As the streetcar rolled along the scenery turned from commercial to a more residential area with beautiful homes. Mansions really.

"I never get tired of looking at the beautiful homes on St. Charles Avenue. I know of a few boutique shops at the end of the streetcar line, close to the university and park," offered Stella.

Rhonda was enjoying the ride and looking at the beautiful homes, one bigger and grander than the next. "It's hard to believe that only one family lives in some of these majestic homes." Rhonda gazed out of the window as they passed the home of Rodney and Charlotte Park.

"You'd be surprised as to what goes on behind some of those beautiful doors," offered Stella. "I know of a few men personally that live in their ivory tower, but come into the quarter every Saturday night to sow their wild oats. Then you'll find them at the cathedral on Sunday morning praying for a crop failure."

Rhonda wanted to ask more, but they exited the streetcar and walked just a few steps to the boutique.

The dresses and apparel were comparable to those found in New York and the ladies spent little time loading up the dressing rooms with their finds. Both women had spectacular figures, so everything they tried on looked great. Rhonda thought to herself, *I'm going to be in a lot of trouble when the bill for this comes in.* To soften the shock of the credit card statement, she purchased a naughty nighty with J.C. in mind.

They left the store and headed back towards the business district. As much as Rhonda wanted to question her about the men she knew from St. Charles Avenue, she decided to wait to avoid suspicion. Rhonda got off the streetcar on St. Charles and Poydras Street, which was just a two-block walk to the hotel. She asked Stella to join her at the hotel bar for cocktails later in the evening. Stella agreed to meet her at the Cabaret Lounge for 8:00 p.m.

***

Rhonda walked into the hotel lobby and was immediately greeted by Net.

"I was just picking up my phone to call you. There has been another murder and it was one of our suspects, Bernard Lampino."

CHAPTER 9

Bada Bing Bada Boom

Bernard Lampino had just left the Joker's Wild bar and headed for one of his goombahs (Steve Colombo) residence in the French Quarter. Usually, he never traveled anywhere without his bodyguard, Lorenzo. Today was different. He had given Lorenzo special instructions to take care of some "family business" while he established his alibi for whatever Lorenzo had been ordered to do. Bernard summoned a rideshare service as he didn't like walking by himself. The car pulled in front of Steve Colombo's dwelling. The rideshare driver sped off as soon as Lampino exited the car. Lampino was an easily recognizable face in the French Quarter so the driver didn't want to linger longer then he needed.

As Lampino reached the stoop of Colombo's residence a person dressed in a dark-hooded outfit jumped from between cars and placed a knife against his throat. Without saying a word, the stranger wasted no time in slicing Lampino's neck from ear to ear. The wound left a large enough gap causing his immediate collapse to the ground with instant death. Blood forcefully squirted from the wound, quickly trickling down each step until it reached the sidewalk. The wound was so deep it wasn't long before he bled out.

The culprit disappeared as fast as he struck and because of the attire it was impossible to determine if the killer was a male or female. Lampino's body lay stretched across the front steps of Colombo's home.

The area was extremely quiet and no one had witnessed this event. Lampino's body lay outside of Colombo's house for hours before a black four-door sedan with tinted windows stopped in the middle of the street. Out jumped a large muscular man who rushed to the side of the victim.

"Boss. Boss, you okay?" yelled the hulk of a man as he reached Lampino. There was no answer and the man immediately realized that he was too late to save his boss. Lorenzo Russo had been a devoted employee of Bernard Lampino for many years. It had been his task to keep Lampino safe but this one time he was assigned another duty, his boss was killed.

Lorenzo kneeled next to his boss and friend in disbelief. After moments of reflection, he banged on Colombo's front door. He continued to knock at the door with the side of his fist but there was no answer. As he contemplated his next move, a police car suddenly pulled behind his auto which was parked in the middle of the street. Flashing lights from the top of the police car were blinding but they arrived with no siren blaring. Two policemen emerged from the car surveying the scene. One checked Lampino's pulse and immediately called for detectives and forensics.

"Can you tell me what happened here?" asked the other officer.

"I don't know. I pulled up and found him like this," Lorenzo offered.

"Tell me your name," asked the officer.

"My name?" There was a hesitation on Lorenzo's part. "My name is Lorenzo Russo. This is my employer."

One officer slightly turned the body to get a good look at his face. "Jack, you need to take a look at this," said the officer.

The two policemen immediately recognized the victim and decided it would be best to let the detectives handle this situation. More police arrived, as well as the assistant coroner, Jennifer Davison. Net and Rhonda finally made their way to the scene just before Deputy Chief Rodney Park arrived. Rhonda began her interrogation of Lorenzo Russo while Net worked with the forensics team.

Russo told Rhonda exactly what he had seen, which wasn't much. He became a little nervous when questioned about his relationship with Bernard Lampino. "I'm head of security for Mr. Lampino. Bernard was a powerful man. Plenty out there would want to see him fail."

"So you're saying the list of suspects could be very long," commented Rhonda.

"Yea, I suppose so."

"Anybody stand out in your mind who might have done this?" asked Rhonda.

Lorenzo shrugged his shoulders as if he wouldn't know. Truth is, he wouldn't tell the cops even if he did know. This situation would be taken care of by the family.

Rodney viewed the body alongside J.C. Net. He did his best to hold back his joy in seeing the dead body of Bernard Lampino. His hatred for him was shared by the smile on his face. Net was concerned that his friend's attitude would be misconstrued by the media that was on hand.

"Rhonda, get Rodney out of here," Net demanded. "Take Rodney's car so I can have the car to meet you later."

Rhonda escorted Rodney back to Park's car and got in the passenger's seat. As they headed towards police headquarters Rodney saw the look of concern in Rhonda's face.

"I know what you're thinking Rhonda, especially after my outburst when Lampino was in our office. I swear I didn't lay a finger on him, even though I'm glad someone took him out. Lampino was part of the Italian connection in the quarter and his list of enemies isn't short."

Rhonda was trying to send a text to Tatiana, when her phone slipped out of her hand. She bent over to retrieve it from the floor and noticed some blood on the carpet. She felt around under the seat, pretending to be searching for a phone, when she felt a sharp object.

When they reached police headquarters Rhonda told Park she needed to call Tatiana and would meet him in his office. Rhonda waited until Rodney went through the front door of headquarters and turned on the flashlight on her phone. Her jaw dropped as she noticed the knife with fresh blood under the passenger's seat. Not wanting to disturb anything, she quickly called Net.

"JC, I just found something in Rodney's car and it doesn't look good for him. It's a knife with fresh blood and was under the passenger's seat. I think we need to bring this to FBI headquarters rather than police headquarters, given the circumstances."

"Bag it and bring it in. It must be a set up. I can't believe that Rodney would be so stupid as to keep a bloody weapon under the seat of his car. Lots of people witnessed Rodney's outburst, so if Rodney had any enemies this was a perfect opportunity to frame him. I'm just about finished here. The coroner's office is about to take the body away, so I'll meet you shortly."

Net turned to Jennifer Davison and asked if he was needed any longer because something had come up at the FBI office.

"I'm ready to bag and carry this guy. Are you sure you don't want to meet me back at the coroner's office to watch the autopsy? You sure would make better company than Hancock."

J.C. was flattered by the attention, but knew his immediate concern was finding the source of the weapon found in Park's car.

**

When J.C. arrived at the FBI office Rhonda was waiting in the conference room. "I'm glad you made it. I was holding off turning the knife in until you arrived."

J.C. took the evidence bag from Rhonda's hand just as his cell phone rang. "J.C., this is Rodney. I don't know what happened to Rhonda, but she never came into our office."

"Rodney, something came up and she had to meet me back at the FBI office. The coroner's office took Lampino's body back to autopsy. As soon as I hear anything I'll get back to you." Net hung up the phone and turned to Rhonda.

"I've had second thoughts about having the FBI run analysis on this knife. I'd like to keep this quiet for now. Hold on for a minute." Net picked up his cellphone and started dialing a number.

"Do you know who this is?" Net said shyly. "Yep, it's me and it has been a long time. I'm actually in New Orleans right now helping the local police on a case. We need to catch up but right now I need a huge favor."

The person on the other end of the conversation was his old friend, Emily Livingston, from when he worked for the Louisiana State Police. Emily was the technical analyst at the main state police headquarters in Baton Rouge but over the years she had developed many connections with various agencies throughout the state of Louisiana. "Of course, I will do whatever you need if I can. All you have to do is ask."

"I've got a bloody knife which may or may not have been used in a crime. I need the knife tested for prints and DNA. I need to find out if it's human blood and if so, whose blood is it. Can you get that done for me?"

"Absolutely. Get that knife to me and I should have your answer in a couple of days."

"Hate to ask but can you run this and have results ready as soon as possible? If this wasn't really important I wouldn't ask."

Emily looked at the clock on the wall. "I'll finish up what I'm working on now and devote my day to getting this done for you."

"Ok, I'm sending it with my assistant, Tatiana Sokolov. She works with me in the Boston office. Just in case the knife has discernible evidence, we want to preserve the chain of custody. I'll have her drive it to Baton Rouge first thing in the morning. I can't thank you enough for doing this."

"It's no problem J.C. We all miss you here and when you finish whatever you're involved with please come and see us."

"I will. Gotta go right now but I will be in touch."

"Is that an ex-girlfriend?" questioned Rhonda.

"Friend, yes. Girlfriend, no. She and I worked together for quite some time. By the way, what happened at the Le Bon Theatre? Did you get the part?"

"No! There was some asshole director who wouldn't even let me audition. He had some kind of chip on his shoulder."

"It wasn't Zack White was it?" asked Net.

"No. That wasn't his name but I don't really remember it. I did meet this nice lady though. She's been around the theatre for a long time so she may know things. I wanted to gain her confidence so I had lunch with her and then she took me to a clothing store in the Garden District of the city. I know you've seen it many times but it is really a beautiful area. And yes, I bought an outfit just for you," Rhonda smiled.

"Oh boy. Looking forward to it. Let me see if I can get Zack White to hire you in some capacity at the theatre. What was the name of your new friend? I'll check her out with Zack."

"She said her name is Estelle but people call her Stella. Really nice lady." Rhonda stood still momentarily staring into space.

"Anything wrong?" asked Net.

"Oh. No," she answered shaking her head. "The time we spend together, well it was almost like she knew me. It's nothing. I guess it's true. Southerners are very friendly."

"Tatty, please take this to the Louisiana State Police office in Baton Rouge first thing in the morning. Be sure to have Emily Livingston sign for the package, so we will have a record of its whereabouts during the entire process. I know you're unfamiliar with this area, so feel free to have an agent with the New Orleans FBI office drive you, but don't go into any details on what you are carrying. If Saul Bernstein gives you any trouble with this, tell him to see me."

"Why can't I tell Saul Bernstein what this is for?" asked Tatiana. "What is this?"

"I'll explain later. If you don't know, you can't tell him. You're better off not knowing."

Rhonda took J.C. by the arm. "What do you say we take the night off and have a nice dinner and relax? Maybe I'll wear my new outfit for you later," Rhonda mentioned with a smile.

"Let's do it!" exclaimed Net. "Why don't you head back to the hotel and do whatever you need to do. I want to stop by the Le Bon Theatre and see Zack White again."

"See you back at the hotel in a little while," Rhonda confirmed.

***

J.C. returned to the little theatre where a dress rehearsal for an upcoming play was taking place. Zack White was right in the middle of all the action, instructing each and every actor what they were doing wrong. White noticed Net standing at the rear of the theatre. He did not like visitors surveying any performance before it was ready for production. "Detective Net, are you here for a reason?" White inquired as he suspended the performance.

"Yes, Mr. White, I'd like to talk with you again." Net showed White a picture of Bernard Lampino. "Do you know this guy?"

"Everyone knows him. He's a regular patron of the theatre. Doesn't miss a show. Personally the guy scares me. He shows up with his bodyguards and expects me to seat them in the best seats despite not having a prior reservation."

"That won't be a problem from now on. Someone killed him today."

"Bernard Lampino?" White seemed legitimately surprised. "Wow! I wouldn't want to be that guy!"

"Why not? Seems he was a pain in your ass. Exactly, where were you earlier today."

"You consider me a suspect?" asked White. "You're joking aren't you? I didn't like the guy but I wouldn't kill him. I'm not stupid."

"So where were you?" Net asked again.

"I was here. Where else would I be? I have a play opening in a couple of days. I practically live here."

"Can anyone confirm that?" asked Net.

"I was in my office reviewing the script. No one is here as early as me. Anyone brave enough to kill the Great Italian will eventually pay the consequences. There will be retaliation from his goombahs. So who got him? The Mexican Cartel?"

"What's their connection?" asked Net.

"Rival gang," answered White. "The whops and the spics have been jockeying for first position in the drug and prostitution trade."

"Are you the only director working out of this theatre?"

"No. The play I'm directing, Quarter Fever, will have its opening night next Saturday. Chris Nelson, the other director, is just starting to cast his play. While my show will have performances Thursday through Saturday, Chris will be holding rehearsals Sunday through Wednesday. We handle it that way so that the building will have someone using it nightly. Gotta pay the rent on this place and French Quarter rent ain't cheap. Why do you ask? If you're looking to begin a new career I'm sure Chris would love to see you in action."

"My acting ability leaves a lot to be desired, but a friend of Estelle, one of your theatre regulars, tried to audition for Chris but was turned away. Apparently he pre-casts all his plays."

"I'm not aware of anyone called Estelle ever being in any of my plays and Chris and I basically use the same cast."

"I think she goes by the name Stella."

"Never heard of an Estelle or Stella in this theatre. If you know of anyone that is interested in backstage work we could sure use the help. The pay isn't very much, but we're willing to train for free. If you run into this Estelle, or Stella, please pass the word that we are desperate for help. The problem I'm having is that everyone thinks they're a star and too good for the grunt work. A play cannot open without a behind the scene cast."

Net felt he had as much information he could get from Zack White so he returned to his hotel in anticipation of spending a romantic evening with Rhonda.

***

When he arrived, Rhonda greeted him at the door but not dressed as he expected. She wore a new cocktail dress that Net had never seen before.

"I'm so sorry but I totally forgot I made arrangements to meet Stella at the bar downstairs at 8:00 pm. I know you're disappointed." She could see it written all over his face.

"I need to tell you something. I asked Zack White about your friend Stella and he said he never heard of her. I got the impression that no one works at that theatre without Zack White knowing them."

"Well, that's interesting," Rhonda responded.

"I think I will join the two of you tonight. She doesn't need to know we are FBI. Maybe we can indirectly question her to see what she knows."

8:00 pm was fast approaching and Rhonda and Net were both anxious to meet Stella. They arrived in the bar about ten minutes early to secure a comfortable table and ordered a glass of red wine while they waited. Their conversation was centered around the questions they wanted to ask their guest without arousing suspicion. The first glass of wine went down very slowly and it was well past the hour before they noticed.

Just outside the lounge door, Stella peeked in and saw the two agents waiting. She stared for a few seconds, but then rushed away.

CHAPTER 10

Runaround Sue

Stella was gone as quickly as she arrived. Her behavior was odd as she seemed to relish the opportunity to spend more time with Rhonda but when she saw Net seated with her, she vanished. The two agents were enjoying their second cocktail when J.C. glanced at his watch. "It's half past the hour and there's been no sign of your friend," he observed. "Let's call it a night and go up to our room. I'm still waiting to see the 'special' outfit you have me thinking about all day."

"That sounds like a plan, just let me finish my wine."

"I'm going to make a trip to the men's room, so take your time. If the waitress comes by ask for our check."

Net got up from the table and headed to the restroom. The cocktail waitress came over and asked if Net would like a refill on his wine. Rhonda said, "Just bring our check please."

The waitress had their bill on her tray and left it on the table. Rhonda looked towards the bathroom door, but didn't see Net. She noticed his wallet and phone case were on the table. Opening his wallet in search of his credit card, she noticed the edge of a worn photograph sticking out from one compartment. Curiosity got the better of her as she pulled out the photograph. Her mouth dropped open and all the color ran from her face.

It was obvious that the photo wasn't recent and the hair color was different, but there was no denying the person in the picture was Stella. Rhonda put Net's credit card on the tray, just as Net returned from the men's room.

"You ready to go up to our room now that I've plied you with wine?" Net laughed.

"Are you sure you want to go to the room with me?" Rhonda took the picture and threw it in front of Net. "I thought you didn't know Stella. If that's the case, how did her picture end up in your wallet?"

J.C.'s face turned red. He didn't know how to answer. He wasn't expecting Rhonda to find that picture. In his wildest imagination he wouldn't have thought the picture of a previous love interest would be Stella.

"I know we are supposedly engaged, but I would really appreciate a separate room. If nothing is available, I will see if I can bunk with Tatiana," Rhonda huffed.

Net looked at the picture in disbelief. "Are you sure the woman in this picture is Stella? I can explain, but this is not the place. Please, let's take this upstairs and I'll tell you about the woman in this picture. Her name is not Stella."

Rhonda reluctantly accompanied him to their room. The elevator ride was very reticent. Not one word was spoken. Rhonda made sure she stood away from Net on the opposite side. Her arms were folded tightly around her midriff. When they arrived at their room she was the first to use her card to open the door. She entered first, allowing the door to hit J.C. in the side as she refused to hold the door until he entered.

"Start explaining," she commanded.

"I'm in shock just as much as you that this picture is your friend Stella. Her name is not Stella. Her real name is Sabrina Keister. I knew her as Susan Griffin."

"Yeah. Okay. And I'm the Easter Bunny," Rhonda declared sarcastically. "Sounds like this is going to be a tall tale."

"Come on. Let me finish. I'm not going to lie to you. This is the truth. I was working for the Louisiana State Police investigating murders in a small town named Keister. I met a reporter named Susan Griffin or so I thought. She aided me in my investigation."

"Did you all have a thing?" Rhonda interrupted. "Why would you have a picture in your wallet?"

"I told you I'm not going to lie to you. I was in love with her and her with me. I thought she was the love of my life."

Rhonda's whole body slumped into the chair where she was seated. Tears began to form but the look on her face was that of heartbreak and anger.

Net continued. "But I was wrong. All the while she was helping me, she hid a dark secret. Her last name was Keister. She planned and committed some of the very murders I was trying to solve. She had a partner and when we arrested him we thought the case was closed. It wasn't until she was long gone before I realized she was just as guilty. I keep her picture, not because of my love for her, but I want to be reminded that I still need to arrest her. This case will haunt me until she is apprehended."

"So you're not in love with her?" asked Rhonda with tears now rolling down her cheeks.

"Absolutely not!" demanded Net. "You are my love. The love of my life. There is no question about that. I want to spend the rest of my life with you."

"Why would she befriend me? Does she know who I am?"

"That's a good question," answered Net. "All I know is this gives me the opportunity to finally end this. She must have seen me in the lounge and decided not to come in. Do you have any idea of how to contact her? A phone number? Where she lives? Anything?"

"No. I don't." Rhonda was unsure how to react to this news. "Why didn't you tell me about her before now?"

"I don't know. I should have. I'm sorry. I guess I was afraid what you would think. I was afraid you would think I was on the rebound."

"Is that what I am?"

"Absolutely not! I will love you forever." At that moment he reached out with both hands to grasp her shoulders as she quickly moved away.

"I'm not sure how I feel about all of this. I wish you had told me long before now. I think for tonight it's best if I stay the night with Tatiana."

There was nothing more for Net to say. He sat on the edge of the bed with his head hanging in disappointment. Rhonda gathered her immediate essentials such as a nightshirt, toothpaste, toothbrush, and clothes for the next day. The nighty that she planned to wear, she tossed into her suitcase which was still open in the corner of the room. She slowly made her way towards the door hesitating before opening the door. J.C. waited for her to say anything but she slipped into the hall closing the door behind her. She tapped lightly on Tatiana's door until she answered.

Tatiana was already in her nightgown ready for bed. She looked at Rhonda and immediately realized something was wrong. "Oh no. What happened?" she asked as she looked at the contents of the bag Rhonda was carrying.

"Do you mind if I spend the night here?" asked Rhonda.

"You don't even have to ask. But what's happened?" She obviously suspected that she and Net had an argument.

"I really don't care to talk about it," Rhonda countered. "I'd like to just lie down and go to sleep."

94

"Not a problem. If you want to talk, I'm here for you." There was total silence in the room for several minutes and Tatiana had almost fallen asleep.

"Have you ever had a man confess to you that someone else was the love of his life?" Rhonda suddenly broke the silence.

"Oh my dear! Is that what he did to you? Is he having an affair? Oh, you poor thing. What a bastard!" There were additional moments of silence. "Wait a minute! We're talking about J.C. Net. No way! That man is totally in love with you. I see the way he looks at you. The way he treats you. No possible way he would step out on you. What did he tell you?"

Rhonda had not been able to get a word in while Tatiana rambled on. "I didn't say he cheated on me," Rhonda interrupted. "When he worked for the state police in Louisiana he fell for another girl. He was in love with her. Now it appears she is here in New Orleans."

"Did he say he wanted to meet up with her?" asked Tatiana.

"Well, not really. As a matter of fact he wants to arrest her for murder."

"Wait, what? Let me get this straight. A girl he loved before he met you committed a murder that she's wanted for and he wants to put her in jail. You are mad at him for this? What the hell are you doing here? You better not let that man get away."

"Well, he didn't tell me about her before."

"So you want his entire life story before you marry him? As long as he loves you and you alone, that's all you need to know. You want a list of every girlfriend he's had?"

"Well, no. He did tell me he loves me."

"Don't need to say anymore. Go to sleep and I would suggest you go strip him naked first thing in the morning," commanded Tatiana.

***

Net sat restless on the edge of the bed. Every few minutes he stood and paced through the room. He couldn't sleep. He didn't even try. Finally, he entered the hallway and stopped in front of Tatiana's room. He thought about knocking on the door but by now it was in the early hours of the morning. The French Quarter rarely closes so he decided to take a walk to Bourbon Street. A few die-hards remained on the street but the area was unusually quiet. Some of the clubs were still rocking with music, mostly jazz but some hip-hop. He looked for a quiet place. Somewhere he could sit and think. There was a small bar he was passing that looked like the ideal place. As he entered, the bartender advised that they would close in about fifteen minutes. That was perfect for him to have a drink and walk back to his hotel. No other patrons besides him were in this place. The cleaning crew had already started tidying up to prepare for tomorrow.

"What can I get you?" asked the bartender.

"Whiskey, neat." Net thought in fifteen minutes he could do some damage to his sobriety.

"Here you go, man," said the bartender as he handed him his drink. "What brings you in here this late?"

"Just looking for a quiet place to get a little drunk."

"Can't say I've seen you before. You a local?" asked the bartender.

"Not really. I'm here on business"

The bartender could tell he didn't want to talk. "Another one?" he asked pointing to Net's empty glass. Net slid his glass forward to be refilled. It wasn't long before the second glass was empty. The bartender said it was last call and asked if Net wanted a go-cup. Net laughed to himself, remembering he was in New Orleans, where it's perfectly normal to walk down the street carrying a drink. Since he was about eight blocks from his hotel, he ordered a whiskey for the walk.

When he exited the bar he could feel the warm humid air hit him and the whiskey was starting to kick in. He headed back towards his hotel, determined to get there before the sun came up and the business district was full of people on their way to work. Net turned onto a side street which he figured would cut a good five minutes off his walk. Being an FBI agent and familiar with New Orleans, he knew if he was totally sober he wouldn't have turned onto such a dissolute street.

No sooner did the thought enter his brain, he felt a hard blow to the back of his head. He tried to turn around to confront his attacker, when a second blow sent him crashing into the gutter. He was drifting in and out of consciousness and all he could feel was agonizing pain and the taste of his own blood running from his head into his mouth. The blows continued and he was kicked repeatedly in the chest and stomach, until everything went dark.

***

The sun came up and a local store owner was on his way to open his antique shop when he saw the lifeless body in the gutter. He quickly called 911 and bent down to check for a pulse. He could hear a faint moan coming from the man, but from the amount of blood in the street and the wounds on his head he knew that his injuries were significant. The police and ambulance arrived at the same time. The paramedics checked for a pulse and immediately put him on a stretcher with a soft collar around his neck. The police informed the medic that his wallet was missing, so there was no way to identify the victim.

"Take him to Charity Medical Center" the officer told the medic. "I'll have a detective meet him there. Judging from his injuries they're probably not going to get much from him."

The medic responded, "I'm not sure he will even make it to the hospital. He's lost a lot of blood and I can see cranial matter from the gash in the back of his head."

The ambulance headed for the medical center with lights flashing and sirens blasting. They arrived and immediately brought Net into the emergency room. The doctor took one look at Net and ordered several pints of O negative blood and rushed him into surgery.

CHAPTER 11

A Dick for a Dick!

Rhonda slept very little overnight. That was not a problem for Tatiana as her snoring was loud enough to keep Rhonda awake. Rhonda moved about the room but she was anxious to see J.C. She gently knocked on the door, assuming he was still sleeping. Getting no answer, she used her key and entered the room. Net was nowhere to be found, but the sheets were disturbed, indicating at some point he was in the bed. "Guess he left for work without me," she whispered to herself. She looked at herself in the mirror and decided that she needed a shower very badly. Stripping down to wash her hair and body she entered the walk-in shower and was enjoying its warmth when she heard a knock on the hotel room door. Hurriedly she wrapped herself in a bath towel and rushed to the door hoping that Net had forgotten his key.

Tatiana stood before her inquisitive about what had happened since Rhonda had left her hotel room. "What's going on?" she asked anxiously.

"Net wasn't here. I guess he left early to go to police headquarters. I was just finishing my shower and about to call him. If you want to get dressed, maybe we can share a cab together."

"That sounds good. Give me about 20 minutes to dress."

Detectives Colin Kennedy and Mike Smith were assigned to the victim assaulted in the French Quarter. They arrived at the hospital and immediately went to the intensive care unit.

"Dr. Jackson? My name is Detective Colin Kennedy and this is Detective Mike Smith with the New Orleans Police Department. We are here about the John Doe found assaulted in the quarter. How is his condition and when do you think we can talk to him?"

"He is one lucky guy. When he arrived I thought for sure he wasn't going to make it. The wounds on his head were deep, but we were able to close him up with staples. I don't anticipate any permanent damage. We gave him three pints of blood and he did sustain two broken ribs and significant bruising over most of his body. He will need to stay here a few days for observation, but all in all he probably can be released by Friday. We still have no clue to his identity, but he has been calling out a name that sounds like Rhonda. He has been in and out of consciousness and has been given some strong pain medication, so I'm not sure he will be able to tell you much."

"Thanks Doc, we won't stay long. It's important for us to speak with him sooner than later, while his memory is fresh," advised Detective Kennedy.

Both detectives went into the intensive care unit and drew back the curtain. Even with the bruises on his face and the bandages wrapped around his head, it was obvious to the detectives that the man in the bed was FBI Agent, J.C. Net.

"I'll call Chief Park. I'm sure he wants to be informed and take part in this interview," commented Detective Smith. Both detectives left the room to make the call to the Deputy Chief.

Net's room was quiet except for the constant beeping of the medical equipment attached to him. His door was opened slightly as someone peeked into his room. Susan Griffin, Sabrina Keister or Stella, whichever name she was entertaining today, quietly entered the room. Almost simultaneously with her entrance, Net's eyes opened wide. He smiled as she approached his bed and she immediately kissed his lips passionately. She began to climb into the bed next to him when he suddenly screamed out and sat straight up in bed. Susan was not there and no sign that she had been there. Two nurses, hearing his scream, rushed into his room finding him awake and alert.

"Was anyone in here with me just now?" he asked.

"No, no one," said one of the nurses. "There is a policeman just outside your door so no one could enter without him knowing. I'll check with him but we didn't see anyone."

Realizing it must have been a dream, Net started to relax. He lay back into his bed but asked the nurse for his clothes.

"You don't think you are going anywhere, do you?" she stated. "While your injuries weren't life-threatening if you don't rest and let your wounds heal you could make them critical."

"I've got work to do. I'll be careful. I won't do anything physical."

"I'll let the doctor know you want to leave and let's see what he says." The nurse poked her head out the door and had a brief conversation with the officer nearby. "No one has been in your room between the time the doctor was here and we came in. Oh look, you have a visitor."

It was at that moment Rodney Park entered. "What happened, man?" asked the Deputy Chief of Police.

"Don't remember much. Someone came up behind me, hit me over the head and evidently stole my wallet, identification, and gun. Anybody contact Rhonda?"

Before those last words were out of his mouth, Rhonda rushed through the door with Tatiana at her side. "Oh my God!" she yelled as she quickly made her way to his side. The perspective of the numerous medical devices operating in the room in addition to the bandages covering his head was enough to alarm Rhonda. "Are you okay?"

"The doctor says I'm fine." Net flinched in pain as he thought Rhonda was about to crawl in his bed. The painkiller he had been given had started to wear off and any movement sent shooting pain to his rib area.

"Obviously, you're not. Where is the doctor? I want to talk with him myself."

"I'm okay," Net reassured her. "I've got a couple of broken ribs and just needed the doc to close some wounds on my head. I'm ready to get back to work." Just as he said that a sharp stabbing feeling crossed his chest. "Okay, maybe not right this minute but soon."

"Let's give these two a little time alone," Rodney suggested to Tatiana. "Come on. I'll buy you a cup of coffee."

"What were you doing out so late at night?" Rhonda asked.

"Couldn't sleep so I decided to get some air but I ended up at a little bar where I had a couple of drinks. I was walking back to the hotel and I took a route I probably shouldn't have and I guess it was a mugging. My badge and gun were taken so we need to notify the bureau of the incident."

"I love you so much," Rhonda stated. "I guess I didn't handle the situation very well. I just couldn't imagine you being in love with anyone but me."

"Not only that," Net began, "this was long before I knew you. Believe me there is no one else for me but you." Net was in obvious pain as he talked.

"I'm going to let you get some rest," Rhonda offered. "I'll be back later.

Rodney and Tatiana sat in the busy hospital cafeteria. Rodney grabbed a cup of black coffee while Tatiana sipped on her favorite, an ice-cold diet soda. "Before joining the New Orleans police force, weren't you a deputy in Keister, La.?" asked Tatiana.

"Yes. I was born and raised in Keister."

"So you worked with Net while he was with the State Police?"

"Yep." Rodney nodded affirmatively.

"So you were there when Net was with this Susan Griffin? What's the story with her?" she inquired.

"Oh yes. They were a hot commodity. I did my best to get her interested in me but she only had eyes for J.C. I guess I ended up being the lucky one since she turned out to be a murderer. That crushed Net but he seems happy now with Rhonda. I know he feels like he won't have closure until she is finally arrested and prosecuted. How do you know about Susan?"

"J.C. told Rhonda about her last night. Seems there were some hard feelings and Rhonda slept in my room last night."

"That explains what Net was doing by himself in an area where he shouldn't have been." Just at that moment, Rodney's phone rang simultaneously with Tatiana's phone. He answered recognizing it originated from his home phone. "Well, where is she? Never came home all night? I'll be there in a few minutes."

Tatiana answered her phone despite not recognizing the phone number. "This is Tatiana."

"Tatiana, this is Emily Livingston. I tried calling J.C.'s phone but there was no answer. I have the results of the lab tests on that knife you asked us to analyze on a confidential basis. I'm texting it to your phone." Her phone beeped denoting the receipt of the text message. Tatiana clicked on the message and scrolled to the DNA match that was listed at the end of the report. The blood seemed to drain from her face as she turned pale, almost ghostlike. She jumped from her chair and raced out of the door arriving quickly at Net's room.

His eyes were closed, so Tatiana did not want to disturb his rest. She sat patiently for some time before thinking of calling Rhonda with the DNA news. She began to dial her phone but thought better of it. "No. Net needs to see this first," she mumbled loud enough that Net began to stir. His eyes opened slightly.

"Net, it's me, Tatiana. Can you hear me? I don't want to disturb you, but I just got a text from Emily Livingston. She sent me the report on the knife you sent her. The DNA matches Bernard Lampino and prints on the handle matched Rodney Park. I need to know if I should send this report to anyone, or do you want to handle it?"

Net moaned a little, then opened his eyes. "That can't be! Rodney Park is not a murderer. Please keep this under wraps until I'm well enough to speak with Emily. Rhonda went back to the hotel to get me some clothes. I need to get out of this hospital and get to the bottom of who's framing Rodney."

Rhonda fought back tears as she went back to the hotel. She blamed herself for Net's injuries. "If only I hadn't acted like a jealous schoolgirl, J.C. would have been in bed with me and not in the quarter." She hurriedly threw clothes in a bag and rushed back to the hospital.

Net was sitting on the edge of the bed, waiting for Rhonda to return with his clothes when the doctor entered.

"What do you think you're doing Mr. Net? Your injuries were not insignificant. I advise that you stay with us at least one more night."

"Sorry doc. I'll take it as easy as I can, but I have a killer to catch before he or she strikes again. Can't do that from a hospital bed."

"I'll have them draw up your discharge papers, but it will be noted that you are leaving against my orders. I'm not comfortable prescribing pain medication, since I know you won't be remaining in bed."

"I can handle the pain, just sign the papers and let me be on my way."

Rhonda came through the door, carrying a set of clothes for Net. He slowly raised himself off the bed and proceeded to dress.

"J.C., I'm so sorry this happened to you. It was all my fault."

"Rhonda, I love you and you have no reason to be jealous of Stella, Susan, or whatever name she's going by now. That was in the past and the only reason I'm interested in her is to bring her sorry ass to justice. Please don't blame yourself for my injuries. I was just in the wrong place at the right time." Dressed and walking towards the exit, Net stopped and held his head in his hands.

"Are you okay?" asked Rhonda.

"Just slightly dizzy from the medication and being in that bed."

"That blow you took to the back of your head doesn't help either," Rhonda offered. "Are you sure you don't want to stay another day?"

It was at that moment Rodney walked up. Seeing his buddy was struggling to get about, he took his arm and helped him along. "I wish you would let my crew handle this case until you are feeling better." Rodney knew there was no use continuing to persuade Net.

"I don't need that," Net snapped at the nurse pushing a wheelchair by him.

"Sir, it's hospital policy that anyone be escorted out in a wheelchair until they reach their car," demanded the nurse.

"I apologize," Net responded as he sat in the chair. He didn't have far to travel as an FBI vehicle was awaiting him by the front door of the hospital. He was in obvious pain in his rib area. His face was battered and bruised and bandages circled the top of his head, yet he told the agent driving to take him to FBI headquarters.

The only one not surprised to see Net enter the office was Tatiana. She knew there was no keeping him down. "Not surprised," Tatiana stated helping to escort him to a chair.

"Take me to the conference room where I can use the telephone," he asked Tatiana. Rhonda followed the two of them until they reached the room as she assisted in helping Net settle in. "Now if both of you can give me some privacy while I do some work."

Tatiana expected this request but Rhonda did not. She appeared surprised as well as disheartened by his demand. "I guess he's still upset with me," Rhonda suggested.

"I don't think that's it, *medovyy*."

Emily Livingston was shocked to hear Net's voice on the phone. "How are you? I was told you were beaten pretty badly."

"Yeah, yeah. That's what they say. I'm okay and back at work. Tatiana told me your findings. Are you absolutely sure?"

"One-hundred percent," answered Emily. The blood was a perfect match on the FBI file for one Bernard Lampino. This guy had a rap sheet two pages long. Many DNA samples over the years on this guy."

"But what about the fingerprints? Rodney Park's? Hard to believe."

"No rap sheet on him but the State Police have his fingerprints on file because of his involvement with law enforcement." Emily paused for a moment. "There was one thing though. Some of the prints were kind of smudged while others were very clear."

"Hmmm," Net thought. "If someone had a knife with his prints on it but they wore gloves, would that have smudged the prints?"

"Possibly. I guess if they rub the gloves on the handle, it might."

"As always you have been a delight, my dear." Net showed his appreciation.

"And you, my friend are always welcome. We miss you."

Net sat quietly until Rhonda suddenly burst into the room. "I know you are still upset with me but please don't shut me out," she grumbled.

"Nobody's shutting you out. I just have a lot on my mind right now. With everything that has happened, I just need a little space." Net appeared very agitated.

Rhonda knew when to let things alone, so she slowly backed out of the room. Rodney Park had just arrived and he approached Rhonda at the moment he saw her. "Maybe you can find out what's going on. He's in a mood," Rhonda stated.

"I'll see what I can do." Park entered the conference room and sat down before Net could offer any resistance. "What's going on?" he inquired.

J.C. sat silently, staring at the table in deep thought. "Tell me about the night Bernard Lampino was murdered."

"You know what happened. You were there." Rodney became curious about the direction of Net's question.

"Where were you?" asked Net.

"What am I, a suspect now?" Rodney answered with a slight chuckle.

Net slid the report from the State Police lab in front of Park. Rodney quickly glimpsed at the findings. "Wow, you found the murder weapon. Had Lampino's blood on it."

"Keep reading," Net demanded.

"Wait my fingerprints on the handle?" Rodney was not so jovial now. "That can't be. I mean it looks like a knife from my kitchen but how could that be? Obviously someone stole it from my house and planted it where it could be found. This is a frame job. Exactly where was it found?"

"Rhonda found it in your vehicle under the front seat," Net disclosed. "She found it quite by accident and gave it to me. I had a friend run it through the lab off the books."

"So everyone thinks I killed Lampino."

"The only ones who know these results are Tatiana and Emily Livingston. Rhonda doesn't know and I plan to keep it that way as long as I can," confirmed Net. "I'm going to hold this information as long as I can but at some point I will have to reveal it." The two men sat in silence for a few moments. "Look, I know you didn't do this. We need to find out who did as soon as possible and I will do everything possible to clear your name. It won't be easy because your hatred of Lampino is well known."

Net opened the office door and called for Tatiana to come in with her laptop and files.

"Have you finished compiling information on the weapons used in all of the killings? You will need to add the recent information from Emily Livingston."

"Yes boss, I haven't added the recent report since you wanted it to remain secret. Four of the victims, Max Cooper, Senator Lawrence, Sidney O'Conner and Sal Siegel were all killed with serrated knives approximately six inches in length. The recent killing of Lampino was also a serrated knife, but the length of the wound indicated a shorter blade. Jimmy Schwartz, the lawyer found in his French quarter apartment was stabbed multiple times in the genital area, and sustained blunt force trauma to his head.

Schwartz's wounds were also made with a serrated knife, but because they were rough jabs it was impossible to determine the size of the blade. Three of the victims had paralytic drugs in their system, along with alcohol and erection medication. The victim, Joseph Carson, found on the riverfront, is not believed to be part of the serial killers victims and an arrest has been made in that case. His file is being closed by this office."

A knock of the office door caught all of them off guard. Rodney peaked out of the office as a secretary handed him a package that was addressed to J.C. Net, care of FBI headquarters, New Orleans. Net thanked her and closed the door behind her. Net, Tatiana, and Rodney looked at each other and at the small box on the table. Net carefully cut the strings on the box and proceeded to slowly open the box.

"Well Rodney, another missing piece of evidence has turned up."

Net passed the box to Rodney, who looked in it and gagged. Between two pieces of tissue paper a man's penis with dried blood was carefully tucked between the sheets. An index card on the bottom of the box stated, "A dick for a dick!"

CHAPTER 12

Shooting Blanks

Net looked at Rodney, then at Tatiana, who looked like she was going to throw up at any minute.

"We need to rush this over to the lab. Tatiana, can you take care of this? It appears that the penis belonged to an African American, which would fit the description of Buck Lawrence. Rodney, please ask the secretary who received the package, no pun intended, to come to the conference room."

"I'll get right on that." Rodney returned moments later. "Net, this is Olivia. She received and signed for the package."

"It was sent by courier service," Olivia began. "The name of the service is Speedy Couriers and they deliver here on a regular basis."

"Olivia, I just have a few questions. Do you know the person who delivered the package?"

"Yes, I'm not sure of his first name, but we call him Buzzard. He has been with Speedy for at least two years."

"Can you get me the telephone number of the courier service?"

"Got it right here in my phone." Olivia offered her cell to Net so he could retrieve the number.

"Good afternoon. My name is Agent J.C. Net with the FBI office. One of your couriers delivered a package to the FBI office a short time ago. I believe he goes by the name Buzzard. Can you tell me the origin of the package and if Buzzard is available to return to FBI headquarters to answer a few questions."

"Just a moment Agent Net and I'll check our records. It appears the package was delivered to our office earlier this morning. Our records indicate that Joe Beckman, who you referred to as Buzzard, actually was in the office and received the package. He is due back from a delivery shortly. I can have him at your office within the hour."

"Thank you very much. I'll be waiting for him."

"Rodney, I think under the circumstances I'd better interview Buzzard alone.

Tatiana passed by Rhonda on her way to deliver the package to the lab. As she crossed her path, she opened the box ever so slightly so that Rhonda could take a peek. "Is that what I think it is?" asked Rhonda.

"That's exactly what it is."

Rhonda made her way to the conference room where Net was now alone. "Where did that come from?" asked Rhonda referring to the box. Before he could answer, "Are you still mad at me?"

"Hell no. We just received that little gift and before I had some things on my mind."

"What are you not telling me?" asked Rhonda. "Is this about Susan?"

"Absolutely not. Sit down. I've got something to tell you. The knife you found in Rodney's vehicle had Bernard Lampino's blood on it. And even worse, its handle had Rodney's fingerprints."

"Oh boy. What are you going to do about that?" she asked.

"Nothing right now," Net stated. "I've talked to Rodney about it and for now I'm going to keep it between us."

112

"J.C., you can't do that. You are obligated to use that evidence and share it with all law enforcement."

"I know and I will, but at the right time. I need to prove Rodney innocent before I consider anything further."

"Promise me you won't hold this information too long because you know the consequences if you do."

"I promise I won't. Now's a good time for you to head over to Le Bon Theatre and try to get employed so you can do some undercover work."

Rodney poked his head back into the conference room as Rhonda exited. "There is one thing you didn't ask me. Did I do it?"

"I didn't need too."

Olivia buzzed the phone next to Net. "Yes, what is it?" he asked.

"Buzzard is here."

"Send him back, please," Net requested.

Olivia escorted Buzzard to the back of the office. Buzzard was in his twenties and his face was covered with piercings in just about every place he could have one. Tattoos covered his entire arms and neck while partially covering his face. He seemed nervous as he took a chair next to the table. "Why am I here? I ain't done nuttin'. I did my time and I've been clean for over two years now. Whatever you think I did, I didn't."

"Relax Buzzard. Okay if I call you Buzzard?" asked Net.

He nodded and shrugged his shoulders as if he didn't care.

"You delivered a package here today and I understand that you also accepted the package at your place of business."

"I not accept nuttin'. Some dude brought it in and asked that we deliver it here."

"Did you know this dude?" questioned Net. "Can you tell us what he looked like?"

"It was some kid. Probably about fifteen years old. I seen him out on the streets before while I'm workin'. You know he's one of dem gutter punks. Has a dog with him always. A mutt. Dirty looking. I think his name is Billy but I think they call him Ugly. Can't think of the dog's name."

"That's good Buzzard. We don't need the dog's name. Can you give us a description of him?" asked Net.

"Greasy blonde hair. Has a tattoo or so. I don't know, maybe it's just dirt. Always looks like he needs a bath."

"Appreciate your help Buzzard." Net handed him one of his cards. "Can you call me if you see him again? In the meantime we will also look for him. You said he hangs out in this area?"

Buzzard nodded his head as Olivia returned to escort him out of the office. He was so relieved he wasn't in trouble this time that he didn't wait for Olivia as he rushed out of the front door.

Net had second thoughts. Rushing to catch up to Buzzard before he disappeared, Net unwrapped the bandages from around his head and tossed them into a garbage can. "Say Buzzard. Do you think you could spend a few minutes taking me to the area where this Ugly person hangs out? You know what he looks like so maybe you can point him out?" Net requested.

Buzzard was reluctant to help Net but he thought maybe this goodwill would go a long way in the event he ran afoul of the law in the future. "Yeah, okay," he responded.

They didn't have far to go. About a half mile away was an underpass of the interstate highway where a number of homeless people had set up residence. Tents formed along this area as far as one could see. The location was filthy and smelled of urine. As Net travelled along, he couldn't help but feel sympathetic for how these people were living. Families with small children who not only hadn't bathed in a long period but probably hadn't had a full meal, were searching for scraps of food in dumpsters around nearby restaurants. He managed to continue on until he reached a lady holding a small girl around three years old. The little girl looked so scrawny, Net could not continue until he handed the lady a twenty dollar bill. "Go buy her a good meal," Net smiled.

Just at that moment, Buzzard nudged Net on the arm. "That's him down there. Wearing the red baseball cap." Buzzard pointed out a young boy about fifty yards away from their position. As soon as he did, Buzzard must have felt he fulfilled his obligation and took off running in the opposite direction.

Net just let him go and proceeded towards the boy Buzzard had pointed too. As he got closer to him, the boy saw him coming in his direction and began to move away. "Ugly, FBI. Can I ask you a few questions?"

Ugly didn't want anything to do with the FBI. People who lived in this area were always wary of any authorities. He continued to slowly move away.

"I just want to ask you some questions. You are not in any trouble. I'm not here to arrest you. Please don't ...run." Before Net could finish his sentence, the young boy took off running. "Shit!" commented Net. With his injuries he knew he could not run after the boy.

***

Rhonda reported to the Le Bon Theatre for her first day on the job. She was assigned to the stagehands behind the scenes. It was their responsibility to place any props on the stage in their proper place before any scene would begin. Today was a dress rehearsal so it was expected each item to be positioned where the actors would be familiar.

Being her first day, Rhonda had no clue, so she had been assigned to follow the lead of an experienced stagehand, Samantha Samuels. Samantha had been with this local theatre for nearly five years and had worked on this particular play for the past three months. The play, Murder in the Neighborhood, was about a woman who was having an affair with her next door neighbor. He was to be shot and killed in the mistress's kitchen by presumably the neighbor's wife. The rehearsal was moving along smoothly as Rhonda looked on with great anticipation of the upcoming murder scene.

The neighbor's wife entered the kitchen from the rear door on the set and pulled a gun from her waistline, firing a shot that stunned the entire crew. A live bullet buzzed just to the right of the actor's head and shattered the glass covering of a picture on the wall behind her. The actor was in disbelief as the gun fell to the floor while everyone stood in shock. Chris Nelson, the play's director, rushed upon the stage and secured the gun from the stage floor.

"Who was in charge of this gun?" Nelson screamed. Everyone was frightened by the occurrence and did not say a word. Nelson repeated his demand.

Rhonda knew that Samantha was the one who had inspected the gun but didn't want to speak up at this moment especially since no one was hurt. "I guess it was me," Samantha finally confessed.

"Well was it you or wasn't it?" Nelson screamed again.

"Sir, if I may interject," Rhonda stated. "I was with Samantha when she inspected the gun and she didn't do anything wrong."

"You're new, aren't you?" Nelson stated. "How in the hell would you know?"

"I beg your pardon sir, but I watched her the whole way. The bullet she used was from the box clearly marked as blanks. Why would you have live ammo around here? I might be new but I know my way around a theatre."

"We don't allow live ammo on the set. Someone must have brought this to the theatre. I think we need to stop rehearsal right now and call the New Orleans police department. Having lost Jimmy Schwartz not long ago I'm not taking any chances. I'd like everyone to remain here until the police arrive."

Rhonda excused herself saying she needed to use the restroom. She quickly called Net and told him of the situation. He told her he could be there in 15 minutes and to sit tight.

Net arrived at the same time as the NOPD. He met with Detective Colin Kennedy and explained to him that they had an agent working undercover at the theatre and the attempted murder may be connected to a serial killer he was investigating. Colin told Net he could take the lead, but would stand by in case he was needed. All of the actors and stagehands were seated in the first few rows of the theatre.

"Good afternoon everyone. My name is Agent J.C. Net of the FBI. I have a few questions for each of you and hopefully you can continue with your rehearsal. My first question is, who was the actor who was supposedly being shot in the play?"

"That would be me, Jay Solomon. I've been in several plays at this theatre, but can't think of anyone who would want to hurt me."

"When you're not doing plays, what is your profession?"

"I work in civil court downtown as a clerk. I've held that position for over 10 years."

"Working at civil court were you familiar with Jimmy Schwartz?"

"Yes, I knew Jimmy pretty well."

A snicker came from someone in the theatre, which indicated to Net that the relationship between Jay and Jimmy was more than casual.

"Who was the stagehand in charge of loading the weapon?"

"That's me. My name is Samantha Samuels. I was in charge of the props, together with Beth Randle, who just started today."

"Ms. Samuels, I'd like to speak to you and Ms. Randle alone. I'd like you to meet in the director's office. Also I'd like Mr. Solomon to remain for additional questions. Detective Kennedy with be taking information from the remaining cast."

Samantha and Beth followed Net into Zack White's office.

"Okay ladies, tell me everything you did this morning involving the props."

"Well Beth is new, so I just showed her where we kept the props and where things needed to be located for each scene. Backstage right is a prop shelf where all of the props are located, with the exception of large items that need to be wheeled onto the set. The gun was where it was always located, so all I did was check to make sure we loaded the gun. The blanks were kept in a box on the same shelf. We've rehearsed this scene over a dozen times and the gun was always loaded with blanks."

"Who would have access to the gun?"

"Everyone in the theatre. It's not like any of the props are valuable."

"Samantha, how long have you been in the theatre and what is your occupation?

"I've been in the theatre for about five years and I work at Orleans Antiques in the quarter. I've lived in the quarter for over ten years, so I know a lot of people."

"Okay, Ms. Samuels, I'm sure you heard the chuckle in the theatre when I asked about the relationship between Mr. Solomon and the deceased Mr. Schwartz. What can you tell me about it?"

"The theatre is a close group of people. When we are in rehearsal for a show, we spent 5-8 hours a day with each other, so our personal lives are an open book. When we are not at the theatre, we're usually hanging at someone's apartment or one of the local clubs. Jimmy Schwartz was both a ladies man and a gentleman's man. To say he was promiscuous is an understatement. But then people that live in the quarter are known to switch partners like changing socks. Jimmy and Jay had a fling, but so did most of the guys in theatre and a few girls."

"What about you Samantha? Did you ever have a physical relationship with Jimmy or Jay?"

"I'm no angel. I've sampled both of them and a few others, but nothing serious. I have a tendency to drink tequila, which as you know, makes your clothes fall off."

"Beth, this is your first day here?"

"Yes, and hopefully not my last. I really don't know any of the cast or crew, except Samantha who I just met today. I'm not sure how much help I'll be."

"Samantha, do you know if Jay had any enemies at the theatre, or from his social life?"

"Even though the cast members were very friendly with each other and shared a love for the theatre, and sometimes their bed, they were also competing for the same roles and sometime the same men. I don't think I should mention anyone by name, but you may want to check out Roberto Lopez. He was up for the same role as Jay and was visibly upset when Jay got the part. He let out quite a few fucks on the way out of the theatre and made a reference that it's not your acting abilities that get you a role in this theatre."

"What do you know about Roberto?"

"He's your typical quarter dweller. Lives somewhere off Bourbon Street and frequents some of the same bars that we all do. At one point he was close to Jimmy, but when Jay started sleeping with Jimmy he went ballistic."

"Okay ladies, please leave your phone numbers and addresses with Detective Kennedy in case we have further questions. On your way out would you please ask Jay Solomon to join me?"

"Mr. Solomon, again my name is J.C. Net and I am with the FBI. I have just a few questions for you."

"Sure, I'm pretty upset, seeing I could have just been killed."

"Do you live in the quarter? How close were you to Jimmy Schwartz?"

"I live on Esplanade Avenue and yes I was close to Jimmy. We dated some and I was shocked that he was killed."

"Do you know if Jimmy was seeing anyone else besides you?"

"Jimmy was not a one man's man. He saw a lot of people casually, but I feel that we had something special. I was with him the night before he was killed. I'm surprised the police haven't gotten around to asking me any questions."

"Maybe they weren't aware of your relationship. What about enemies? Do you know of anyone who would want to hurt you?"

"Jimmy had hundreds that wanted him dead, but I'm just a quiet clerk."

"Anyone in the theatre who may have been jealous of you either because you got the starring role, or because of your relationship with Jimmy?"

"There was this one guy, Roberto who was pissed when I landed the role. He and I were always after the same parts, so I'm sure he's not thrilled with me. I don't think he would resort to violence, but there is nothing more vicious than a scorned queen!"

"Thanks for your help. Please leave your phone number and address with Detective Kennedy."

Net left White's office, just as Chris Nelson, the director entered the office, followed by Samantha and Beth.

"Are you finished with these two? I'm going to give the cast and crew an extra hour break for them to regain their composure." Chris turned to Rhonda. "You and what's your name?"

"My name is Beth Randle, Zack White hired me to work on the crew."

"Wait a fucking minute, I know you! Aren't you that arrogant bitch that got pissed off when I wouldn't let you audition for a part?"

"I was upset at the time, but I'm content just to work backstage."

"Well, maybe I'm not fucking content to have you part of my play. I think I'll discuss this with Zack White personally."

Beth (Rhonda) was not happy about Nelson's attitude towards her. She felt it would be appropriate to ignore his comments as if she didn't give a rat's ass. "Samantha, do you know of any place nearby where we can grab some lunch?"

"Sure Beth, I think we need to get you away from Chris."

Net walked into the theatre and spoke with Detective Kennedy. "When you're finished getting information from the crew, we need you to bag all of the evidence and send it to the lab. You may want to have a crew dust for fingerprints around the prop shelf, but giving the number of people with access to the area it may be useless."

Samantha and Beth walked over to a sandwich shop near Jackson Square. Samantha ordered a shrimp po-boy and a root beer. Beth settled on a salad and iced tea. As soon as they were seated, Samantha turned to Beth. "How did you manage to piss off Chris Nelson on your first day," she laughed. "Not that I'm a fan of the little prick, but usually it takes a week or two before he curses you out. Anyone that can piss him off so fast is a friend of mine."

"I tried to try out for a part in this play, but he had precast the role and got pissed when I called him on it. Today has been pretty stressful. Do you have any ideas who would want to hurt Jay?"

"Besides Roberto, the only other person I can think of is Chris Nelson. I know he wanted to get with Jay before Jimmy was killed. Now that Jimmy is out of the picture, Jay got the lead. Chris doesn't do anything without expecting something in return. Actually, Roberto would have been better in the part, but Chris had no interest in a Latin lover."

"I guess working at the theatre is like acting in a soap opera. Everyone is sleeping with everyone and they all have motives for killing everyone," Beth (Rhonda) noted.

"You are 100% correct," Samantha agreed. "Well I guess it's time to get back to the theatre. You'd think they would give us the rest of the day off because the police will certainly have the stage area still closed for their investigation. Nelson will keep us going even if we have to work outside. Speaking of the police, how about that FBI Agent. What was his name? Net? He is some good-looking. Girl, I could curl up next to him and lick him all over."

Rhonda became very embarrassed by the conversation. "Well, yes. He is very attractive."

"Come on, Girl. Tell me what you would do to that body of his. You don't need to be shy around me. Maybe you'd like to have a threesome with him and me."

"Can we change the subject?" Rhonda requested.

"Sorry, didn't mean to embarrass you. Even if it never happens, it's damn nice to dream about."

Chris Nelson was waiting outside of the theatre for the group to return. "I talked with Zack White about you, Randle. He said to leave it alone. Don't know what you've got on him but I'll be watching you very closely."

"Looking forward to it," Rhonda snapped back. As Samantha predicted, rehearsal proceeded outside. There wasn't a whole lot for Samantha or Beth to do since no props were to be used.

CHAPTER 13

The Reprimand

Net knocked on Rodney Park's door. Mildred answered the door and ushered him into the study.

"Mr. Park will be with you in a minute. Would you care for a cup of coffee or something cold to drink? I know it can get pretty hot in New Orleans."

"I'd love just a glass of water Mildred."

"Yes sir." After returning with his water Mildred stated, "Now if you excuse me, I was just going to give Ms. Charlotte her medication."

Net proceed to look around the room as he waited for Rodney Park. The study was filled with Mardi Gras memorabilia from Charlotte's reign as queen and various other society functions. One particular photograph caught Net's eye. It was Rodney in a tuxedo with Charlotte on his arm. She was wearing a white formal gown with blue feathers in her hair and a beautiful blue necklace around her neck. Net pulled out his cell phone and took a picture of the photograph just as Rodney entered the room.

"That's a great picture of you two. What a beautiful dress and jewelry Charlotte's wearing. I don't think I've ever seen a necklace like that before."

"Yes it was very pretty and expensive. I should have known better than to buy that for Charlotte. She's pretty careless when it comes to jewelry.

In fact I think she lost that necklace shortly after that picture was taken. It was at the King's Club dinner of the carnival club. We both got a little tipsy and the next morning the necklace was gone. Now while I appreciate your fashion sense, please tell me that you found something to clear me," said Rodney.

"I wish I had good news, but you know the lab report came back and your prints were on the knife and the blood matched Lampino. Some of the prints were smudged, so several people may have handled the knife. I'd like you to show me into your kitchen to see if all your knives are accounted for."

"Sure, J.C., just follow me. The knives are usually kept in the second drawer of the kitchen island."

Rodney opened the drawer and proceeded to take out all the knives in the drawer. He lined them up in order on the countertop and noticed there was a gap between the longest serrated knife and the paring knife.

"Mildred, do you have any idea what happened to the knife that would be next in line?"

"No Mr. Park, I haven't used any of those knives in ages. Ms. Charlotte is constantly dieting, so I use mostly the small knives for paring fruit and vegetables."

"I know this doesn't look good, J.C., but I swear I had nothing to do with the Lampino murder."

"I know, but now we have to find a way to prove it. I went out on a limb sending the knife to Baton Rouge instead of the local lab. I'm sure they will have questions for me. I can't keep this information secret any longer. I'm going to send the report to the local FBI office. I just wanted to meet with you in person and prepare you for what might happen."

"When Charlotte's father finds out about this he will have my ass."

"I think your father-in-law is the least of your problems. I hate to ask this, but do you know a good criminal lawyer? When the word gets out that you are the prime suspect you will want to have someone ready."

"Because of my job, I really don't want to use anyone local, especially since the mayor and the DA, Patrick McQueen run this city. My job with the police department could be put in jeopardy if we end up hiring someone who's under their control. Do you know anyone good who practices in Louisiana?"

"I just had a thought. Net, do you remember the guy from Keister, Ernest Washington? If you recall, he was Sly Washington's brother. He has experience as both a prosecutor and criminal attorney. That's the only name I can think of right now. Given the makeup of New Orleans, it wouldn't hurt to have an African American attorney on my case."

"I only met him a few times, but he seemed competent and professional. I know lots of great attorneys in Boston, but they probably aren't licensed to practice here. If you'd like we can call him together before I leave."

Rodney picked up the cell phone and searched for information on attorney Ernest Washington in Keister, Louisiana. "Mr. Washington please," he didn't hesitate to call.

"May I ask whose calling and the nature of your business with Mr. Washington?"

"My name if Rodney Park. Used to work with Mr. Washington a few years ago in Keister. I may need his help on a delicate matter,"

"Pants, is that you? I heard you went all big city on us and married a debutante in New Orleans."

"Yes Ernest, I'm deputy chief of police here in New Orleans and my only claim to society is that I married the mayor's daughter. Unfortunately this isn't a social call. I'm sitting here with J.C. Net, who's now with the FBI. Do you mind if we put you on speaker phone?"

"J.C. Net, it's been a long time. How are you my friend?"

"I've been better Ernest. To get right to the point, Rodney is in some trouble here and we're hoping you can help us out. A local gangster type was murdered recently and it appears someone is trying to set up Rodney. The murder weapon was found in Rodney's car. I managed to send it to the lab in Baton Rouge instead of New Orleans, but the results came back positive for the victim's blood and Rodney's prints. We just learned a knife that fits the description of the murder weapon is missing from Rodney's kitchen. I'm going to turn over the findings to the local FBI office, but Rodney is going to need an attorney ready to act fast."

"I'm only a country lawyer, but I will help out all I can. I have two partners in my firm now, so I can move things around here and be in New Orleans in a few days. Any chance you can give me just one day before you turn over the information J.C.?"

"The best I can do is hold it until the end of tomorrow. I've been staying at a hotel on the riverfront. I can book you a room starting tomorrow. We really appreciate your help. How is your wife Crystal and your brother Sly?"

"Sly is doing well. He has a job at the local feed store. Mostly helping customers to their trucks and loading grain, but he seems happy to be useful. He still lives with us, so Crystal won't be making the trip. Pants, do not talk to anyone without my being present. I'll start packing immediately. By the way Net, did you ever capture that Susan Griffin person you were after?"

"That's a story we can share when you get here. I feel much better knowing you're willing to help Rodney. I'm afraid he may be in for a rough time, given his position as deputy chief of police. We both know how the court of public opinion is ready to think the worst of anyone in uniform."

"Okay guys, I'll see you by the end of tomorrow."

Just as they hung up the telephone, Charlotte entered the room.

"Did you take your medicine dear?" asked Rodney.

"I took it, but I still don't like the way it makes me feel."

J.C. noticed how pale Charlotte looked and how her hair and clothes were a mess.

"I heard you weren't feeling well Charlotte. Hopefully you can get well soon and maybe join Rhonda and me for dinner."

"Charlotte, do you know what happened to one of the knives that missing from the kitchen drawer?" asked Rodney.

"I very seldom go into the kitchen. Now if you will excuse me, my medicine makes me very tired and I must go lie down."

"Okay dear. I'll come check on you soon. J.C. is there anything else you can think of for now?"

"I'm headed back to FBI headquarters. I need to explain to Rhonda what's going on and plan my course of action on how to turn over the information without looking like I was trying to hide something. I'll call you in the morning. In the meantime, you may want to explain things to Charlotte and possibly give your father-in-law a heads up. It will be better if he learns what's going on from you and not the press."

J.C. gave Rodney a slight hug. "It's going to be okay Rodney. We will figure this thing out."

***

Traffic was unusually heavy traveling down St. Charles Ave. Cars were bumper to bumper moving at an extremely slow pace. Net wondered if some of the streetlights ahead were out of sync but as he gradually moved forward, he could see blue lights flashing in the distance. NOPD had a heavy presence a couple of blocks away. Even passing by, Net was unable to determine what the commotion entailed. Uniformed police officers were everywhere, while some were entering and exiting a home on the avenue. Of course every passing driver rubbernecked whatever was going on and just as Net passed officers were escorting a male, hands cuffed behind him, from the premises. He strained his eyes through the sun's glare to see if he could recognize the individual in custody. He wasn't sure but the man certainly resembled Biff Holder, the bartender from the Joker's Wild. There was just no time for Net to stop. He had to get back to the FBI office to see Rhonda and file his report from the lab findings on the knife.

Tatiana and Rhonda were seated in the kitchen enjoying a cup of coffee when Net entered. "I need to talk with you," Net stated with reference to Rhonda.

"I think I will leave you two alone," Tatiana softly declared as she tiptoed away.

"What now?" Rhonda sighed.

"Well you know about the knife with Rodney's fingerprints and Bernard Lampino's blood on it. We've contacted an attorney to help Rodney."

"And you still haven't turned over that evidence? Damn!" Rhonda exclaimed. "Never would have thought Rodney could have done such a thing?"

"No. He couldn't have!"

"You are going to report this, aren't you?" she asked. "You know you have to."

"I don't want too. This is my friend." It was obvious Net was anguishing over this decision.

"Who else knows about this?" questioned Rhonda.

"Tatiana, Rodney, Emily Livingston, you and now Ernest Washington."

"Who?"

"Washington is the attorney that Rodney and I both know."

"I know you like this guy but you have to file that report and arrest him for murder. He has motive and the evidence points to him being guilty. If you don't do it I will."

J.C. wasn't particularly fond of Rhonda's mindset but even though he didn't like it, he knew what he had to do. He walked away from Rhonda and into Saul Bernstein's office. Without saying a word he slid the report across the desk in front of Agent Bernstein.

Bernstein studied the report with the use of his reading glasses. He looked up at Net, sliding his glasses to the edge of his nose. "How long have you known this?" he queried.

"Not long," answered Net nervously.

"Let's see. You broke regulations by finding this evidence and not reporting it. Then you sent it secretly to the state lab in lieu of the FBI and when you received the report you covered it up until now. I'd say that's enough for disciplinary action including possible termination. You broke all the protocols. Did you at least not discuss this with Deputy Chief Park before you came to me?" Net lowered his head and looked away without an answer. "Okaaay. I guess I got my answer. You are officially off this case. I will discuss this with your boss, Sam Huddleston, but as far as I'm concerned you can go back to Boston."

Net didn't say another word before leaving the room. Rhonda tried to stop him as he walked past. "What happened?" she inquired. "Where are you going? Tell me what's going on."

"Well, I guess we're going back to Boston. I'm off the case."

"I'm going to talk with Bernstein," Rhonda insisted.

"Absolutely not!" demanded Net. "I didn't tell him you found the knife. He thinks I did. I don't want you involved because of my decision."

"You can't take the full blame for this," she urged.

"I need to face the consequences of my decisions. It is what it is. I'll probably be suspended but I don't think Huddleston will fire me." Net paused for a moment of reflection. "I don't know maybe he will have to. Whatever happens, happens. I need some air."

Rhonda knew she needed to give him some space and let him do what he needed to do.

***

Net walked around the French Quarter and even stopped in at the Joker's Wild for a drink. Sitting at the bar, he ordered a beer. A female bartender served him his beer and asked him where he was from. "I'm originally from Louisiana but living in Boston now."

"You here on business or just a vacation?" asked the bartender. "What's your name, honey?" It appeared obvious that she was beginning to flirt with J.C.

"Business, I guess."

"Well you don't look too happy. Can't be going to well. You have a name that goes with that handsome face?"

"Jamison." This was Net's real first name but no one really knew that.

"Well Jamison, my name is Lisa. Listen, I get off in about two hours if you want to hang around." Lisa was an attractive girl in her twenties with long, flowing, black hair. Her pale face made her appear fragile but she had an extremely solid body.

Net stared at her for a few moments almost appearing to be contemplating her offer. "I'm sorry, what did you say?"

"Oh, it wasn't important." Lisa realized Net's mind was elsewhere. "If things don't work out for you and her, you know where to find me."

"Who? What are you talking about?" She didn't have to respond. Net finally realized what she was saying. "You know you could help me with something," suggested Net.

He now had her attention again. "Biff Holder. I met him in here the other day. Do you know where he is?"

"I don't. He called in and said he would be out today and asked me to sub for him. Didn't say when he would be back." Lisa looked dejected. "Now I know why this guy has no interest in me," she mumbled to herself as she walked away to serve another customer.

Net finished his beer and rushed out of the door before she could return. A couple of hours had passed since he departed from the FBI office. He returned to gather Rhonda before they headed to the hotel.

***

Rhonda was waiting for him with a big smile on her face. "Bernstein wants to see you."

"Oh boy, just what I need. More shit from him." Net slowly walked into Bernstein's office ready to get this whole ordeal over and done with.

"Sit down Net," Bernstein commanded with a stern look on his face. "I don't know who you have naked pictures of but the director of the FBI called me personally and told me not to take you off this case. Actually he ordered me. So, despite my objections, you're back but I'll be watching you closely."

Net walked out without saying a word but once his back was turned, he had a sly smile across his face. Bernstein was no longer a fan of Net and obviously the feelings were mutual.

Rhonda was awaiting his return. "Well what happened?" she asked with a smile.

"I don't really know. The FBI director called him and told him to let me continue." Rhonda's big smile gave her away. "Did you do something?"

"Well, I just made a call to your childhood friend, the honorable senator for the great state of Louisiana, Senator Greg Slidell. I told him what was going on and he was more than happy to assist you."

CHAPTER 14

All in the Family

The telephone rang in Mayor Hebert's office.

"Mr. Mayor, this is Saul Bernstein with the FBI office. Unfortunately this isn't a social call. We have reason to believe that Rodney Park is involved in the murder of Bernard Lampino. We have enough evidence to warrant an arrest and I'm making a courtesy call to you on how to handle it. I know Park is married to your daughter, Charlotte, so I'm trying to limit publicity."

"Thank you Agent Bernstein. I am not aware of any evidence against my son-in-law or his connection to Lampino. While I don't believe Rodney is capable of murder, I know you have to follow the evidence. I would appreciate it if you would allow Rodney to come down to police headquarters and turn himself in. I will have to make arrangements for him to be suspended from the police department, pending the outcome of the investigation."

"I have been informed that he has obtained legal counsel from another part of the state and his lawyer will be arriving tomorrow."

"I only ask that you wait to question him until his attorney arrives. Charlotte, as you can imagine will be very upset, so anything you can do to limit her exposure in this matter will also be appreciated."

"That will be fine Mr. Mayor. I can only give him until 10:00 tomorrow morning to turn himself in. If he is not in my office at that time I will have no alternative but to have him picked up. Hopefully we can clear up this matter quickly, but I don't mind telling you that the evidence is more than circumstantial."

"Thank you and I'll make sure he is there. Bye." Mayor Hebert hung up the telephone and immediately called Rodney Park. "Look you son of a bitch. Did you fucking kill Lampino? I've managed to arrange for you to turn yourself in to Saul Bernstein at the FBI headquarters by 10:00 a.m. tomorrow. If your sorry ass is not there by that time I'll make sure you never work in law enforcement again. You are a disgrace to Charlotte and my entire family."

"Glad it's not your decision if I'm guilty or not, asshole," Rodney exclaimed. "I didn't fucking do it but you would like nothing better for me to be guilty."

"You mother fucking better be telling me the truth that you're innocent and your fancy lawyer better be able to prove it."

Hebert was never fond of the man who his daughter had picked for his son-in-law. He gave him the job of deputy chief of police to be sure his daughter would be well taken care of.

Charlotte needed all the help she could get. As a young girl she was one of the brightest children in every school she attended. The older she grew, the more anxiety issues manifested. Her mother had her own issues, spending time in various psychiatric facilities around the southern United States. Depression, bipolar disorder, and anxiety ran in Reba Hebert's family. Reba had attempted suicide on two different occasions. Her issues were well hidden from the public as she had been diagnosed with these disorders before Clyde was in the political limelight. Reba was confined to a hospital in another state, so she was never mentioned during any of Clyde's campaigns or by the media. Most people assumed his wife passed away and he didn't make a point of telling them otherwise. Charlotte, on the other hand, had been the media darling as the mayor's only daughter and was well-known throughout the city.

Now it was feared that she was following the same path as her mother, Reba. Clyde could not easily hide her as he did her mother.

Shortly after the mayor hung up the telephone with Rodney, Charlotte Park knocked at his door. Clyde opened the door, surprised to see Charlotte. "I just talked with Rodney. He told me about what is going on."

"I was going to call you. What do you know about Rodney's dealings with Lampino? I don't mind telling you that it doesn't look good for him or for our family. If you want to leave him I'll have the best divorce lawyer in town draw up the papers and he can be removed from your house before the weekend."

"Why on earth would I want a divorce? Rodney is the only person who hasn't treated me like I'm an insane child. I came here to tell you that I expect your help in proving his innocence. I can see from my welcome that you have already tried him and are ready to have him executed. My entire life I've had to live in my mother's shadow. I know I have my issues, but I feel I have things under control. Everyone, especially you have been waiting to lock me away, just like you did mom. I will kill you and myself before I allow you to shove me far away in an institution like you did her. When was the last time you even visited mom? You let everyone assume she's dead and forbid me to mention her in public. Well let me tell you something. If you don't support me in proving Rodney's innocence, I'm going to tell the whole world about how you sent my mother away so you could become mayor."

"Obviously Charlotte you don't understand the gravity of the situation. I've had reports that you have slipped out of the house on numerous occasions and returned at all hours, totally incoherent. I have covered for your escapades, even though the word on the street is that you head down to the quarter for booze, pills and God knows what else. Does that sound like someone who has things under control? If you tell anyone about your mother, not only will it be bad for my career, but you will lose your place in society. You'd better think long and hard before you open your mouth. I have been getting reports from Mildred that you haven't been in compliance with your medication. Based on that and what Doctor Howser reported, I wouldn't have any problem getting an interdiction."

"Just try it you bastard and I'll show you what crazy really is!"

Clyde Hebert watched in disbelief as Charlotte's face grew red and her hands began to tremble. She picked up a vase off of the coffee table and threw it across the room towards his head.

"I hate you, you fat mother fucker. I could kill you now with my bare hands. I do take my medication. If I decide to go out at night it's none of your fucking business."

"Calm down Charlotte. You're making yourself upset. Come into the living room and lie down a few minutes. I'll make you a cup of tea and we can discuss this quietly. The last thing I want to do is rile you up."

Charlotte reluctantly went into the living room and lay on the couch as Clyde went into the kitchen to make her tea. Once out of sight, he called Dr. Howser and told him to come over immediately and bring a sedative for Charlotte.

Clyde handed her a cup of tea and tried to calm her down. Within 15 minutes, Dr. Howser knocked at the door. Clyde answered the door and showed the doctor to where Charlotte was laying down.

"I should have known he would call you Dr. Howser. My dad thinks I'm nuts."

"No one thinks you're insane Charlotte. I'm just here to give you something for the stress you're under. This is just going to make you relax."

Doctor Howser gave Charlotte an injection and within five minutes she was fast asleep.

Clyde Hebert called Mildred and told her that Charlotte had an episode at his house and that Dr. Howser had sedated her. He asked her to please come and pick her up and bring her home. He informed her that Rodney would be away from the house starting in the morning and that he was going to rely on her to take care of Charlotte. He didn't go into any details about Rodney, since he knew it would be all over the news within days.

Mildred arrived at Clyde Hebert's house and with the mayor's assistance they placed Charlotte in the back seat of the car. Mildred drove to the Park house and ushered Charlotte in through the rear door. Charlotte was still groggy but managed to allow Mildred to help her into bed. Mildred covered her up and dimmed the lights. She assumed that Charlotte would sleep for several hours, so she thought this was a good time to do a little shopping.

***

Mildred arrived home and immediately went to check on Charlotte, who was sound asleep in her room. She prepared a sandwich and placed it by Charlotte's bedside with her night medications. It was past 7 o'clock and Mildred assumed Mr. Park would be home any minute. She left a note on the kitchen table saying she would be back by 7 a.m., and left through the rear exit.

***

Mayor Hebert was visibly shaken by the latest events. He fixed himself a cocktail and tried to relax on the living room couch. His home was void of any noises that would be made by people, but being an older New Orleans home it had its own creaks and squeak. It wasn't long before his eyes closed and he was sound asleep. The sun had set and the house was in total darkness. A neighborhood security service hired by the area residents patrolled the area, and as customary they paid particular attention to the mayor's home. One of the security guards noticed an unusual flash inside the home immediately followed by another.

"Hold on Ed. Did you see that?" asked the guard who saw the flash.

"See what? I was watching that person in that hoodie crossing the street. Might have hit them if I hadn't noticed."

"Stop the car. I think we need to check out the mayor's house."

"What did you see?" asked Ed, the guard who was driving.

Before Shane, the first guard would answer, he jumped from the car and climbed the front steps of the home. He knocked and rang the doorbell but there was no answer. Ed moved around the front of the home trying to peer through any window. He shone his flashlight through the window and saw the shattered vase still on the living room floor. "Shane, we need to get in there. Bust open that door," Ed yelled.

It took several blows but the two guards managed to breach the door and enter the home. The mayor was still on the sofa but wasn't responding to their voice. "Mayor, are you okay?" As soon as that question was asked, they knew the answer. An exorbitant amount of blood had already covered the sofa and floor. Shane placed his two fingers on the mayor's neck checking for a pulse. His head dropped, shaking it from side to side signifying they were too late.

***

Rodney arrived home around 7:30 and went into the kitchen looking for Mildred. He saw the note and went upstairs to check on Charlotte. He knew she was quite upset about the accusations against him, but wasn't aware that she paid a visit to her father. He turned on the lamp by her bed and was surprised to find Charlotte was gone. Not knowing what to do and not wanting to call her father, Rodney went downstairs and poured himself a drink. He turned on the TV and set on the couch waiting for Charlotte's return. The stress of the last few days took it toll and by the time he fixed his second drink he was fast asleep.

Rodney awoke startled by the loud banging on his door and the ringing of his bell. He groggily got up and opened the door. Three NOPD officers were standing at the door.

Surprised by their appearance he asked. "Oh God no, has something happened to Charlotte?"

"Sir, we ask that you step aside and keep your hands where we can see them."

"What is this about? Is my wife okay?"

"We are not here about your wife. We are here about Mayor Hebert. He was found dead in his home tonight. We need you to come downtown with us now to answer some questions."

"The mayor is dead? That can't be. I talked to him earlier today. He was upset about the accusations against me, but I convinced him of my innocence and he believed me. Colin Kennedy, you know me. You know I would never hurt Mayor Hebert."

"I'm sorry Deputy Chief Park. I have my orders to bring you in. We are aware that you made arrangements to turn yourself in tomorrow on the Lampino matter, but given the recent events we can't wait until morning."

"Can you at least give me the courtesy of making a phone call first? My attorney is in route to New Orleans, but I'd like to notify J.C. Net at the FBI office."

"I'll give you five minutes to make your calls, then we have to go"

Rodney picked up his cell phone and immediately called J.C. Net.

"J.C., this is Rodney. Things have gone from bad to worse. My father-in-law has been killed and they are taking me in as a suspect. When I got home I noticed Charlotte is missing. Her cell phone was still on her nightstand, so I have no way of getting in touch with her. I don't know what to do."

"Okay Rodney. Let them take you in but you know not to answer any questions until Ernest Washington arrives. I'm going to call him as soon as we hang up and let him know what's happening. I will see what they have on you and will meet you at the lock up. If you'd like I can have Rhonda come to your house and wait for Charlotte."

"I would appreciate it if Rhonda would come over. Charlotte was upset about the accusations against me, I don't want her to be alone when she learns about her dad."

"Okay, I'm going to drop off Rhonda and head over to the mayor's house. Can you leave a key under the mat for Rhonda? When is your housekeeper due back?

"Mildred left a note saying she would return at seven in the morning. I have a gnome on the porch that I can put the key under. Thanks man. I'd be screwed without you."

Colin Kennedy escorted his boss to the patrol car parked in front of the house. The press had already received the word of the mayor's death and had gathered outside the Park home. Kennedy protected Park from any embarrassment by not handcuffing Rodney as they passed the press.

Even so, the media shouted so many questions to not only the deputy chief of police but also the detectives who accompanied him. Officer Kennedy repeatedly responded "No comment" as they continued to their vehicle. By the time Net arrived with Rhonda most of the reporters had departed.

***

As Kennedy and Park arrived at Police Headquarters, some of the same media greeted them. For the most part, they just ignored their questions as they entered the building. Rodney was placed in an interrogation room in the far back of the office. He remained by himself for hours before Deputy Kennedy was joined by Deputy Mike Smith in the room. "Well, this is awkward," declared Kennedy. "Chief, we know you were going to turn yourself in for the murder of Bernard Lampino tomorrow morning. But with the murder of the mayor, we felt we needed to expedite your appearance. It's common knowledge that you and the mayor did not like each other."

"I had nothing against the mayor. He didn't like me for whatever reason. He didn't think I was good enough for his daughter."

"Well, he made you deputy chief," countered Smith.

"Let's get something straight. I worked hard for this job before and after I was given the position." Park was annoyed by Smith's statement.

"Chief, we're behind you. I hope and believe in your innocence. But even you have to understand our position. We found the Lampino murder weapon in your vehicle with your fingerprints and the same type of knives in your kitchen, with a serrated blade knife missing from the set," Kennedy stated.

Smith unexpectedly slammed his hand on the table in front of Park. "Admit it you hated Lampino for fucking your wife and the mayor was going to fire you. You killed both of them."

Park let out a slight chuckle. "You think this good cop, bad cop, routine will break me? Colin you know me better than that."

The three stared at each other when Kennedy's phone rang. He didn't immediately answer it as it rang and rang.

"You going to answer that?" asked Rodney.

Kennedy let it ring just a couple more times before he finally answered. "Kennedy," he answered. "Oh really. You'll take care of that? Let me know what you find out." His mood totally changed after taking that phone call. "That was FBI Agent Caden Caruso. A search warrant was authorized by Judge Scott Post to conduct a search of your home."

"You won't find a thing," Rodney interrupted.

"A gun matching the description of the gun used to kill the mayor was found hidden in the pocket of your coat hanging in your closet. The weapon will be sent for a ballistic match by the FBI. Oh by the way. It had recently been fired."

"I'm not saying another word until my attorney arrives," demanded Park.

"I think that is very wise." Smith began providing his Miranda Rights. "You have the right to remain silent. You have the right to have an attorney present during questioning…"

CHAPTER 15

Undercover

Tatiana reported for her undercover work at the Joker's Wild. As far as anyone would know she was just a new server for the bar. She didn't know how to make many drinks so bartender was out of the question. Not being a fully-trained agent she was to observe and report back to Rhonda or J.C. if she saw anything or anyone who looked suspicious. She had hoped to get close to other employees which was something she was very good at. Barbara was the other server who worked the same shift as her. Biff Holder had still not returned to his bartender duties, so Lisa was behind the bar. Tatiana hoped he would return soon as he seemed to know more about what was going on there.

"Hi, I'm Tanya," she introduced herself to Lisa. She had already met Barbara.

"How can you make any money here? I don't see a crowd."

Lisa smiled at Tanya and told her the crowd didn't arrive until after 10:00 p.m. and it was mostly street people and fellow quarter rats.

"The people who come in here are working people. So they tip well," said Barbara.

Lisa replied, "I've only been working since Biff left, but the tips aren't bad if you don't mind the characters."

Tanya's eyes got wide. "I've heard that several people who frequented this place have turned up dead. You think it's safe to work here?"

Barbara shook her head. "The people who were killed weren't the nicest people on the street. I also heard that they arrested this Park guy for at least one of the murders."

Lisa agreed. "I know that Park's wife comes in here sometimes, usually stoned out of her mind. I guess when she doesn't get what she needs at home she comes to the other side of the tracks. Everyone knows he had it in for Lampino because he fucked his wife many times. Of course, Lampino had a lot of people who probably celebrated his murder," Lisa laughed.

Tanya pushed a little further. "Lisa, whatever happened to the guy whose place you took, Biff? He didn't end up like Lampino, did he?"

"I'm not sure, but rumor has it that he was picked up on a domestic violence charge and is lying low until it's cleared up. Apparently it had something to do with a director from the local theatre group that he was servicing. He thought it was an exclusive arrangement, but guess he learned otherwise."

People started entering Joker's Wild and most of the tables became full of drinking customers. Tanya was busy serving drinks when she noticed two men sitting at a table near the rear exit. It wasn't long before she realized why they looked familiar. They were the two Russian men from the airplane. She remembered they had mentioned the word bomb and that they got off the plane in Atlanta. She didn't want to wait on them in case they remembered her. She turned to Barbara and told her she needed a smoke and that she would be back in five minutes.

Bourbon Street was coming alive with tourists and locals, moving down the street to the music coming out of the clubs. She took out her cellphone and dialed Rhonda but the call went directly to voice mail.

"This is Tatty. I'm going under the name Tanya in this bar," said Tatiana. "I have some information for you about Biff and rumors about Rodney. Also, the two Russians from my flight to Atlanta are here at Jokers. Please tell me what you want me to do. I don't know if they'd recognize me in my waitress attire, but not sure if I should chance it."

Tatiana returned to the bar and started waiting tables in another section. When she glanced towards the table with the Russians, she noticed that they were joined by a woman that Tatiana recognized from photographs as Susan Griffin. Knowing she couldn't sneak out for another smoke, she purposely spilled a beer on herself and went to the bathroom to clean up. She again tried to call Rhonda, but the call went directly to voicemail again.

"Rhonda, this is Tatty again. I'm pretty sure that Net's ex, Susan is meeting with the Russians. Please advise as soon as you can how you want me to proceed?"

Within seconds, Tatty received a text from Rhonda saying she would be there in 15 minutes.

Tatty walked out of the bathroom and the table with the Russians was empty. Without any warning she raced to the street in time to watch the two foreigners disappear into the large Bourbon Street crowd. There was nothing more she could do so she reentered the bar and proceeded to wait the tables as though she had never left.

"Did something happen?" questioned Barbara. "I saw you run out but I covered one of your tables so Lisa wouldn't notice."

"Thank you so much," Tatiana exclaimed her appreciation. "It was nothing. I thought I saw someone that I hadn't seen in years but it wasn't her."

Rhonda arrived at Joker's Wild shortly after. Tatiana motioned for her to sit at a particular table which was located in her service area. "Can I get you a drink?" Tatiana asked her new patron.

"I'll have a club soda with a twist of lime."

Tatiana did not linger around the table so she would not call attention to Rhonda. She returned moments later with the drink and held a brief conversation with Rhonda. "I know Net was wondering about Biff Holder and why he was arrested. Seems he was taken into custody on a domestic abuse case. He evidently had a physical altercation with a director from that theatre you are working."

"I want to know about Susan Griffin. What was she doing with the two Russians?"

"I'm sorry but I didn't handle that well. I saw the Russians and I panicked because I thought they might recognize me and blow my cover. I asked the other waitress to take that table but within a couple of minutes they were gone. I tried to follow them but lost them in the crowd. I wasn't able to hear any of their conversation."

"Just as well. If you were recognized, it might have not ended very well for you," Rhonda suggested. "But I wonder what connection Susan Griffin has with those two guys?"

Tatiana didn't feel comfortable lingering around Rhonda's table for very long. There were a couple of drunks nearby clamoring for another round of drinks. "What can I get you guys?" inquired Tatiana.

"What's your name babe?" asked one of the men.

"Me? My name is Tanya."

The other man attempted to put his arm around her but Tatiana pulled away. "Now, what can I get you?" she asked again.

"A couple of beers babe and an introduction to that lucky lady sitting right there." He motioned his hand towards Rhonda.

"Can't introduce you to someone who I don't know," countered Tatiana. "She looks like someone who wants to be left alone."

"Why would someone that looks like her come to a place like this unless you're looking for some action?" With that said the first man stood and approached Rhonda. "Hey babe. You looking for some company? Let me buy you a drink."

"Thank you but that's not necessary." Rhonda was trying to be polite as she recognized he probably had a little too much to drink. Even with the decline of a drink, the man sat next to her. "Look, I really just want to sit here alone and enjoy my drink and this club. No offense. I'm sure you are a nice guy but I'd rather be by myself."

The man didn't get the hint. "This ain't a place a nice girl comes to by herself so let's just get to it. How much do you want?"

"I beg your pardon?" Rhonda felt maybe she had stayed to long. She finished her club soda and began walking towards the door. "Besides, you couldn't afford me." The moment she said that she knew it was a mistake. She tried to exit the premises without any incident but the man followed her outside the bar. When they reached the street, he grabbed her arm. Her immediate reaction was to pull her blazer open showing her holstered gun.

"Okay lady!" the man exclaimed holding his hands up as though he was surrendering. He backed away and returned to his friend inside the bar.

***

Rhonda returned to FBI headquarters and told Net what had happened.

"We know that Susan was at Jokers Wild and that Susan knows the Russians that were on the plane with Tatty. Tatty also learned that Biff was in a domestic disturbance with one of the directors from the theatre. I think I'll follow up with the theatre lead and have Tatty keep working at Jokers. How are things going with Rodney?"

"Things are not looking good for Rodney. The knife you found under the seat of his car matches the murder weapon and also a set of knives in Rodney's home. They found a gun in a coat pocket in Rodney's room that matches the caliber of weapon used in the mayor's murder. It's being tested now. Even if Rodney was the killer, which I don't believe for a second, he's too smart to leave that kind of evidence around. Ernest Washington, his lawyer, was able to post the one million dollar bail established by the judge, using the Park house as collateral. Rodney is just staying at his house since he's been relieved of all police duties. I told him we'd stop by later tonight to check on him. Apparently Charlotte is not taking any of this well. He told me she stayed out all night before he was arrested. I'm trying to follow up on the serial killings and leave Rodney's problems in his attorney's hands. Do you remember Buck Lawrence, the victim with the missing penis? Josh Hancock was able to match the DNA from the penis delivered to me as belonging to Buck Lawrence. I'm going down to Lawrence's church on Decatur Street and see what I can learn. Go back to the theatre and we'll meet up at the hotel around 8 o'clock. Send Tatiana a message to report back to the hotel after her shift at Jokers is over. Love you and please, stay safe Darling, ok?" He gave her a quick hug and dashed off.

***

Net arrived at the New Horizon Fellowship Church just as a prayer meeting was ending. He walked up to the pastor and introduced himself.

"Hello, my name is J.C. Net and I'm with the FBI office in charge of investigating the death of Pastor Lawrence."

"I'm Pastor Isaac Green. Not sure how much help I can be, but you're welcome to come inside to my office. I don't want my congregation to see me out here talking to you. You have FBI written all over you and my people don't place much faith in any law enforcement."

Both men went into the church office and Green offered him a cup of coffee.

"What can you tell me about Lawrence? I heard he was a ladies man and was also under investigation for tax evasion."

"Old Buck did have a way with the ladies. Rumor has it that he fathered over 20 kids in the city, but none with his wife. Now as far as tax evasion is concerned...Our church is a tax-exempt non-profit entity. If Buck had any tax problems it was in his personal life and had nothing to do with our church. I'd appreciate you letting your FBI folks know that our church is clean."

"Do you know of anyone who would want to kill Lawrence?"

"I know at least a dozen people wanted him dead, but I can't name anyone who would actually do it. Lots of jealous boyfriends and husbands had it in for Buck. I think it's something about the pastors' uniform that makes the ladies feel like getting with Buck is making them get closer to God. Hell, I've even had a few ladies throw themselves at me, but I'm more afraid of my wife Ethel than any jealous husband."

"Can you give me the names of any of Lawrence's children or women he's fathered children with?"

"It's not like he kept track of any of them. I think he believed that after he donated the sperm it was up to the baby mamas to raise them. I do know of two young men in our congregation who Buck claimed as his own. They were at his repast and funeral. They might be able to help. If you leave me your information I'll send you their numbers."

151

"Thank you pastor. If you can think of anything else please contact me."

As Net departed down the steps of the church, his cell phone rang. "Agent Net," he answered.

"Agent this is Special Agent Caden Caruso. This is a courtesy call to let you know that we are re-arresting Deputy Chief Rodney Park for the murder of Mayor Clyde Hebert."

"On what grounds?" shouted a surprised Net.

"A gun was found in his home that tested positive for the gun that killed the mayor. The district attorney has authorized his arrest and will now ask the court to rescind his bail."

"Do me a favor. Don't process the arrest papers until I can get there and talk with him. I'm on my way."

***

The weather had changed to misty and chilly conditions. Someone wearing a dark color hoodie entered a building located in a desolate area of the warehouse district. Most of these buildings were vacant with many undergoing renovation. All the streetlights were out. Only a sparse light could be seen from a window of this building. It was in very poor condition and likely would be torn down in the future. Even so, this building was occupied by a few tenants who couldn't afford to be anywhere else or were in hiding. As this person tapped on a second-floor apartment, she pulled the hood from her head revealing Susan Griffin. The door to this apartment opened slightly. "It's me, Mrs. Van, Stella."

Mrs. Van opened the door wide to allow Stella to enter. "He was a perfect angel tonight, dear. He fell asleep on my lap."

"Always good to hear that, Mrs. Van and I thank you so much for watching him again."

"It's my pleasure. Keeps me young, ya know. Good night, sweet boy," Mrs. Van stated patting him on the head.

"Okay. Let me get him in his bed. Stella picked up her son and nestled him against her shoulder. He stayed asleep until she entered her apartment next door. The room was pitch black but she managed to locate the rocking chair where she held her son in her arms. Facing a window, there was a picture of J.C. Net on the sill that could be seen from the reflection caused by the light of the moon. Staring directly at this picture with tears in her eyes, she began singing a children's song to help send him back to sleep. *"Sweetest little boy, everybody knows, don't know what to call him but he's mighty like a rose. Looking at his momma, with eyes so shiny blue, makes me thing of heaven..."*

CHAPTER 16
Pretty in Pink

When Net arrived at police headquarters he was met by Ernest Washington. Ernest gave Net a big hug.

"Man it's been too long. I love seeing you but the circumstances suck. Whomever is framing Rodney is doing a great job. I was just going to talk to him, hopefully you'll join me."

"That's why I'm here Ernest."

Net and Washington went into an interrogation room where Officer Colin Kennedy and FBI agent, Caden Caruso had escorted Rodney Park in handcuffs.

"This isn't necessary. Please remove the cuffs so I can freely speak to my client."

The police officer looked towards Net, who nodded his approval. The cuffs were removed and both officers left the room.

"Well, it's good to have three of Keister's finest gathered together, but I didn't think it would be my ass on the line," said Rodney.

Ernest Washington gave Rodney a hug.

"I'm not going to lie to you man, whomever is setting you up is good. Who in the hell did you piss off and who would have access to both your

155

car and home? The knife found in your car and the gun in your home had to be planted by someone who has it in for you."

"Everyone knew I hated Lampino, but not enough to kill him. My wife Charlotte had some issues awhile back and ended up sleeping with Lampino. I blame myself for this, since I should have made sure she was better taken care of."

"I think you better come clean with Ernest about Charlotte's problems and her family issues," said Net.

"My wife's mother has been confined to a mental institution since before I married her. Actually, I've never met her in person. Charlotte had some issues in the past, but they were mainly due to her lack of medication. She has a great doctor now, Jeff Howser. I have a caretaker, Mildred Monroe who makes sure Charlotte takes her medication as prescribed and I trust her to care for Charlotte."

"Well, we can't rule anyone, or anything out including you, Mildred and Charlotte," insisted Washington. "What can you tell me about your relationship with your father in law?"

"Gee, I thought you were here to defend me. To prove me innocent," stated Rodney."

"You must be totally honest with me. You know anything you tell me is confidential. Guilty or not I will do my best to defend you."

"It's my job to find the truth," added Net. "That's what I'm going to do. But you need to be prepared for anything that might happen."

"As far as my relationship with Clyde is concerned, I respected him, but there was not any love between us. He thought Charlotte married beneath her station and never let an opportunity go by to remind me of that. I wasn't crazy about him, but had no reason to kill him. Hell I wouldn't have the job I have, or had, without him."

"There's no way they will give you bond now, so the best I can do is request that you be housed away from the general population, due to your position. I'll be working as hard as I can, with help from J.C. Net to clear this up as soon as possible. In the meantime, if you think of any other suspects, please get in touch with us."

The men all got up and hugged each other. Ernest Washington knocked on the door window and Colin Kennedy came in and handcuffed Rodney and led him away.

Ernest made an emergency telephone call to the night judge on duty to arrange for Rodney to be placed in a private section of the jail, under protective custody. Timing was of the utmost importance, so Net was also on the phone with his lifelong friend Senator Greg Slidell.

"Senator, we have a situation here in New Orleans…my friend Rodney Park has been charged with murder—" Net began.

"J.C., I've heard about that situation. You know I would do almost anything for you but this is just a little over the limit of what I can do," the judge interrupted.

"Greg, I'm not asking for you to step in and convince the judge to release him on bail, even though I do think he is innocent. I'm asking that you make arrangements to place him in a cell away from the general population."

"I can do that. The warden is a friend and supporter of mine. I'll make the call. Talk with you soon."

"Thanks Greg. Hate to ask but we need this done right away. Even a minute in the general population could be deadly for a cop." Net gave a thumbs up to Ernest who was still on his phone awaiting the judge's response.

"Glad you were able to pull some strings. The judge I was waiting on doesn't pull any punches. Odds were against him doing any favors for us. Never had the pleasure of standing before him in the past," Ernest responded sarcastically. "Not much more we can do tonight. I suggest we get a good night's sleep and hope Rodney is protected in that prison."

**

Rhonda and J.C. didn't sleep very well during what was left of that night. Still, they were both up early the next morning. "Let's have breakfast downstairs," suggested Rhonda.

Their hotel room had a sizable walk-in shower, so J.C. decided to take advantage of the opportunity and joined Rhonda under the wonderful pressure of hot water. There had been little time to appreciate this occasion together since they had returned to New Orleans. Steam from not only the hot water but from the passion within the shower resulted in a dense condensation covering the shower glass door. Only the silhouettes of their bodies could be seen sandwiched together against the wall of the shower. When they stepped from the shower both were clean and seemed satisfied after their few moments together.

"Do we still have time for breakfast?" asked J.C.

Rhonda looked at her watch. "Absolutely. I don't have to be at the theatre for another couple of hours. Those theatre people are not early risers. They hit the Quarter scene after rehearsal and party all night."

The couple decided to sit outside in the courtyard area to enjoy their breakfast. Net convinced Rhonda to try grits properly this time. She ordered the grits as a side to a couple of scrambled eggs and bacon. It was the grits she tried last as she was concerned about their taste and texture.

"Put a little butter in the middle of those grits and stir it around until it is melted within," suggested Net.

A spoonful of the grits was placed in her mouth by J.C. because she was taking too long to try them. As she moved them around her mouth and then swallowing, a big smile spread across her face. Net knew that meant she liked them as she quickly finished the rest in a flash.

While they waited to sign their bill, Net noticed T.J. talking across the street. "Hey, T.J.," yelled Net.

As soon as he heard his name, T.J. began to run down the street with Rhonda and J.C following.

"Put the charge on the FBI hotel bill," Net yelled at the waitress who was on her way to their table with their bill.

Rhonda chased behind T.J. while Net took an alternate route through some side streets. She followed as close to T.J. as she could but he was a little too fast for her. After several blocks, T.J. cut through an alley to evade his chaser but as he came through the other side, J.C. was waiting. Net lowered his shoulder as T.J. plowed into his side which sent T.J. to the ground and Net bent over in obvious pain. The collision allowed enough time for Rhonda to catch up and place handcuffs on T.J. still on the ground.

"J.C., are you okay?" she asked concerned about his pain.

Net put his hand up indicating he needed a minute before he could respond. He was still feeling the consequences of the beating he took at the hands of the mugger. "I'm okay. Just need a couple of seconds."

"Why you after me?" screamed T.J.

"Who said we were after you? We only called your name because we wanted to talk with you and you took off running like you were up to something," answered Rhonda. "So why did you run?"

"Don't know. You guys lookin' to pin some of them murders on someone and T.J. knows you feds would like to take T.J. off the street."

"We're not going to pin anything on you unless you are guilty," commented Net who was still recovering from the blow he took. "I think we'll take T.J. to the station for questioning and we'll see what happens from there."

"I need to go to the theatre from here but I called for a police car to pick you two up and here they are now," Rhonda said as a patrol car pulled by their side.

Net and T.J. proceeded to police headquarters.

***

"Can we use one of your conference rooms?" ask Net. "My friend here T.J. and I need to have a little talk in private."

Colin Kennedy showed Net to a conference room and closed the door.

"Can I get you a cup of coffee, or something cold to drink?"

"Fuck no! I don't want to spend any more time here than I have to. I didn't do nothing and you have no reason to hold me here."

"No one is charging you with any crime, at this point. We just need you to tell us what you know about the murders in the quarter, the Lampino murder and any connection between that and the murder of Mayor Hebert."

"Man that shit is fucked up. A few of the ladies that I have a business arrangement with dated Lampino on a regular basis. I know for a fact that he was known to rough up the women, which could have put a target on his head, but I swear it wasn't fucking me. Now as far as that mayor dude's concerned, I had no idea that his daughter was the same woman I know as Carla. She sort of worked part time in the quarter. I wasn't exactly her sponsor, she more or less freelanced, but if she got in a jam, she had my number. Blew my fuckin' mind that she was married to the deputy police chief. Just goes to show ya that if ya not giving a bitch the right stuff at

160

home she's gonna find it on the street. I will say one thing, that bitch was some high class pussy. When she was on the street, she was always dressed to kill. I didn't mean that literally." T.J. gave out a loud laugh, pleased with his own sense of humor.

"When and where was the last time you saw Carla?"

"I haven't seen her in weeks. Bitch used to strut her stuff down Bourbon Street and had men falling all over themselves buying her drinks at the Kitty Club and Jokers. I'm not even sure if she charged for her services. I do know that she would get so fucking drunk that she didn't know where she was. Out of the goodness of my heart I poured the bitch into a cab a few times when her ass was falling in the gutter. Still can't believe who she was. My fucking mind is blown."

"What about any connections she might have to any of the victims?" asked Net.

"Look, I don't want to answer any more questions without an attorney present," T.J. responded.

"We're not looking to hook you up on any charges for the services you provide. I just want to get this killer."

"Well, this bitch Carla or whatever her name really is, should be a prime suspect. I know for a fact she did Buck Lawrence. If I'm thinkin' straight, I kinda remember seeing her the night old Buck got his penis whacked."

"How do you know about Lawrence's penis?" inquired Net.

"She done chopped it off, didn't she? I think I heard it somewhere on the street," revealed T.J.

It was obvious to Net, T.J. was only willing to provide so much information. "Interesting that you know about Buck Lawrence and you used the term 'she' when describing his assailant. None of that is public knowledge. I'll ask you again, where did you get that information?"

"I don't know, man. I just heard it. Even if I did know, you don't squeal around here. That could be bad for your health."

"Give me your number, T.J., so I can contact you whenever I need to. And I expect you to answer. Don't even think about leaving town."

"Ya mean I can go?" T.J. asked.

"Get outta here." Before Net could finish, T.J. was out of the door. Net sat alone pondering what evidence he did have when a female officer interrupted his thoughts.

"Agent, there's a lady out here who says she has to see you. Says her name is Aurora?" There was a pause in the officer's statement as though she didn't believe that was her real name.

Net stared at the officer for a moment. "Oh, okay, yeah. Send her in." Remembering that she was Lorena's next door neighbor, Net hoped that she had some pertinent information for him. "Aurora, take a seat," Net offered.

"I ain't staying," Aurora declined. It was obvious she was not comfortable being in a police station. She rocked back and forth constantly looking over her shoulder. "Here. Thought you might want to see this." Aurora handed Net a flash drive and began to walk towards the door.

"Hold on, Aurora. What is this?" asked Net.

"I don't know. My neighbor gave that to me."

Net knew she wasn't telling the whole story. "What's on this?" he said holding up the flash drive. "What's on this? You must feel it's important that you brought it over here."

"My neighbor said it's some dude breaking into Lorena's house. That's all I know. She doesn't want to be involved."

"Who doesn't? What's your neighbor's name?"

"Dude, did you just not hear me? Are you deaf? She doesn't want to be involved." With that statement, she quickly departed from the police office rushing through the door without looking back.

Net did nothing to stop her as he knew where he could always find her. He inserted the flash drive into the side of a laptop that was sitting on the table before him. A video began showing a person wearing a dark-colored sweatshirt with a hood approaching the walkway to Lorena's side of the double of her home. Without hesitation, the person ripped through the yellow crime tape blocking the front of Lorena's home. It was difficult to tell whether this person used a key or was able to pick the lock as he entered the home with little trouble. Just as the door opened, he turned around and the camera caught a clear view of a man as he looked about to see if anyone had seen him. He remained inside for approximately twenty minutes until he could be seen leaving. He had a small package in his hand as he hurriedly continued away from her house. From the angle of the video, it wasn't hard for Net to determine which house the video came from. He wondered whether this same camera might have caught sight of the killer. Without acknowledging the video to the police, Net rushed to the FBI office so Tatiana could run facial recognition on this mysterious man.

Rhonda had arrived at the Le Bon Theatre with the hope that her new friend, Stella, would show her face once again. It wasn't surprising that she wasn't there but there was a familiar face in the crowd. Josh Hancock was in attendance auditioning for a part in a play. COVID 19 had claimed the health of one of the performers who wouldn't be able to return anytime soon. By coincidence, the open part was that of a doctor and Hancock felt he was the obvious replacement. He spotted Rhonda on the opposite side of the stage and began to joyfully waving to her.

Rhonda rushed over to his side and took him by the arm. "Keep quiet!" she exclaimed. "I'm here undercover and I can't have my cover blown. As far as you know I'm just an acquaintance or someone you just met."

"Wow! How exciting. Maybe I can help you."

"No, Josh. This isn't a job for rookies. It could be dangerous. Anyone of these people could be a killer."

Hancock looked around and thought he didn't want to be the next victim. "You can count on me. I will stay out of your way, Agent. Oops! Sorry."

"Please don't call me agent," Rhonda hissed as she looked around to be sure no one was within ear length. "Are you here for a part in the play?"

"Yeah," he snapped. "I've been trying for a part in this theatre for years and they keep passing me by." It was obvious Hancock was holding a huge chip on his shoulder because he had not been selected in the past. "Pardon my French, but these fuckers have bypassed me numerous times. Well, I'm the only one here for this part this time so we'll see what excuse they will have."

Just at that moment, Chris Nelson walked in and immediately started screaming at everyone on stage. Both of his eyes were blackened as though he had been in some sort of fight. He had a split lip and a contusion on the side of his neck. "Are you here to try out, or are you just putting the moves on that employee?" asked Nelson referring to Hancock. "She's not one to be associated with if you want to be successful with me."

"Good luck," whispered Rhonda as Hancock moved away.

The cast spent the next two hours listening to Nelson screaming at each one of them, not singling any particular person out. Hancock spent that time stumbling through his lines and constantly being humiliated by Nelson. All in all, he wasn't as bad as Nelson would like one to believe but at the end of the rehearsal Nelson told him not to call, they would call him. Hancock knew what that meant and stormed away from the theatre.

Rhonda saw the interaction between Nelson and Hancock and tried to comfort the doctor as he rushed away. He would have none of it and never gave her a passing glance. "Why do you have to be such an asshole?" Rhonda asked Nelson not being able to hold her tongue. "The guy did his best. Why don't you encourage him instead of degrading him? I guess you insult everyone around you." Rhonda was referring to the injuries about his face.

"I beg your pardon." Nelson got directly in front of Rhonda's face pointing his finger close to her nose.

Rhonda took his finger and bent it backwards until he dropped to his knees begging for her not to continue. "From now on, you will treat me and anyone else with respect."

Nelson nodded his head vigorously and she let go. It was only seconds before he regained his cockiness and he informed her she was fired and never wanted to see her on his set again.

Rhonda decided it best to just leave and not push matters any further. She would contact Zack White later and determine if she would still have a position at the theatre.

***

Joker's Wild served lunch every day before it turned into the sleazy barroom it was noted for.

Tatiana had the early shift this day and Rhonda decided to check in with her before proceeding back to the FBI office. "What can I get you?" asked Tatiana who was playing her part very well.

Rhonda hadn't finished breakfast that long ago so she just asked for a cup of coffee. There were too many people in the bar for them to have a conversation including Biff Holder. He had returned behind the bar and was barking out orders to all the servers. "You know I think I'll have my coffee at the bar," Rhonda instructed Tatiana.

"What are you having?" Biff asked Rhonda.

"Oh, I ordered a coffee from your waitress. I just wanted a seat at the bar." Rhonda was a little flirtatious by touching Biff's hand which he quickly removed from the counter and walked away. She noticed his right hand was bruised and battered. Tatiana placed the cup of coffee in front of Rhonda but it was Biff who returned with cream and sugar. As he placed the items before her, she again grabbed his hand, and gently caressed it. "What happened?"

Biff would have none of it and jerked his hand away from Rhonda. "Things happen," was his response as he walked away.

Rhonda wanted to get Biff talking but she soon realized that she was the wrong gender to do so. The lunch rush began to subside and Tatiana strolled over to where Rhonda was seated.

"I think you're wasting your time. J.C. would have a better opportunity."

"I'm thinking you are correct," answered Rhonda.

Just at that moment, there was quite the noise, laughter, coming from the rear area of the room. T.J. appeared with a "lady" on each arm strutting as if he owned the place. He wore a pink leisure suit with matching hat and bright orange shoes. He was obviously parading his available merchandise through Joker's Wild to see if any customers would have any interest. The first person he spotted was Rhonda seated by the bar. "What's up Agent?" he yelled loud enough for even those outside could hear him. His attention was suddenly diverted to a table of young men that seemed to want to negotiate his price.

His statement immediately caught the attention of Biff. He stared at Rhonda for a moment and began to approach her. He removed her cup and advised her that those seats were reserved for alcohol drinking patrons. Rhonda paid her tab and decided to move on. "Do you know her?" he shouted at Tatiana.

"I have no idea who she is," responded Tatiana. "Just a lady who wanted a cup of coffee."

Biff went about his bartender duties and was preparing to finish his shift. Lisa had just shown up as his replacement. "You're late," Biff snapped as Lisa began to take over.

"Sorry. She just lied to you," Lisa concluded trying to change the subject.

"What are you talking about? Who lied to who?"

"That Tanya chick just lied to you. She was getting cozy with that FBI agent in here the other night."

"What do you mean, cozy?"

"She definitely knew her. They were chatting about something. Before that Fed arrived there were a broad and a couple of foreigners seated at the same table. Tanya seemed to have some interest in them."

"Interesting. You think they were hooking up?" asked Biff.

"Didn't look like that to me. I think Tanya was feeding her some dirt on whoever was seated at that table because that Fed left right after they had that conversation."

"Sooo, Miss Tanya, is either an agent or an informant," pondered Biff. "Watch what you say to her but let's keep an eye on her. I think the boss might be interested in this."

CHAPTER 17
Gentlemen Prefer Blondes

A dense fog rolled in from the Mississippi River and engulfed downtown New Orleans during the late afternoon hours into the evening. The Le Bon Theatre was in total darkness except for the flicker of a small light coming from a back room. The theatre was located deep in the French Quarter in an area that had little traffic and almost no pedestrian activity. Barely seen, a dark figure lurked around the outside of the building, disappearing in the gloomy darkness of the night.

Chris Nelson was spending late hours in his office which was often the case. Searching through papers on his desk, he seemed frustrated with his project. The aroma of a fresh pot of coffee encouraged him to take a break. Pouring his coffee, he sensed a presence behind him and he swung around facing someone dressed in a dark hooded garment. "What are you doing here?" he exclaimed. "Thought I told you not to come back. You're not welcome here anymore. Now, get the fuck out." He turned his back momentarily to finish preparing his coffee and felt something he wasn't expecting. The cold steel blade of a knife was pressed across his neck and only a second later, his neck was gushing blood down his side. Dropping his coffee to the floor, he quickly grabbed his neck, gasping for air but before he hit the ground he was dead.

This stranger quickly exited the building carefully avoiding any cameras as though he or she knew their location.

***

J.C. arrived at their hotel deciding to make it an early evening. Rhonda was nowhere around so he assumed she was working with Tatiana trying to find a connection between all the victims and suspects. Net had eaten so much good food since he had been in New Orleans that he felt a night with no rich cuisine might be just what he needs. He laid on the bed to relax and it wasn't long until he was sound asleep. The noise of the door opening woke him so he expected Rhonda to walk into the room. He was extremely surprised to see Susan Griffin approach him before he could react. He searched for his gun before he realized it was across the room sitting on a small table.

Susan dropped her coat on the floor revealing a low cut sexy dress as she sat on the edge of the bed next to Net. "I've been waiting for this moment for a very long time. I've missed you so much." She began to nimble on his ear and ran her fingers down his side.

Net seemed reluctant at first but he did put his arm around her and pulled her even closer. "I've missed you too," announced Net in a surprising fashion.

Susan pressed her lips against his and he responded in a similar way. She climbed into the bed next to him and held him as tight as she could. She continued to kiss him and he did not fight her off. Susan began to remove her dress at the same moment Net was removing his shirt. "Don't you have a girlfriend?" she suddenly asked.

It was at that moment that the door to the room swung open and Rhonda entered. Startled, Net sat straight up in the bed and looked about him. He realized he was alone.

"What's wrong?" questioned Rhonda as she observed Net rubbing his eyes and looking as if he didn't know where he was.

"I guess it was a dream," he responded as he regained his wits about him. He wasn't sure he remembered everything in this dream.

"What dream?" asked Rhonda. "What was it about?"

J.C. began to remember most of the dream but felt it wasn't a good idea to explain it to Rhonda. He didn't really understand what had happened himself. He knew Rhonda was the love of his life and didn't want to destroy the relationship he had built with her. Still he was bothered by his actions. "I don't remember what happened. You know it was one of those occurring in your sleep but you don't recall anything when you finally wake up."

"Well, you look like shit. Looks like you were run over by a truck."

Ordinarily Net might have been insulted by that statement but he was more concerned about the actions he took in his dream than anything else. "Come lie down by me and let's get some sleep." Net patted the mattress by his side.

Rhonda was asleep in minutes after lying in the bed while Net lay wide awake for the remainder of the night. Morning arrived quickly for Rhonda but not so for Net. The night seemed to drag on forever as he tried to resolve his actions in his dream. Probably seeming like a nightmare to him, he dug himself out of bed and into the bathroom to have his morning shower. Just as he lathered himself to its peak, his cell phone began to ring. Trying to rinse the soap from his face before he rushed to answer his phone, his foot slid across the tiled floor as he caught himself on the vanity. Managing to regain his balance, he caught his phone on the final ring.

"Did I wake you?" asked Tatiana.

"No, just in the shower. What's up? I'm naked and dripping all over the floor."

"Well, that was a commentary I didn't need to visualize. On second thought, hehe." Tatty was glad no one could see her at this moment as her face turned as red as could be. "I've got some information for you. I searched and searched for an ID on that person in the video you gave me. Finding no match, I did some digging in areas where, well, let's just say you don't want to know about. This individual is Steve Colombo."

"Where do I know that name from?" Net asked.

"He was the man that Bernard Lampino was going to see the night Lampino was murdered."

"Interesting. My understanding is this Colombo guy was also affiliated in the mafia with Lampino," suggested Net.

"Wait. I have more. I checked some of the crime cameras around his home at the time of the Lampino murder and I found him moving in a great hurry away from the scene one block over. I don't think his name is Colombo despite what I found."

"What does that mean?" asked Net.

"The profile I found just doesn't look right. Information is very sketchy and there is very little background on him prior to two years ago. So I..." There was a long pause in her story.

"So this is where you don't want me to know what you did," suggested Net.

"Correct. I did a little more digging and I would suggest you use this information but keep it to yourself. You don't want to answer any questions about how you came about this knowledge. I don't know his real name but he is definitely a federal informant against organized crime."

"Are you sure about that?" inquired Net.

"Are you really asking me, of all people, that question? You do know who you are talking too? I also noticed many phone calls between him and Lorena Gonzalez. I'm looking into that connection."

Net began shaking his head. "How stupid of me to ask that question." Net suddenly checked his phone. "I've got another call coming through. Keep looking for any connection with the victims and our suspects. Talk with you soon." Net switched over to his incoming call. "This is Agent Net."

"Agent, I'm not sure you remember me but this is Mildred, Ms. Charlotte Park's caretaker."

"Ok, yes, I know who you are," responded Net.

"I didn't know who else to call with Mr. Rodney in jail and everything but I haven't seen Ms. Charlotte in over a day. Previously she was coming home in the wee hours of the morning, drunk and completely out of it. The death of her father and Mr. Rodney's arrest has hit her hard. I called Dr. Howser, but all he did was up the dosage of her medication. Just a moment. I hear a noise at the front door." Mildred placed the open receiver on a table in the foyer while she opened the front door in time to see a taxi driving away from the premises. Charlotte stumbled up the steps to the front door barely keeping her balance as she entered her home. "Ms. Charlotte, where have you been? I was worried about you. You need your medication."

"Fuck off, Mildred," Charlotte ordered as she pushed past Mildred approaching the stairs inside her home. Charlotte was wearing the blonde wig she commonly wore when she went out. Her clothes were askew and Mildred recognized that she was wearing the wig backwards.

"Agent, are you still there?" Mildred asked as she retrieved the phone.

"Yes, I'm still here Mildred. I heard everything. I'll ask Rhonda to stop by and check on her in a little while. Probably best to let her sleep it off for a while."

"I don't normally stay overnight but maybe I should," commented Mildred.

"Probably not a bad idea, but you don't get paid for that kind of service do you? I'll get Charlotte to pay you whatever you earn."

Net's phone began to ring again. "Mildred, I need to run. Just keep doing whatever you're doing and I'm sure the Parks will be grateful." The caller ID on Net's phone showed the call was coming from Orleans Parish Prison. "This is Agent Net."

"Agent, this is Warden Jeff Dallas at OPP. I regret to inform you that Rodney Park was beaten badly today in the recreation yard before guards could get to him. He's been rushed to University Medical Center. I don't know his current condition but he was in grave condition when the ambulance arrived. He was still alive when they departed."

"What the fuck, Warden?" screamed Net. "How did that happen? He was supposed to be under constant surveillance and protected from the general population of the prison."

"His cell is in isolation but I guess no one suspected this would happen in the yard."

"What did you think would happen? What kind of buffoon are you?" Net couldn't talk to this guy any longer as he hung up the phone. He raced out of the bathroom and began to put on the first clothes he could find.

"What's going on?" asked Rhonda. "I heard you screaming at a buffoon?"

174

"Rodney's been hurt and rushed to the hospital. I need to get over there. I need you to go to the Park's home and check on Charlotte. Mildred can fill you in." Net headed towards the door in a rush.

"Call me when you have news about Rodney. Be careful," Rhonda urged.

Rhonda and Net departed for their respective destinations. Net reached the emergency room entrance of UMC flashing his FBI identification to the police detail at the door. Registration was just inside and Net inquired the whereabouts of his friend.

"Are you family?" the registration nurse asked.

He again flipped his ID open and she immediately referred him to the third room behind a closed curtain. "Anybody here?" asked Net as he peeked around the curtain. Covers on the bed were pulled back and blood stained the sheet and pillow but there was no sign of Rodney. Net backed away and stopped a nurse walking past. "Do you know where they have taken Rodney Park?" he asked.

She wasn't familiar with this case but she instructed him to follow her to the nurses' station where she could find his answer on the hospital computer. "It appears he has been taken to surgery."

"How is he? What are they doing to him?" Net wasn't sure what to ask so he was hoping the nurse would give him a rundown on Rodney's injuries.

"I better let the doctor talk with you as I really don't know his condition. I'll make a note in the computer that you are here. This may take a while so I would suggest you go to the waiting room."

***

Rhonda was greeted by Mildred at the front door of the Park residence. "Mildred, how is she?"

"She's been sleeping for a while now. She needs her medication but I'm scared to wake her."

"Let's go see," suggested Rhonda who began to climb the stairs followed by Mildred. Rhonda opened the bedroom door and was immediately greeted with the stale smell of alcohol.

"Wow," said Rhonda, waving her hand in front of her nose. "Let's see if we can get her up. Charlotte, it's Rhonda. I'm just checking on you." Charlotte rolled over on her side away from Rhonda in order to remain asleep. Rhonda was persistent with her attempts to arouse her. "Charlotte, you must get up and take your meds and get something in your stomach."

Rhonda picked up her medicine bottle, containing large white pills, on the table next to the bed. Reading the prescription it said to take one in the morning with breakfast. "Come on, Charlotte. You have to get up and take this pill. It's way past due. Mildred can you fix Ms. Charlotte something to eat."

"Yes, ma'am. Immediately."

Charlotte began to come around and sat up in the bed even though her head kept nodding up and down. "Rhonda, what are you doing here?" she asked. Her eyes were very blurry but the more she rubbed them, the clearer they became.

"Everybody was worried about you so I thought I'd come check," responded Rhonda.

"Why was everyone worried? Because I slept late?"

"No. You disappeared for a while and no one knew where you were and when you arrived home you were pretty drunk and your clothes were in disarray."

"Well, someone is telling a fib. I've been here the whole time." Charlotte paused for a moment and thought before she said anything further. "I actually don't remember the last couple of days."

"You remember nothing?" asked Rhonda. Charlotte shook her head. "Well, alcohol and drugs mixed together can sometimes do that to some people. Do you remember the news about your father?"

Charlotte's head dropped lower but then rose with a smile on her face. "Yeah, the bastard got what he deserved."

"Charlotte, you don't mean that," offered Rhonda.

"Oh yes, I do. The man was a tyrant and put my mom away because he was embarrassed. She didn't need to be placed with lunatics. She needed some affection from her family. He would have done the same to me if Rodney hadn't come along." There was another pause in her thoughts. "Poor Rodney. He finally had enough of that bullshit and killed his ass."

"You think Rodney actually killed your father?" asked Rhonda.

"Of course I do. But I won't say that in a courtroom under testimony. Who else would have done it?"

"Did he say anything to you to make you think he did it?"

"Oh, I see what you're doing. I'm not saying another word."

"Charlotte, believe me, J.C. and I are on your and Rodney's side. We want to help you. J.C. is convinced Rodney did not do this."

"And what about you Rhonda? Do you think he did it?"

"All I know is I support J.C. and if he believes it, then I believe him."

Rhonda's phone rang and she told Mildred she would take the call in the other room.

"How is Rodney? I'm here with Charlotte and I can tell you she believes Rodney killed her father. She's in pretty bad shape."

"Rodney is in surgery right now. Do you think Charlotte is well enough to come to the hospital? It doesn't sound very good. Hold on here comes a doctor."

The doctor slowly made his way down the hall to the waiting room. His surgical mask hung from his neck covering his blood and perspiration stained scrubs. He wiped his brow and thinly gray hair as he reached the waiting room. "Are you family of Rodney Park?" the doctor asked Net.

"I'm not family but a very close friend," Net responded.

"I can only discuss his condition with his immediate family."

Net showed the doctor his FBI credentials and implored him to provide any details he could.

"Well, I'm Dr. Jacob Steinberg and I just performed a craniotomy to relieve pressure on his brain. Apparently Rodney was hit on the head with a rock by another prisoner."

"So he's coming out of surgery?" asked Net.

"No. He has a long way to go. I'm a neurosurgeon and my part was successfully performed. He was apparently stabbed several times in the abdomen area and another surgeon suspects he is bleeding internally. Quite honestly it is touch and go. Keep him in your prayers and let's hope for the best."

"How did anyone get access to Rodney?" Net mumbled as he returned to the call with Rhonda. "Did you hear all of that?"

"Yes, I heard everything. Poor Rodney. I won't tell Charlotte anything right now. Maybe by the time we get there, you'll know more."

"He was supposed to be well guarded and kept away from other prisoners. When I leave here I'm going to have a long talk with the warden. I have a feeling that someone was paid to look the other way when Rodney was in the exercise yard. Ernest Washington just walked into the waiting room, so let me talk to him."

"If you can give me an hour or so, I'll get Charlotte showered and dressed. It's obvious she got really drunk last night, but I know she'd want to be there for Rodney. I'll call you when we're on the way. I love you."

"Love you too." Net sat back down and positioned himself for the long wait.

Except for the continuous beeping of medical equipment, the operating room was in total silence. Rodney lay on the table surrounded by six doctors and numerous attending nurses. Blood not only stained the sheets covering him but also the attire of the medical staff. The lead surgeon occasionally barked out orders for the staff to perform but the mood in the room was extremely tense.

A CRNA (Certified Registered Nurse Anesthetist) sat near Rodney's head monitoring all of his vital signs when suddenly the regular beeping sound turned into a continuous alarm warning the staff of his failing health. "Doctor, the patient's pressure is 60 over 40 and declining," warned the CRNA.

Just at that moment, Dr. Lindsay Perry, the attending surgeon, announced that she had found the bleeding artery and was attempting to cauterize it to stop the bleeding. "Just give me a couple more minutes Rodney. Hold on man. Hang in there."

The medical staff held their collective breath as the doctor feverously worked to save Rodney's life. The heart rate was quickly restored to a sinus rhythm as the anesthesia machine signaled a return to the normal beeping sound. There was a sigh of relief as the scrub tech wiped the sweat from Dr. Perry's forehead. "You guys can do the close," Dr. Perry suggested to the resident surgeon assisting her with help from the circulator (registered nurse).

Dr. Perry began to remove her gloves when suddenly the warning alarm once again began to sound out. The medical equipment showed a flat line indicating there was no heart action. Perry rushed back in and called for the crash cart. The circulator (registered nurse) quickly charged the paddles for the resident to administer the charge on Rodney's chest. There was no sign of life.

CHAPTER 18
Hospital Food Sucks!

Dr. Lindsay Perry, looking exhausted, walked slowly down the hallway of the hospital corridor stopping several times along the way to answer questions from the nursing staff. Rhonda had arrived with Charlotte as they waited impatiently in the waiting room. Perspiration dripped from Perry's face as it seemed like an eternity for her to arrive. Charlotte, Rhonda, Ernest, and J.C. all jumped from their chairs at the sight of Dr. Perry. "He made it through the surgery but the next twenty-four hours will be critical to his recovery. He's not out of the woods yet."

"So by tomorrow we'll know if he will survive?" whimpered Charlotte.

"He's very weak but he's a fighter. If he makes it through the next day, I'll be very optimistic about his recovery. Right now, I just don't know. We managed to repair his injuries but like I said, he is just so weak. And we need to continue to monitor the pressure on his brain. Dr. Steinberg provided relief but we need to be sure that doesn't return. For the time being, we are going to keep him in the ICU where he will get the best of care."

"Thank you Doctor. Is there anything we need to do?" asked Net.

"Go home and get some rest yourselves," answered Dr. Perry. "And pray. Pray a lot. There is nothing more you can do here. I'll have the nurse contact you if there is any change."

Ernest got up from his chair and started pacing around the waiting room. "I've spoken to the police department and they are having a guard positioned around the clock at ICU. I'm not leaving this hospital until he gets here. The warden was apologetic, but I told him that shit won't cover it. He better pray Rodney makes it, or I'll fucking sue him and his entire department. When I'm finished with him he'll be lucky to get a job as dog catcher."

There was no way any of them were going to leave. They returned to their chairs except for Charlotte who decided to lie on the only sofa in the room. She was so tired, probably from the night before, that she actually fell asleep for a short while. Net took the opportunity to visit the hospital cafeteria and purchase coffees for everyone. By the time he returned Charlotte was awake and seemed more alert than before. She began to ask questions that had already been answered by Dr. Perry. Net and Rhonda glimpsed at each other as if to say, "Wasn't she there when Dr. Perry answered that?" However they understood Charlotte's condition and appeased her with the same answers.

Hours went by and there had been no word from any doctor or nurse which J.C. felt was probably good news rather than bad. He asked an occasional passing nurse if there was any information but they didn't seem to have anything new.

Suddenly and surprisingly, Charlotte stood and announced she was leaving. "I'm tired of waiting around this shit hole. I've got things I could be doing." With that disclosure, she abruptly departed.

"Wow. I thought, maybe, her medication was working. Guess it wasn't," stated Rhonda.

Two of New Orleans finest showed up just as Charlotte was making her exit. "I'm Officer Gregory Owens and this is my partner, Lara Moore. We were sent here to guard a prisoner."

"We don't need you to guard a fucking prisoner, you need to protect a suspect that someone is trying to kill," shouted J.C.

"I'm sorry, this is just what the assignment read."

Ernest Washington got up in Gregory Owens' face. "This man, Rodney Park is innocent and if anything happens to him while y'all are on duty, I will personally blame you. This man is the deputy chief of police in this city and deserves respect."

"Yes sir. Lara and I will make sure he is protected."

***

Josh Hancock had been under a lot of pressure to find evidence from the bodies of all the victims. He decided to clear his head and take in some entertainment at the Kitty Club. It was a slow time at the club so he didn't stay long before he decided to walk down to Joker's Wild to see what was happening there.

Lisa was serving drinks today as Hancock bellied up to the bar. It wasn't very crowded here either but he decided to have a drink anyway. He was a Long Island Iced Tea man and had a tendency not to stop at only one. A lady with long blonde hair was seated next to him but her back was turned so he couldn't get a good look. "You come in here often?"

She couldn't believe he used that corny line on her and she swung around to see who he was. Josh was a fairly good-looking guy, although very strange, but he did not recognize that he was talking with Charlotte Park. Not sure if it was the blonde wig or the makeup she was wearing but she looked very attractive to Dr. Hancock. "If you're going to buy me a drink, you better have a better pick up line than that." Before Hancock could respond, she ordered herself a cocktail and told Lisa to put it on his tab.

"Well, I just haven't seen you before in here so I was just curious if this was your first time," Hancock stated.

"Honey, this isn't my first time for anything," she countered with a wink. She placed her hand on his upper thigh as he nervously changed the position in his chair.

Hancock wasn't used to a female aggressor. He was usually the one making the advance. Having lost his composure, his tea went down very quickly. Lisa immediately brought him another which he wasn't sure he wanted but drank it anyway.

"Well, are we getting the fuck out of here?" Charlotte abruptly asked. She didn't wait for his answer as she took him by the hand and pulled him towards the door carrying a large red bag. He passed a hundred dollar bill to Lisa but Charlotte didn't allow him to wait for any change. Charlotte escorted a reluctant Hancock to the Chez Royal Hotel.

Upon seeing Charlotte, the clerk behind the front desk didn't hesitate to toss her a key to one of the hotel rooms. "Usual room," the clerk advised. "Don't mess it up."

Hey, wait just a second," came a voice from the other side of the lobby. T.J. appeared at that moment and approached the couple. "I told you, any tricks you perform I get a cut."

Josh Hancock looked at Charlotte like he was surprised by T.J.'s statement. "You're a hooker?" he questioned.

"I ain't no hooker," Charlotte exclaimed. "Do I look like a hooker? I don't owe him shit."

"Are you charging me for sex?" asked Hancock.

"Look, are you horny or not? I'm not going to wait all night. I can find me another man at a moment's notice."

Hancock thought for a minute and pictured what he thought Charlotte would not only look like naked but also what she told him she would do to him in bed. "Let's go." He took Charlotte by the hand and pulled her towards this old elevator in the lobby.

The elevator smelled of perspiration and urine and the carpet was worn to the point of holes through to the floor. The door rattled close and the elevator trembled as it lifted to the second floor. About fifty percent of the second-floor hall lights were burnt out or weren't working and the carpet wasn't any better than the elevator. The door to the room was difficult to open even with a key and the deadbolt could not be used because it no longer lined up with the hole in the frame.

Hancock sat on the bed listening to the flushing toilet in the bathroom. He slowly began removing his clothing as he awaited Charlotte's appearance. To his surprise and delight, she entered the room totally naked. Her flowing blonde hair touched the perky nipples of her breast. Surveying what he was in store for, he quickly removed the rest of his clothes and slid under the covers on the bed.

Charlotte wasted no time in joining him, disappearing under the sheets. "Oh my Lord!" Hancock groaned with an expression of satisfaction on his face.

After a few minutes, Charlotte emerged from under the covers in order to fulfill her desires. Hancock made numerous attempts to kiss her but each time she turned away. Finally, being finished and without a word, she turned away from him and told him to go to sleep. Hancock spent most of his day around the dead so this encounter was not something he expected.

185

He'd expended all of his energy and it was only minutes before he was sound asleep.

Footsteps from above floors could be heard as well as outside his room but it was a loud boom that startled him. Charlotte was no longer next to him. The curtains were drawn closed and with no light on, the room was pitch black. He could barely see a dark silhouette in the far corner of the room. "Is that you?" he asked realizing he didn't even know her name.

The figure moved closer and climbed on the bed. He suddenly felt a sharp pain as he grabbed his side feeling something that was wet. The pain continued as this person was now close enough for him to see someone wearing dark clothing and a mask covering their entire head. Just as a knife was about to be plunged into him for a second time, there was a banging on the door.

"Your time is up!" screamed the desk clerk from the hotel.

Holding the knife dripping with blood, the stranger bolted from the bed, through the door, shoving the hotel clerk to the side.

"Hey, what are you doing?" screamed the clerk. Other guests began opening their doors as they heard the ruckus in the hallway.

Before anyone could react, the unknown person was down the stairwell and out the door.

The clerk flipped on the light in the room and found a naked Hancock standing with his blood-covered hand over a wound in his side. The clerk rushed in to assist him and reached him just as he collapsed from the amount of blood he had lost. He helped Hancock to his feet just long enough to get him back in bed. Curious onlookers had now come into the doorway as the clerk tried his best to put pressure on the wound to keep it from bleeding out. "Someone, please call 9-1-1!"

Charlotte, red bag firmly in hand, had been unable to find a taxi to take her home so she continued to walk through the French Quarter with the hope of finding one. Something must have occurred because there was a large police presence on the street ahead where a crowd had gathered. In order to avoid the mess, she moved one street over where there was less gridlock. It was dark and few people could be seen. She was suddenly grabbed from behind and shoved against the wall of a store she was passing.

"Where's my cut, bitch?" T.J. pushed himself tightly against her body smashing her into the wall. His hand covered her mouth. "I told you I get thirty percent of anything you take in so hand it over or you ain't gonna be working these streets much longer." He relaxed his hand just long enough for her to talk.

"I didn't get any money. You can check me out. I've got just enough for me to get a taxi ride home."

T.J. searched her pockets, purse, and red bag. When he opened the red bag, he asked, "What's all this shit?"

"Just a change of clothes," she responded. "That's all. Just clothes."

"Well I don't see no money. Why you give him a free ride? If he didn't have no money, I don't know why you did him." T.J. decided to release her when he saw others walking towards them. Relieved, Charlotte rushed to the nearest hotel hoping to find an available taxi. On her way, she stepped in front of a cab causing him to slam on his brakes.

"What are you doing lady? I could have killed you!" yelled the driver.

"Take me home," she demanded.

"Where is home, ma'am?"

"Just drive uptown on St. Charles. I'll tell you when we get there."

Traffic was light so it wasn't long before they reached the vicinity of the Park home. "Drop me off here," instructed Charlotte.

This was about a block away from her home. Mildred was waiting for her on the porch as Charlotte walked up and for a change Charlotte didn't seem drunk.

"Ms. Charlotte, where have you been?" scolded Mildred. "I worry about you when you do this. You look awful." Mildred commented about Charlotte's appearance and was trying to reposition her wig as it was hanging by a pin. "You go ahead and put on your nightgown and get in bed. I'll bring up a warm glass of milk with your medication."

***

Net arrived at City Hall first thing in the morning where police headquarters was also located. There was a podium and microphone set on the top of the steps leading into the building. There was a dozen or so media members lingering around outside of the building waiting for a press conference which had been scheduled. One of the reporters spotted Net and rushed to interview him. As he did so, many of the others joined them. Numerous questions were shouted at Net but he informed them repeatedly that he had no comment.

Their attention was suddenly diverted to the Chief of Police, Lauren Tabassco- Johnson, the first African-American head of police in the city. The chief took to the podium to make a statement. "There have been many questions concerning the recent murders in the city. I am pleased to advise that we do have a suspect in custody."

"Who is it Chief? Give us a name," demanded a media member.

"At this point, I'm not going to provide any names as we are still collecting evidence. I'll leave that to the authorities to provide. Oh, I see FBI Agent J.C. Net over there. Maybe we can convince him to provide more details of this investigation. Come over here agent." Lauren Tabassco- Johnson pointed to Net standing to the side of the steps.

Net slowly moved in front of the podium, not particularly happy about being put on the spot without warning. The group of media had now grown to about twenty people. Cameras were snapping and filming whatever he was about to say. Before he could even begin, once again the reporters shouted questions at the same time.

Net stood there silent for a moment. "I really have no comment because this investigation will continue as far as I'm concerned."

"So, what does that mean agent? Are you not satisfied with the arrest that has been made?" shouted some of the media.

"The evidence points to the person we have in custody but we want to be sure is not just circumstantial. Because of this I'm not going to name anyone."

"Rumor has it that Deputy Chief Rodney Park is the one in custody," announced a female reporter in the back of the crowd.

That statement took Net by surprise and when he looked up to see who asked the question, he was shocked to see Susan Griffin standing there smiling. He rubbed his eyes and when he looked up again, all reporters standing before him were all Susan Griffin. As he refocused on the crowd, he realized that Susan was nowhere to be found. His mind was confused. "I have no further comments," he stated as he walked away.

The reporters continued to yell questions as Net disappeared into the building and Lauren Tabassco-Johnson returned to the podium. She held her hand high to settle the crowd. "Everyone, please. One at a time." She had no more answers to provide them and eventually the media disbursed in different directions.

***

While Net traveled to police headquarters, Rhonda returned to UMC to check on Rodney. She entered through the emergency room door when she overheard nurses discussing Josh Hancock's injuries. "Pardon me," she began. "But did I hear you correctly that Dr. Hancock has been injured and is in the hospital?"

"Yes ma'am. He came into the ER early this morning."

"Is he still here? What happened to him?" asked Rhonda as she flashed her credentials in front of the nurse.

"You can see him for yourself. He's in bed 3 on the right side," replied one of the nurses. "I believe the doctor is with him now."

Rhonda peaked through the closed curtain of ER room 3 and found Hancock sitting on the edge of the bed while the doctor was securing a bandage to the side of his stomach. "Are you okay, Josh?" she asked.

"Except for this hole in my stomach, I'm fine," responded Hancock. "I took a couple dozen stitches and the doc here patched me up. He says I'll be as good as new in a few days."

The doctor excused himself from the room while Rhonda had many questions. "What happened to you?" she asked.

"I was attacked in the French Quarter. I guess it was a mugging. Somebody wearing all black and a mask, stabbed me with a knife and ran off."

"Did they take anything?"

"Not really. I think they were just scared off." It was obvious Hancock was not going to tell the whole story of the prostitute and hotel room to Rhonda.

"You were damn lucky if that's all that happened." Can you provide any description of your assailant?"

"I already told the cops but I really didn't get a good look."

"Well, I'm glad you are okay." Rhonda walked away feeling like he wasn't being truthful but there was nothing more she could do if he was unwilling to cooperate. She took the elevator up to the ICU and was greeted at the door by the officer outside of Rodney's room. She again flashed her badge and entered the room. Rodney lay there still unconscious, attached to many medical machines including a ventilator to help him breathe. Rhonda stood there for a moment staring at his comatose body. Afterwards she stepped back in the hall and asked the guard if he had any visitors today.

"No one but you and the doctor," he replied.

Just then she saw Dr. Lindsay Perry standing by the nurses' station. "Dr. Perry," she called out.

"Hello agent. What can I do for you?"

"Can you give me an update on Rodney's condition?"

"I'm sorry to say there's really no change. He did make it through the night and that is a positive. But I would have liked to have seen a little more alertness from him by now. His vitals have improved but we are watching that pressure on his brain. We may have to go back in."

"Please keep us updated on his condition Dr. Perry."

***

Charlotte stepped out on the balcony of her two-story home overlooking St. Charles Ave. Street cars passed by up and down on what New Orleanians called the neutral ground. This was the wide median between each way of the avenue. A breeze was blowing just enough to ruffle through her hair, causing her to continuously push it from her face. Students were riding bikes to get to their classrooms at the nearby universities of Loyola and Tulane. Charlotte enjoyed the scenery of the day until Mildred appeared at her side.

"Can I fix you something to eat Ms. Charlotte?" asked Mildred.

"No, I think I'll just have a cup of coffee. What did we do last night Mildred?"

Mildred looked at Charlotte like she was speaking a foreign language. "Don't you remember?"

"Everything is a little hazy. Actually I really don't know. Wasn't I here all night?"

"No Ms. Charlotte. You went out but I don't know where or what you did. Did you go to the hospital?"

"Mildred, why in the world would I go to the hospital?" Charlotte giggled.

"To see Mr. Rodney!" Mildred exclaimed.

Charlotte looked confused. "Why would Mr. Rodney be at the hospital?"

"He was beaten into a coma in the jail, Ms. Charlotte," Mildred asserted.

"Coma, jail? What in the shit are you talking about?"

"Ms. Charlotte, Mr. Rodney was arrested for the murder of your father and was being held in jail. He was beaten badly by other inmates."

"What did you say? What happened to my father? Why didn't someone tell me all of this?" Charlotte burst into tears. "I just spoke to my father today, nothing is wrong with him!"

"Ms. Charlotte, your father was shot two days ago. They found a gun that matched the caliber in Rodney's coat pocket. He was arrested and sent to jail. Apparently, some inmates hurt him really bad and he's in the hospital fighting for his life. We told you all about this Ms. Charlotte. You even went to see Mr. Rodney in the hospital."

"No one told me a fucking thing. Mildred, go get the car and take me to the hospital immediately!"

CHAPTER 19

Smile for the Camera!

Net met Tatiana at FBI headquarters. She had reviewed and compared the angles of the video on the flash drive Aurora presented with all the possible locations near Lorena's home.

"The only possible location of this video camera, Boss, is across the street from Lorena's place and one house down on the right," Tatiana advised. "I took the liberty of doing a property search for that address and it belongs to a Margaret Simons. Ms. Simons is over seventy years old, but it's still worthwhile sending someone to interview her."

"I agree. I've been trying to narrow down the list of suspects, victims, and the locations they all have in common. Most of the victims were Johns and/or tied to the mafia, and definitely vendetta killings. The Le Bon Theatre, Kitty Club and Jokers Wild all seem to be the common denominators. You may be the perfect person to interview Ms. Simons, given her age and being female. Why don't you go see her this afternoon while I go back to the hospital to check on Rodney? Lauren Tabassco-Johnson is out there trying to fry Rodney in the press and I need to steer her in another direction. We need to bring Steve Colombo in for questioning, but I don't want him picked up until after you speak to Ms. Simons. I don't want him to lawyer up before we have more information. Call me on my cell after your interview and I'll see where we go from here. As always, please be careful."

***

Net arrived at University Medical Center just in time to greet Charlotte and Mildred entering together. "Is there any new information on Rodney's condition?" asked Net.

"We are just getting here too. Haven't heard a thing," answered Charlotte. She rushed to the elevator and pushed the close door button several times. "I'm very nervous. Why didn't anyone tell me what was going on?"

Net looked at Mildred with a puzzled look. She shrugged her shoulders as if to say that Charlotte has no clue on all that's happened.

Charlotte rushed to Rodney's bedside and grabbed his hand in hers. "Oh my poor dear. Please wake up. I don't know what I would do without you."

Mildred and Net sat in silence while Charlotte spoke softly to her husband. "Why would someone do this to you?" she whimpered as she looked about his battered and bruised face. "You said my father is dead too?" she asked Mildred as she burst into tears.

"Yes ma'am. Mr. Rodney—" Mildred started until Net interrupted her.

"Let's not get into the details right now," suggested Net. "But yes, Charlotte your father has passed away. Rhonda and I will help you with anything you need. Just let us know if you would like us to make arrangements for his funeral."

"I think my father made all of his arrangements so we didn't have to make any decisions."

Just at the end of her statement, Rodney's legs began to squirm and there was a groaning sound as his eyes fluttered open. His eyes focused on Charlotte seated beside him and he attempted a tiny smile.

"Rodney, are you okay?" she screeched as she squeezed his hand tighter.

Net jumped up and looked into the hall for a nurse or doctor. He had the attention of a nurse very quickly who immediately paged for the doctor. The nurse joined them in the room and checked Rodney's vitals and tried to get him to talk. He was still very groggy from not only the medication but he had been asleep for several days.

"What happened?" Rodney murmured in a very hoarse voice. "Can I have some water?"

The nurse smiled and said, "You're going to be okay." Charlotte poured a glass of water from a pitcher that was sitting next to the bed. "Just give him a little at a time. Don't want to overload his stomach."

Dr. Perry walked in and seemed surprised by the latest development. "Well, you finally decided to join us," she quipped. She examined his heart rate and cognitive functions and began to smile. "Things are looking very good but you have to understand you will have a slow recovery. I know you can't go back home but I'm willing to sign off on a prison rehab facility for you to be placed in for the time being."

"What are you talking about? A prison facility? Why would he be assigned there?" Charlotte became very anxious and agitated. She bounced from her chair directly face to face with Dr. Perry.

Perry stepped back only to have Charlotte counter with a step forward. Net decided to intervene and tried to pull Charlotte away from the doctor. "Charlotte, the doctor has nothing to do with this. Let us sit down and we'll explain. Mildred, did you bring any of Ms. Charlotte's medication with you? I think she needs something to calm her."

"Yes sir. I always do."

***

Tatiana gathered her notes and was leaving to visit Ms. Margaret Simons. She called and arranged to meet at her house at 3:00 p.m. As she headed for the door, Rhonda walked in.

"Where are you headed Tatty?"

"J.C. wants me to interview the lady on Lorena's block who sent him the video."

"I have some time on my hands Tatty, do you want me to join you?"

"Please do. Interviewing witnesses is not my usual job. I know she isn't a suspect, but I would be more comfortable if you come along."

Rhonda knocked several times on Margaret Simons' door before she finally answered.

"I'm sorry ladies, have you been waiting long? I was in the kitchen making tea and didn't hear you knock. I heard you are here about the video I gave to the young woman across the street. A young policeman knocked on my door a few days ago asking if I was aware of the horrible murder across the street. I didn't have much to tell him, but then I remembered that movie tape thing my youngest son put on my front door. I didn't know who to call, so I gave it to Aurora. As far as the murder of that sweet girl is concerned, I sleep in the very back room and don't hear much of anything going on outside. That's why my son, Raymond decided I need that thing on my door. Lordy, I have no clue what help it can give you."

"Thank you Ms. Simons. I just have a few questions. Do you recognize the man on the video? We have identified him as Steve Columbo."

"Let me look closer at the photograph dear. That looks like the gentleman caller that Ms. Lorena entertained often, but these old eyes could be fooling me. There was this nice dark-haired man who would wave to me when I was sitting on my porch. Right after that poor girl was killed I saw him go into her house and carry out a satchel. He was looking around kinda nervously, but when he saw me on the porch he slowed down and told me to have a nice day. The guy in this picture could definitely be him, but I can't be sure.

"We may need you to come downtown and look at some men in a line up, but for now we just want to thank you for your cooperation. If you think of anything else about the man in the photograph, please call me."

Rhonda handed Ms. Simons her card and they both headed for the door.

"I think we have enough information to bring Steve Columbo in for questioning. If you head back to FBI headquarters Tatty, I'll put in a call to Net."

***

J.C. and Rhonda decided to meet at Lorena's house. Colombo must have been looking for something and it would be beneficial if they could discover what it was before questioning him. The yellow police tape across the door was torn and they found the front door unlocked. Inside the house looked trashed. Someone had definitely been searching for something. Whoever was there before them made their job a lot harder with everything tossed about, not to mention, they may have found what they were looking for. Rhonda started in the living room while Net took the bedroom. Clothes were flung across the bed and covering the floor. The drawers to her dresser were all open and mostly empty. The items of clothing were predominantly what you would expect to find in the bedroom of a prostitute. Silky dresses and pants with lacy lingerie littered the floor. But it wasn't until Net came across thongs and pasties that he would initiate a feeling of embarrassment.

"I think we are looking for a needle in a haystack," Rhonda stated. "We really don't know what we are even looking for." She sat down on the edge of the bed looking defeated.

"Let's get Tatiana searching for any connection that Colombo had with Lorena," suggested Net.

"J.C.," Rhonda began. She never called him J.C. so he knew something was up. "How strong do you feel about Rodney's innocence? I mean, are you really convinced he didn't kill the Mayor and Lampino and maybe others?"

"I'm 100% positive he is innocent. If I thought he was guilty, I wouldn't be here right now. I'm determined to find the real killer. I hate to say it but I'm not so sure it's not Charlotte. Her necklace was found at one of the scenes. She has access to Rodney's vehicle, his closet where his clothes are hung and she seems to have had issues with her father. Her memory loss is either very convenient or she really doesn't know what she is doing. Isn't she bipolar? It could explain a lot about her disappearances at night and the rumored sexual activities she seems to enjoy."

"All of that is interesting and I guess could be true but I just don't know. I think the one thing we can agree on is that one of them is a killer."

CHAPTER 20

All That Jazz

The day started gloomy and very humid as a large crowd lined the French Quarter streets in preparation of Mayor Clyde Hebert's funeral. A jazz band would lead the horse and carriage transporting the mayor's casket for citizens of New Orleans to pay their respects. A mass would begin at St. Louis Cathedral in Jackson Square and then parade through the Quarter until they reached his final resting place. Every pew in the cathedral was filled to capacity with a large contingent also outside. The archbishop of the New Orleans Archdiocese was the celebrant of the funeral services. A eulogy was performed by the mayor's closest and oldest friend, Patrick McQueen, who happened to be the local district attorney.

Charlotte sat quietly in the first pew flanked by Mildred and a few close friends. Her mood never seemed to change as she stared in the same direction the entire service. Mildred handed her several tissues but Charlotte just clutched them in her hand, she never did seem to have the need to use any.

After the conclusion of the mass, the procession, led by several motorcycle policemen, slowly began their march through the streets of the city. The brass jazz band took one deliberate step at a time while playing the funeral dirge "Just a Closer Walk with Thee", as hundreds of mourners walked behind the carriage carrying the casket. The mayor was loved and respected by all members of the community and people from all walks of life showed up to pay their respects.

Net and Rhonda were late arriving and joined the enormous crowd lining Royal Street. While the ceremony continued in front of them, Net had focused his attention on the gathering across and around him. He suddenly fixated on a female in the rear of the crowd. He hesitated for a moment because he recognized it was Susan Griffin. He wasn't sure if his eyes were playing a trick on him once again. Rhonda noticed his attention trained across the street and she too recognized Susan.

"Net, it's her. Across the street!" Rhonda and Net burst through the crowd attempting to cross but police officers standing along the route detained their passage through the procession. "Let him through!" screamed Rhonda flashing her FBI credentials in the face of the officers. "We're FBI!" They backed away but by the time Net was able to fight through the crowd there was no sign of Susan.

J.C. ran up and down the street but there were so many ways she could have disappeared including alleys between some of the structures. The same policemen who obstructed his path, joined them in their search but to no avail. Susan had once again managed to evade his attempts at her capture. After exhausting their search, Net and Rhonda joined the mourners following the procession to St. Louis Cemetery No. 1. This cemetery is one of historic significance so only close friends and family members were allowed inside. As they followed the pallbearers to the mayor's final resting place, an above-ground vault, the group passed the grave of voodoo queen Marie Laveau which is a main attraction during a guided tour of the cemetery.

Net and Rhonda were not included on the list of close friends and family. It was especially noticeable that Charlotte was not among the guests entering the cemetery. Net wanted to check on Rodney again and decided that he and Rhonda would head back to the hospital.

***

They were both surprised to find Charlotte seated by Rodney's side and not attending her father's burial. Mildred was also there but sat to the side of the room away from the Park couple. Rodney was more alert than the last time they were there and Net had some questions for him. "Good to see you feeling better, old man. If you're up to it, I'd like to ask you some questions about what happened to you in prison."

"Better? Don't know about that. They cut my painkillers back some so my head may be clearer but my pain certainly hasn't subsided. What do you want to know?"

"Do you know who did this to you?" asked Net.

"Not really, but I can guess. I was jumped from behind and basically knocked out. I didn't see who it was but there's a few guys in there I helped put away. If they knew I was a cop, it really could have been anyone."

Net was disappointed but understood and expected this. "I'd really like to punish those guys for doing this to you."

"Well, when you are a lifer, what more can you do to them?" Rodney shrugged.

"Rodney, glad to see you alert and awake," Rhonda said as she approached his side. "Have you thought anymore about the evidence they have against you? How did that gun get in your coat pocket and the knife under the seat of your car?"

Net suddenly interrupted as he didn't like the direction Rhonda's questions were going. "I don't think Rodney should be answering any of those questions without his attorney present." Truthfully he didn't want to ask any questions related to the murders with Charlotte present. "We're going to let you rest now and we'll talk about this later."

Net took Rhonda by the hand and led her out of the door. "What the hell were you doing asking those questions?" Net exclaimed. "What were you thinking in front of Charlotte?"

"I know. I know. It was out of line. I just thought I could get him talking," Rhonda suggested.

"I'll tell you again. Rodney did not do this!"

"I'm sorry. Don't be mad." Rhonda had fallen behind an irritated Net. She quickly sped up to catch him and grabbed his hand. He clutched her hand in his which signified that all was okay between them.

***

Officer Colin Kennedy and FBI Agent Caden Caruso arrived at Steve Colombo's home to question him. There were numerous knocks on the door but there was no answer. Caruso walked to the side of the French Quarter home and peered through the window. There was no sign of activity but he could see what appeared to be the legs of an overturned chair in the center of the front of the house. "Colin, I don't see anyone inside but there is a chair on its side."

"I think that's good enough for us to enter, don't you?" Kennedy smiled. It was no effort on their part to go inside as they found the front door unlocked. Drawing their pistols, they entered calling out to Colombo that the police were entering his home. Caruso went right and Kennedy left as they searched for anyone who might be there. The two met in the middle where Caruso had seen the chair. Not only was the chair exactly as he described but when they looked up they found the dangling body of Colombo hanging from a rope around his neck. The rope was attached from the balcony railing. Apparently the chair was used for him to disembark with the rope around his neck.

Kennedy called and requested a forensics team and the coroner to meet them at Colombo's home. He then called Net with the news. "Agent, we are over at Steve Colombo's and found him dead. Apparently a suicide. He hanged himself. We are looking to see if he left a note or anything that would give us a clue why he killed himself."

Kennedy and Caruso began looking around Colombo's shotgun home. Everything was in its place and the whole house was spotless. Even in the drawers of his dresser, each item of clothing was folded perfectly. In the kitchen, every can or box of food were positioned in the cabinets, label forward and type of food arranged together.

Kennedy discovered a sealed envelope resting on the kitchen counter. Nothing was written on the outside but Kennedy felt it was important to open. There was a letter inside, not addressed to anyone in particular. Kennedy sat in a nearby chair and began to read. "If you are reading this letter, you know I am dead. I decided to take my own life after I learned that my own daughter was murdered. I somehow feel that if I had been a better father things might have been different. I don't know who the person was who took the life of my sweet Lorena but I will rest easy knowing they will eventually pay for their crime. Lorena had her issues and I can't help but feel they were mostly my fault. I cannot go on living knowing I played a part in the manner her life turned out to be. With that in mind, I end my life as swiftly and abruptly as I can. Signed Steve Colombo."

"Net, this is Colin Kennedy. Colombo left a suicide note so I don't think there's any question that he committed suicide. We'll see if forensics turn up anything else but I think at this point we can conclude this was not a homicide."

"Were you able to find anything he may have taken from Lorena's house?" asked Net. "Strange he ransacked her home just after her murder. He was definitely looking for something."

"Nothing stands out but we'll spend some more time looking before the coroner and forensics arrive."

Kennedy and Caruso searched the entire home. Nothing seemed like it didn't belong or was out of place including no indication that Lorena was Colombo's daughter. There were no pictures of her or references for any other family members for that matter. The coroner and forensics teams just arrived so the two detectives were about to pack it in when Caruso noticed something odd. There was no television, DVD player or computer for that matter yet there was a DVD sitting on the mantle of the fireplace. Maybe the evidence they were looking for had been sitting right in front of them the whole time. Caruso carefully bagged the DVD and took it with them.

***

Tatiana was back at her job at the Joker's Wild. The bar was relatively quiet but both Biff and Lisa were on duty behind the bar. Tatty sensed a coldness between the two as neither said a word to each other. "Everything okay?" she asked Lisa.

"What do you mean? Between that queer and me? You noticed huh," Lisa offered quietly. "I had a date with a guy named Chris Nelson the other night. He's a play director at the Le Bon Theatre. Nelson must swing both ways because I had no idea that he and Biff were an item. You never would have known it had you seen him in my bed."

Biff walked over and grabbed Lisa by the arm as Tatiana went about her waitress duties. "I told you not to talk with that bitch," Biff warned. "Something's not right about her."

"I'll talk to anyone I fucking please," Lisa demanded as she pulled her arm away from him. "Just because you are pissed at me because I slept with your boyfriend, you can't tell me what to do."

"You've been warned!" Biff stated as he walked away.

David Gold, a Quarter resident and regular in the Joker's Wild walked in at that moment. "Hey, I know everyone knows this guy, but Chris Nelson was found dead in his office last night," he announced so everyone could hear.

Biff dropped a glass that shattered on the floor as he fell to the floor on his knees, while Lisa turned in shock. Tatiana rushed over to assist Biff and found that a shard of glass had already pierced his right knee. She helped him to a table and compressed a clean towel against his wound to curtail the bleeding.

Lisa didn't like David Gold. She called him a jackass behind his back but she was curious what other information he had. "David, what happened? Chris had been coming in here for years."

"I don't really have any details. I saw all the cops over at the Theatre and I asked someone. Evidently, the cleaning staff found him."

"Was it a heart attack or something?" she asked.

"The word in the crowd outside the theatre was, he was stabbed."

***

Net arrived very quickly at the theatre soon after word had reached police headquarters. Like some of the other murders, Nelson's throat had been slashed. No murder weapon had been found by the forensics team onsite. They dusted for prints but it was pointless because so many different people were in and out of his office. Blood samples were taken but most of the blood was confined where the body was found. Nothing appeared out of place and whether anything was missing would have to wait until the morning when the theatre crew would report to work. They would be familiar with the office more so than the police. Officers interviewed the cleaning crew that found his body but they knew nothing more.

***

Rhonda reported the next morning for her job at the theatre. Most of the staff had not heard the news and Rhonda pretended as though it was a shock to her. "Hey, didn't you just have a fight with him the other day?" yelled one of the actors in the direction of Rhonda. "Yeah, I thought he fired you and told you not to come back," commented another. The agent suddenly felt the pressure of the crowd moving in her direction. She had the feeling this staff might automatically determine her guilt and turn into a lynch mob before too long.

Zack White exited the building and saw Rhonda in the middle of this turmoil. He rushed to her aid and as long as he was with her no one dared to touch her.

"Maybe it's time that you reveal yourself as FBI. These people really didn't like Nelson but their jobs depended on his existence. Without him they are out of work so things could get very emotional."

White led Rhonda away from the gathered crowd and into his office. After making sure she was secure in his office he decided to address the theatre employees. By now the group seemed larger as time went on. "Ladies and gentlemen may I have your attention," he yelled but they were so loud his words fell on deaf ears. He repeated himself and along with the help of a few, he caught their attention. "For those of you who worked with Chris Nelson, I'm so sorry for your loss. This is a terrible tragedy. I want everyone to know that their jobs are secure and as we say, the play

206

must go on." There was a modest cheer among some of them. "This is not a time for celebration but one for trying to find the person who did this awful thing."

"We know who did it!" screamed someone in the crowd. "You escorted her away."

"No. No. You are wrong. This lady's name is Rhonda Bordelon and she is an undercover agent with the FBI."

There was a sudden sense of uneasiness amidst the crew. "Why was an FBI undercover agent here at the theatre," yelled another.

"Let me answer that question." Rhonda reappeared at Zack White's side. "The FBI felt it was important for me to be here as some of the victims have had ties to this theatre. I'm sorry if you feel deceived by this but believe me the whole purpose of my being here is to discover who committed these crimes."

"Well, that didn't help Chris Nelson did it?" shouted a stage performer.

"Unfortunately, no, it didn't. Let me do my job and I promise you we will get the person or persons responsible for this."

Net had been working with a forensics team looking for any evidence they could find when Rhonda joined him inside Nelson's office. "Well, obviously Rodney could not have done this," Net told Rhonda.

"No, but it doesn't clear him from the two murders where weapons were found in his possession."

"Okay, let's say he did it. Why didn't he just use his gun when he killed Lampino?" asked Net.

"Let's not get into this now. It will just end in an argument. We'll agree to disagree for now. If we can solve this one, maybe that will clear Rodney as well."

Josh Hancock and his assistant Jennifer Davison both arrived at this crime scene. It was very unusual for both of them to come together. "Hey, Net. What you got here?" asked Hancock.

"Well, looks like we got a dead body," snapped Net sarcastically as Jennifer, amused, gave a slight chuckle.

Hancock looked at the covered body on the floor and pulled the layer back for him to view the body. "Ha!" shouted Hancock. "Somebody finally gave this bastard what he deserved. This looks similar to the others. Slashing of the throat causing him to bleed out." Hancock walked away shaking his head leaving the dirty work for Jennifer to finish.

"I can't do much here at the theatre. Let's bag him and send him to the morgue. It looks like Hancock and I will have our work cut out for us. Lampino's buddy, Steve Columbo is already in a drawer waiting for us."

"Thanks Jennifer. Please give me a call when you have results," requested Net "As always, please keep the results secret until I get a chance to review them. I know Rodney wasn't involved with either of these killings, but Lauren Tobassco-Johnson and Patrick McQueen both would like nothing more than to pin these on Rodney."

CHAPTER 21

Parental Guidance

What a difference a few days make. Ernest Washington entered Rodney Park's hospital room to find him sitting in a chair next to the bed, eating lunch.

"Damn man, you look a hell of a lot better than last time I saw you. I almost wish you weren't healing so fast. The DA, McQueen is pushing to have your case set for trial as soon as they release you from here."

Doctor Perry walked into the room and looked over to Washington. "I'm as surprised as you are about Rodney's progress. His vitals look great and I see no reason to keep him in this unit. He will need physical therapy to strengthen his legs, but that can actually be done at an out-patient facility. Given the fact that he is still under arrest we can arrange for him to be sent back to prison, hopefully in a safer section and he can be sent here for therapy."

"Doctor Perry, do you think you can give me one more day before you release him? I'd like to file a motion for a change of venue, even though my chances are slim. I have the motion drafted, but didn't expect Rodney to heal so fast. I can file as soon as the court opens in the morning and ask for an emergency hearing."

"I can give you until noon tomorrow Mr. Washington. That's when I will be making my rounds and approving discharges."

The visitors increased by four shortly after Dr. Perry's departure. Charlotte and Mildred arrived at the same time as J.C. and Rhonda.

"I'm glad you're here Ernest," stated Net. A couple of suspects we hadn't ruled out yet are no longer suspects. Steve Colombo and Chris Nelson are dead."

"Well, that's good news!" Realizing what he just said, Washington looked about the surprised faces of the others in the room. "Not that they're dead, that's not what I meant. I meant that Rodney could not have killed them! This doesn't totally clear him of any wrongdoings, but they can't pin these two on him." Washington decided to stop talking before he landed up with his other foot in his mouth.

"It helps," answered Net. "But he still had motives and weapons in his possession from the others. We have to be able to explain that. Steve Colombo apparently committed suicide, so that doesn't help Rodney, but Chris Nelson was murdered by his throat being slit open. Ernest, I'll go over with you how these two fit in."

"My, what a clusterfuck!" offered Charlotte. Charlotte seemed a little more relaxed than usual. She was dressed in a designer suit, with matching shoes and bag, looking like she was headed to high tea at one of the fancy hotels, nothing like she would be seen in during some of her escapades in the French Quarter.

"You know I saw a picture of you on a table in the foyer of your home wearing the most beautiful necklace that would have gone perfectly with that outfit," Rhonda suggested. "I wish you would have worn it."

"I know the exact necklace you are referring to," answered Charlotte. "Now that you mention it, I haven't seen it in a while. I should really look for it."

The necklace was obviously very valuable so Rhonda couldn't comprehend Charlotte's lackadaisical attitude towards it. She knew it was in police custody so maybe Charlotte was playing along with her game. "Regardless, you look very pretty today," Rhonda admired.

"Why, thank you. You are such a dear."

Rhonda stepped back for a moment and consulted with Mildred who was sitting in a chair pushed against the back wall of the room. "Ms. Charlotte seems to be in such a good mood today. She actually seems normal."

Mildred was taken aback by Rhonda's statement. "Why, yes, agent. She is doing very well today. She is finally keeping up with her meds on a regular basis."

Ernest decided to break the awkward silence. "We have some good news all. The doctor said that Rodney is well enough to start rehab. Tomorrow he will be transferred back to jail, but this time it will be under close supervision. He will be transferred here three times a week for therapy, but within the next few weeks he should be ready to stand trial and clear his name. J.C., I'd like to meet with you later this afternoon to discuss trial strategy. I'm trying to get the case moved to Baton Rouge, but I doubt McQueen wants to let this one go. This is the type of case that could pole vault him to the governors' mansion."

The door to Rodney's room opened and Josh Hancock stuck his head in. "Well, where was my invitation to this party?" Josh entered the room and surveyed all the people present.

J.C answered, "This is one party you don't want to be part of. Do you know everyone here? This is Rodney's wife, Charlotte, her caretaker, Mildred and his attorney, Ernest Washington. Of course you know my partner, Rhonda Bordelon."

"Hi everyone. I was called down here to pick up a few unfortunate souls and thought I'd check on Rodney."

Josh looked over at Charlotte. "I'm sorry to stare, but you look so familiar. Have we met somewhere before? I know you've never been to my office and I doubt we travel in the same social circles, but for some reason I know we've met someplace."

Mildred glanced towards Charlotte and got an uneasy feeling. "Ms. Charlotte, I think it's time we start heading home. Mr. Rodney needs to get some rest."

Charlotte stood up to leave and shook Josh Hancock's' hand. "I assure you Dr. Hancock that if we met somewhere before I would have remembered you."

Charlotte gave Rodney a kiss on the cheek and she and Mildred headed out the door."

"Josh, how are the autopsies coming on Colombo and Chris Nelson?"

"My office should have the results by morning. Jennifer finished with the autopsies, but we're still waiting for the toxicology reports. I should have them before noon tomorrow and will fax them to you at FBI headquarters."

"Thanks Josh. Rhonda and I are headed back there now. We have some evidence to review from Colombo's home."

Everyone left the hospital room except Ernest Washington.

"Since Colombo and Nelson died while I'm in custody that should clear me from being a suspect in those murders, right?"

"Yes," chuckled Ernest. "At least McQueen can't pin those on you. We do need to start planning our defense. Since you are well enough to start therapy, it's just a matter of time until we get a trial date. My first question is how in the hell did a knife from your kitchen end up under the front seat of your car, with Lampino's blood on it?"

"I wish I knew! I'm not very handy in the kitchen or familiar with kitchen items, so that knife could have been gone a long time. It may have been thrown out in the trash and someone took the opportunity to dig it out to frame me. I've been in law enforcement long enough and I'm smart enough to know not to hide a murder weapon in my own car! Everyone knew I hated Lampino and I can't say I'm upset over his death, but I didn't do it."

"That's the first thing you have to stop saying. Even if everyone knew your feelings towards Lampino, you don't need to keep reminding them. Do you remember where you were and who you were with when you heard of Lampino's murder?"

"I was at my desk in police headquarters when the call came in. I'm not sure who could collaborate this since my door was closed. I don't know if the coroner determined the time of death, so maybe when we have this information I can pinpoint my whereabouts."

"We need to throw some shade on you by compiling a list of other people who could have killed Lampino. What are your thoughts?"

"Gee, where should I start? Lampino was part of the underworld of the quarter. Nothing went on in the quarter without his knowledge. His group was like a branch of the service, with him being a four star general. He had many lieutenants who answered directly to him. He was involved in prostitution, drugs, gambling and even shook down the local merchants for protection money. My thoughts is that one of his lieutenants figured he was due for a promotion."

"I think this is a good place to start. If we can find a way to explain the knife I believe the remaining evidence is circumstantial. Now for the more difficult task, your father-in-law, Mayor Hebert. Apparently he was much loved in the community and was a shoe-in for reelection. Explain your relationship with him and your relationship with your wife, Charlotte. I've learned that she takes medication daily. What kind of problems does she have and will she be able to support you at the trial? McQueen will want to try the cases together. He wants to get the biggest bang and a two for one trial will garner lots of publicity."

"Hebert wasn't crazy about me, but we showed each other mutual respect. I married his daughter who was his only child. Never met his wife. I'm not sure of her current condition. She had some mental issues and has been in a hospital for a long time. Neither Clyde nor Charlotte mention her very often. For all I know, she could be dead. Charlotte and I met at LSU while we were both in grad school and reconnected several years later when I attended an LSU football game. We were married shortly after, so I didn't know a lot about her family until we moved to New Orleans. It was shortly after our marriage that I learned Charlotte had some mental issues, but seemed to have them under control with medication."

"What type of mental issues Rodney?"

"I really am uncomfortable talking about them."

"Rodney, this is your life on the line, so believe me McQueen will know every aspect of Charlotte's problems."

"She has a tendency of not always taking her medication, or mixing her meds with alcohol. I don't completely understand her exact diagnosis. You would need to speak with Dr. Howser. I know I've heard him say something about bi-polar disorder. When she does have one of her episodes she will leave the house in the middle of the night. I'm not sure where she goes since she usually waits until I'm asleep. I do know that on one occasion she ended up at Lampino's place. I guess that is another motive for me killing him."

"When she returns from one of her 'episodes', does she remember anything?"

"No, nothing, which is why I don't want her to take the stand."

***

Net and Rhonda arrived at FBI Headquarters and were immediately approached by Tatiana. Holding the DVD found in Colombo's home, she quickly placed it into Net's hand. "I suggest you take this into the conference room and watch it."

"Well, what's on it?" asked Rhonda.

"I'd rather not say. You just need to see it." Tatiana was blushing as she walked away from them.

Puzzled, Net and Rhonda proceeded into the conference room and placed the DVD into the computer. A video started showing an unoccupied bedroom which lasted about thirty seconds before Lorena entered the room wearing a thong and bra. Music was playing in the background as she proceeded to remove what remained of her clothes. As she stood before the camera au naturel, she began to touch herself in places that made Rhonda look away. Her tongue circled her lips before she wet each finger of her left hand then slowly rubbing her vagina until she was aroused. Net, on the other hand, his interest was intrigued. Rhonda slapped him on the side of his head to draw his attention away from the video.

"Hey, it's evidence!" he announced trying to come up with an excuse to what he was really thinking.

The scene quickly changed from Lorena being alone to a male joining her on the bed. The face of the male was blurred so he could not be recognized, but it was obviously a middle-aged white man with a portly build. He grabbed Lorena by the hair and pushed her head onto his penis. After several minutes of groaning Lorena then rolled over on her stomach and the man in the video started having sex with her from the rear. Lorena got up from the bed and grabbed a paddle from her dresser. It was obvious from her glassy eyes and staggering movements that she was high on something. She started paddling the man's backside as she screamed, "Take that mother fucker!" At this point another male voice was heard entering the room and the video cut off. Tatiana appeared in the doorway with her hands covering her eyes. "Has the porn started yet?" she asked.

"Oh, yes. And I think Mr. Net is enjoying it a little too much," Rhonda answered as she shut off the computer and removed the video. "I think we need to figure out who Lorena's partner in the movie was and who entered the room at the end. Tatty, is there any way you can do facial and vocal recognition on this tape. I know it's a longshot." She looked towards Net.

"I think we'd need 'ass/penis recognition, not facial'," chuckled Net. "So Lorena was not only into prostitution and drugs, but she was also making pornography," stated Net. "Explains the letter we found from Colombo. Anybody have any idea who the male was in that video? Was it Colombo?"

"I couldn't look at it," explained Tatiana. She blushed again at the very thought of the video contents.

"I know you couldn't." Rhonda accused Net of not even looking at the man. "But no, I didn't see any identifying marks. Judging from the build of the body, I'd say it wasn't Colombo."

"I'm glad I caught all of you all together." Patrick McQueen surprised them by entering the room. McQueen had been the district attorney in New Orleans for the past twelve years and was the first African-American DA in the city. He had the reputation of being a bulldog in the courtroom and his record was almost spotless. He was a former athlete who'd played football at Tulane University and then attended law school at LSU. Despite his athletic career ending in college, he had kept in shape by running marathons around the country. "Let's discuss the case we have against Rodney Park."

Net, Rhonda, and Tatiana all looked at each other as if he was looking at the wrong people to help him.

"Look, I know you have personal feelings with regard to this but we still have a job to do and I expect your cooperation," stated McQueen.

"Cooperate? Sure, we'll cooperate but you won't get me to believe that Rodney is guilty. I'm going to continue working this case as though we are still looking for the killer," declared Net.

McQueen shook his head in disgust. "Then I'll have no alternative but to ask you to step away from this investigation. As a matter of fact, I'm going to insist that you no longer have anything to do with it. Let NOPD handle the investigation from here on out." McQueen moved close to Net where they became face to face.

"You can ask or insist all you want but I'm not going anywhere. If I find any new evidence I'll be happy to share it but my main focus will be to prove Rodney Park innocent. You get in my face one more time, you'll never do it again."

McQueen backed away guardedly. "Do the two of you feel the same way, Agent Bordelon, and I'm sorry but I don't know your name?"

"Yes, I'm with Agent Net," suggested Rhonda.

"The name is Tatiana Sokolov and me three."

Without another word McQueen was gone. The FBI threesome momentarily sat in silence. "Well, let's see if we can find out who that was with Lorena in the video," Net said.

"I'm scheduled to work at Joker's Wild later," Tatiana commented. "Do I still go?"

"Let's see how the day goes and decide later," answered Net.

"I'll go back to the theatre and see if I can find out anything more," suggested Rhonda. "They know who I am now so I'm not sure how forthcoming anyone will be."

The three went their separate ways but Net stayed behind to make some phone calls. His first was to Josh Hancock. "What's the status of the Colombo and Nelson autopsies?"

"Jennifer performed the procedure on Colombo and according to her notes there was no reason to think this was anything other than a suicide. Nelson was a different story. No question that the cause of death was a knife to the throat. But I can tell you that the knife was different from the one used on the other victims and not the same as the one in evidence that was found in Park's car. Oh, we did confirm Colombo and Lorena were related. A couple of other things, the person who killed Nelson was shorter than him which we determined by the angle of the knife. The other thing is the killer appears right handed because the cut was from left to right."

"Check the other victims to determine if there is any relation between any of the others," Net requested. "When you have something, give me a call."

Net noticed Caden Caruso through the glass window of the conference room. "Caden, you need to go pick up Biff Holder and bring him in for questioning. I want this one myself."

Net sat back in his chair and studied the suspect board before him. He reviewed each name listed and tried to reconcile any motive they may have. Listed were Rodney Park, Charlotte Park, Zack White, Chris Nelson, Biff Holder, Bernard Lampino, Steve Colombo, and the final name he recently added, Susan Griffin. He stood before the board and placed a red X across the pictures of Nelson, Lampino and Colombo. He had no real reason to include Susan Griffin except for his past with her. As far as he knew, she had no ties to any of the victims, yet he could not eliminate her from suspicion.

***

Mrs. Van was on the floor playing with toy trucks while babysitting Susan Griffin's son. Mrs. Van knew Susan by the name of Stella. The boy was two years old but didn't talk very much except for the few words that he knew. Stella had set up a regular schedule for him to adhere to. After playtime, he had lunch and watched television for one hour, taking a nap afterwards. His favorite lunch food was peanut butter and grape jelly which Mrs. Van always kept in abundance. He liked his sandwich made with small rolls because it was easier for him to handle with his small hands. He didn't make his television hour as he fell fast asleep in Mrs. Van's arms immediately after lunch. She didn't mind as she loved holding him. Her son never gave her any grandchildren so this was always a treat for her.

There was a tapping at the front door followed by the sound of the door creaking open. "Mrs. Van? It's Stella. How is he?"

"Come in. Come in. He's asleep on my lap."

"I'm so sorry that I left him here for so long. You must think I'm a horrible mother."

"Nonsense, my dear. I've enjoyed every minute. I was a little worried when you didn't show up last night to get him. They must be working you awfully hard at that theatre,"

"Yes, the theatre. Right." Stella helped herself to a cup of coffee which had been kept warm by the kitchen stove. Returning to the living room, she sat down next to Mrs. Van and caressed the top of her son's head, then kissed his cheek. The attention to her son was interrupted by the vibration of her cell phone making her leg quiver until she removed it from her pocket. Checking the caller ID, she answered her phone using a language that was unfamiliar to Mrs. Van.

CHAPTER 22

Suspicious Minds

It was a new day and one that Rodney Park should have been ecstatic to reach. After all, he was being released from the hospital. Most patients went home from here but not the deputy chief of police. He was being transferred to a prison rehab facility to further his recovery from the beating he took while in jail. While he could function on his own, movement of his limbs and speech pattern had not totally returned. He remained confined by handcuffs attached to his bed and any movement away from his room had to be supervised by law enforcement. His discharge from the hospital also meant that Patrick McQueen would push for an early trial.

Despite this being a hospital prison, the district attorney made sure that an officer was assigned to sit outside of Rodney's room. While there, he was to undergo speech and physical therapy each day to assist in his recovery. It was expected that he would be ready to return to prison within a week.

Supervisory Special Agent J.C. Net was the first to visit Park. "You don't look very comfortable," Net commented.

Rodney held his arm as high as he could showing the handcuff around his wrist. "Does this look like I'd be comfortable? This place sucks. Let's just say this isn't paradise. Quite the opposite."

"Ernest will be here soon. We need to start establishing a defense. Is there anything you haven't told us?"

"Nothing I can think of. I didn't do this."

"I know you didn't. I'm a little hesitant to bring this up. Where was Charlotte at the times Lampino and the mayor were killed?" questioned Net.

"You think Charlotte framed me?" Rodney was rather insulted by this line of questioning. "We don't have the perfect marriage but she wouldn't do that. She wouldn't have killed her father."

"When she was questioned, she didn't seem unhappy that he was dead," Net offered.

"No question they had their ups and downs but kill him, no. She couldn't have done that."

"Rodney, somebody is framing you. She had the best opportunity to do so. She has no alibi not to mention she doesn't even know where she was. You've told me she disappears at night and no one knows where she goes. The one thing you do know is she slept with Lampino."

"That's more of a motive for me, not her!" Rodney exclaimed. "Leave my wife out of this. I'm telling you now, if you continue to do this I will plead guilty and it will be over with."

Net received word that Biff Holder had been brought into the FBI office. He felt things were becoming heated between him and Rodney Park so his departure couldn't come at a better time. "Get well, brother." He patted Rodney on the leg as he left without any further words spoken.

***

Biff was a naturally nervous fellow but being in the FBI office had his anxiety sky high. He was seated in a conference room on his own but it didn't stop him from speaking out. "I don't know why I am here," he yelled, assuming there were agents watching him through the one-way glass. He wasted much of his energy before Net even arrived.

"Mr. Holder, please take a seat," Net requested as he entered the room.

"Hey, I know you. I talked with you that night in Joker's Wild. Do you have an undercover agent working there with us?" Biff demanded an answer.

"Biff, may I call you by your first name? You're here to talk to us about the murders of Chris Nelson and Bernard Lampino." Net totally ignored his question about the undercover agent.

"What are you talking about? I got nothing to do with any of that."

"No one said you did have anything to do with the murders but you may know something that we don't. Maybe there's something you don't even realize you know. That's why you're here. Maybe we can jog your memory."

"Don't you pigs already have somebody in custody?"

"We do for Lampino but he was in custody when Nelson was killed. Wasn't Nelson your boyfriend? Weren't you arrested for domestic abuse of Nelson recently? That in itself is a motive."

"Oh, I see now. You're looking to pin that murder on someone and I was the most convenient. So why not try and get me on both. That will clear your buddy."

"You worked for Lampino didn't you?" asked Net.

"Well, he owned Joker's Wild so I guess I did. I ain't saying another word until I get a lawyer."

"Fine. If you insist on getting an attorney, we'll reschedule this meeting for Thursday at 10:00 a.m. in my office. If you fail to appear at that time, with legal counsel, we will issue a subpoena for you to appear in court to answer questions."

Biff left Net's office and headed directly to Jokers Wild. It was apparent to Net that he was going to warn all of the employees that the FBI were snooping around the club. Net decided to have Tatiana show up for work at the scheduled time, hoping this would make her appear to not be part of his office.

Net's phone rang. The caller ID said E. Washington. He was afraid this call was not going to be good.

"Hi Ernest. Hopefully you have some good news?"

"Sorry J.C., I just received a call from McQueen's office and they plan on setting Rodney's trial for three weeks from this Monday. That doesn't give us a lot of time to set up a defense. Just as I expected, Judge Kathy Jeffers, a loyal supporter of Mayor Hebert has denied my request for a change in venue. It looks like we will have to pick a jury from the locals. Do you by any chance know of any jury consultants in this area? I've used a firm in Shreveport that really helped my case. If necessary I can have him fly down."

"Crap, that's short notice. Any shot at a continuance based on Rodney's medical condition?"

"Not a chance. Rodney has made remarkable progress and the doctors are saying his physical therapy sessions may end soon. He is still seeing an audiologist regularly, but that will not preclude him from rendering a defense. I would like to meet with you at your FBI office and we can put all our cards on the table. I'm afraid that Charlotte will not be much help in the case and Rodney doesn't want us to even question her. Maybe we can get the testimony we need from her through her caretaker, Mildred. Can we meet tomorrow around 9:00 a.m.? Time is obviously of the essence."

"Yes, let's plan on that. I'll have Rhonda and Tatiana there also. They have worked all the murders with me and hopefully we can plan a defense."

Biff arrived at the Joker's Wild immediately noticing Tatiana already waiting tables. He joined Lisa behind the bar whispering something into her ear. Both looked directly at Tatiana as they were talking but she was too busy to notice. As the day continued, it was very noticeable to everyone in the bar that Biff and Lisa were keeping to themselves as though they did not trust anyone. It was business only when they did speak to Tatty.

"How many beers did you say you needed?" asked Lisa.

"Four. And I also need a bourbon and coke and a gin and tonic as well," responded Tanya (Tatiana). She was beginning to notice the lack of communication with them when her phone began to ring. She recognized that the call was from Net but with Lisa lurking about she wanted to keep that a secret. "Hi, Mom," she began. "What's going on?"

Net was alerting her to his conversation earlier with Biff Holder wondering if she was working with the FBI. "Be careful and if you have any worries about your safety, we will pull you out right now."

"No, Mom. I'm doing okay. I'm at work right now and my boss is giving me the look to get off my phone. Can I call you back later?"

"Sorry Lisa that was my mom. She's worried about me working in the quarter with all the murders happening. I guess no matter how old I get, I'll always be her baby."

Lisa gave her a grin, but was still keeping her distance. Lisa went up to Biff and suggested that they ask Tanya to meet them for a drink when they got off.

"Let's invite Tanya to meet us at the Kitty Club when we get off at 2. We can see how she acts away from Jokers and maybe she'll slip up once we get a few drinks in her."

"Not a bad idea," said Biff.

The crowd was starting to pick up at Joker's as the night moved on. In walked a face familiar to Tanya, Peg, aka Sunshine. She walked up to Tanya and gave her a hug.

"Fuck, you still working here? I thought you'd have high tailed it home to East Jesus by now."

"I'm still here, but it's colder in this bar than in South Dakota. Speaking of cold, I'm getting a cold shoulder from Biff and Lisa tonight for whatever reason. Maybe they are not happy with my work. Since Lampino's death, Biff's in charge and I'm afraid he is about to fire me."

"Let me go talk to them and find out what's up. They know me and will trust what I say." Sunshine walked over to the bar and spoke to Lisa and Biff for a few minutes. She returned to Tanya, holding a bourbon in one hand and a cigarette in the other. "Things are cool now Tanya. For whatever reason they thought you were undercover for the cops or something. I told them that I knew you and was trying to set you up with T.J. for protection. They want us to meet them at the Kitty Club when the shift ends at 2. Business is slow tonight, so I just as soon take a night off and get fucking wasted. I have a date set for 11 at the Chez Royal, but the old bastard doesn't last more than fifteen minutes tops so I should be able to meet y'all there around 2."

Tanya didn't want to blow her cover by refusing the invitation, so agreed to the meeting. She made an excuse to go to the restroom and called Net with her plans.

"I don't like this at all," Net worried. I think you've done enough and should pull yourself out."

"Is that an order, sir? You're the boss but I want to stay in. I've given them nothing to suspect me. They are not trusting anyone right now.

There must be a reason for their paranoia. Let me do this please. I promise I will be careful."

"I will agree to this on one condition. I will have backup planted at every inch of that club. You won't be there alone. I can't be there because they know who I am. Any sign of trouble, they will pull you out whether it blows your cover or not."

There was a noise just outside the bathroom door. "Need to go," whispered Tatiana as she disconnected the call. She quickly opened the bathroom door and saw Lisa walking away.

CHAPTER 23
Blondes Have More Fun

The night was relatively quiet in the Joker's Wild so Biff Holder decided to close early. A dense fog from the river had rolled in and covered the French Quarter which is the reason many people stayed at home or in their hotel rooms. It was 1a.m. and the Quarter was usually rocking and rolling about now. On a normal night, tourists filled the streets and would party until they couldn't party anymore. The plan for Biff, Lisa, and Tanya was to still have a drink at the Kitty Club before they went home. The club was a twenty-four hour establishment but the patrons became more hard-core the later it got. Once the last guest left the Joker's Wild, it would take the crew about fifteen minutes to close everything for the night. Biff and Lisa finished first but Tanya had the arduous task of making sure the kitchen and bathroom were clean. The two bartenders told Tanya that they were ready to relax with a cocktail made by someone else and they would meet her there.

Tanya (Tatiana) performed her job to perfection. She was not about to leave until her work was properly done. The bathroom had been cleaned but dishes in the kitchen had to be put away. A noise from the front of the bar drew her attention. She peeked through the kitchen door but didn't see anything. "Is there anyone here?" she called out. There was no answer.

She was sure she heard something so she walked around to investigate. The front door was locked so she began to think she was just hearing things. It wasn't unusual for rats to run about in French Quarter buildings. It was easy for rats to dart from place to place as walls for each property were built side by side. Tanya turned to continue her chores when she was startled by an animal jumping directly in front of her face onto the top of the bar. Her heart pounding in her chest, she couldn't readily identify the creature until she heard a slight "meow" coming from a cat. Because of the rat population, many businesses utilized cats to patrol their premises after hours to discourage rats from entering.

Tanya was convinced it was the cat that she heard. Finishing her work, she turned off the remaining lights and locked the door behind her. The fog was thick. It was hard to see more than a hundred feet in front of you. There were still some die-hard partiers, drinks in hand, strolling down the street but they were few and far between. Tanya set out in the direction of the Kitty Club. She wasn't quite sure how far she had to walk before she would find it but she knew which direction.

About half of the nightclubs were still open and with each one she passed, an employee, standing in front of each club, would try to entice her to enter their establishment. She just kept moving along as quickly as she could. Suddenly, the fog seemed to become eerily denser as she could barely see more than five feet in front of her. A cold hand emerged from the fog grabbing her arm and pulling her into a dark alley. Before she could yell, the hand covered her mouth preventing her from making any noise. Next she felt the cold steel blade of a knife across her throat as she felt she was about to gasp her last breath.

The raspy voice of a man told her if she screamed he would slice her throat open. He was dressed in a dark hooded sweatshirt with his face covered entirely by a ski mask. He demanded her jewelry and money but warned her not to return to the Joker's Wild. She realized this was not just a commonplace robbery. This guy knew who she was or had followed her.

"What are you talking about? I work there. That's my job," she responded to the man in the mask.

"We know who you are and what you're doing! Stay away from Joker's Wild if you value your friends' and your life." With that thought he released her from his grip and ran away disappearing into the fog and darkness.

Tatiana was noticeably and understandably upset over this event. She stood in this dark alley for several moments until she realized she was still in a vulnerable position. She hurriedly rushed from there and quickly reached the Kitty Club.

Entering there was no sign of Lisa or Biff but she was relieved when she saw Caden Caruso and Colin Kennedy seated on opposite sides of the stage seemingly enjoying the show. Maybe enjoying it a little too much. They hadn't noticed Tatiana enter the club even though she strolled through the area looking for a seat. She finally sat alone at the bar when someone touched her shoulder from behind. Because of her recent encounter, she jumped spilling a portion of her beer across the bar.

"Whoa, take it easy, sister. It's just me."

Tatiana turned to face Peg's smiling face while expressing a huge sigh of relief. "Sorry, I wasn't expecting anyone. I guess I was deep in thought."

"Well, where in the hell are Biff and Lisa? Hey, Jay. Give me my usual," Peg yelled at the bartender.

"I have no idea. They left long before me and were supposed to meet me here. Haven't seen 'em."

By the time the latest show ended, Kennedy and Caruso noticed Tatiana sitting by the bar so they moved closer as they saw her interacting with Peg. They weren't close enough to hear their conversation but they could act quickly if necessary.

Biff and Lisa finally arrived and they seemed surprised when they saw Tanya seated at the bar. After a quick glimpse at each other, they slowly made their way over to Tanya and Peg. "Surprised to see you here, Sunshine," Biff commented on Peg being present.

"Tanya invited me to join this party. I had an early date and when that ended I headed over here."

"You're more than welcome to join us," Lisa offered. "We just wanted to get together with Tanya to get to know her better."

"What is it you want to know about me?" asked Tanya. "I lead a pretty simple life. No family, very few friends."

"Where are you from?" asked Biff. "How long have you been in New Orleans?" Lisa nudged Biff in the side remembering Tanya mentioning the phone call from her mother.

"Not long. Joker's Wild is my first job since I moved here. I've lived all over but you should be able to tell from my accent, I spent most of my time in East Texas, near Dallas/Fort Worth." Tatiana had tried to cover up her Russian accent with a southern one but she was afraid she had forgotten that from time to time.

"Nice, I grew up in the Dallas/Fort Worth area," Lisa announced. "Then you must have hit the Margarita Mile."

"No, I can't say I have," responded Tanya.

"Oh, too bad. I guess I just like to drink," Lisa laughed.

Tatiana was beginning to get a little nervous about these questions. She never spent any time in the Dallas area so if their questions continued in that direction, they would know she was lying.

"You know one thing I wanted to ask you, who was that lady you were talking to in Joker's the other night? You seemed to know her. Somebody said she was FBI."

"My, my. Is this some kind of interrogation or something?" asked Peg.

Tatiana now realized what this whole outing was about. They wanted to know if she was undercover for the FBI. "I have no idea who you are talking about. I try and talk to all my customers so I can make the big tips."

Neither Biff nor Lisa seemed to be buying what she offered. Tatiana was becoming very uncomfortable with this whole setting. She looked around to see if Kennedy and Caruso where still close. "I'm not much of a drinker and I need to get up early tomorrow, so I'm going to call it a night," Tatiana stated.

"We'll give you a ride," offered Biff.

"Not necessary. I don't live far away." She didn't want them to know where she lived, especially since she was staying in a hotel. All she wanted was to get away as quickly as possible. Suddenly, she felt a tap on her shoulder which sent her jumping from her chair.

"Is that you Tanya?" Colin Kennedy had noticed her awkward body language and had come to her rescue. "I haven't seen you in quite some time."

"Oh, Jack is that really you?"

"Guys, this is an old boyfriend Jack. We dated when I lived in Dallas. What are you doing in the Big Easy? I miss your smiling face. Would you like to stay for a drink so we can catch up?"

Colin could sense she was nervous, so played along.

"I'm in town for a sales convention. I'd love to stay for a drink, but I have an early meeting at the convention center. Can I give you a lift so we can catch up?"

"That sounds great. I'll see the rest of you tomorrow at work. I really want to catch up with this big guy." She gave Peg a wink and smile, indicating that she wanted more than a conversation with Jack. Tanya grabbed Jack by the hand and rushed him through the door. She let out a loud sigh of relief as they walked away from the Kitty Club.

"Thanks for coming to my rescue. Can you drop me off at my hotel?"

"No problem. Just let me send Caden a message that I'm giving you a ride and I'll meet him back at headquarters. I could tell they were hovering over you and you were uncomfortable. They didn't hurt you, did they?"

"I don't want to talk about anything right now. Just get me to the hotel and I'll talk to Net. The least amount of people that know, the better."

Colin pulled up to the hotel and waited for her to go through the door before pulling off.

Tatiana stopped in the downstairs bar and got a scotch and water to take up to her room. She was still shaky from the mugging and the reaction from Biff and Lisa. She went directly to Net's room and knocked at the door. After several minutes, Rhonda opened the door, half asleep.

"Is everything alright Tatty?"

"No, I think I need to tell you everything that happened tonight."

Tatty went into the room and sat in a chair by the window. She took a long sip of her drink and proceeded to tell Rhonda about the person grabbing her in the quarter and the interrogation from Lisa and Biff. She mentioned that Colin Kennedy came to her rescue and brought her back to the hotel. Rhonda listened to Tatty and decided she better wake up Net.

"Tatty, I think you better not return to your job at Joker's. Putting yourself in danger is above your pay grade," chided Net.

"I really don't want to quit. I proved tonight that I can handle myself and if you can arrange for Colin Kennedy to shadow me I know I can convince Biff and Lisa to trust me."

"Well, let me think about it. If you do go back, I will have you protected."

Tatiana returned to her room leaving Net and Rhonda alone.

J.C. lay down in his bed and patted the top of the mattress for Rhonda to join him. Both were still tired but Rhonda couldn't help herself but bring up the subject of Susan Griffin again.

"Do you still have feelings for her?" she asked."

"Who?"

"You know. Susan Griffin."

"Not that again? I guess any time you have a close relationship like we had, you never lose all feelings. But I'm with you. I love you more than anything. I want to spend the rest of my life with you. The love I once felt for her is gone. Doesn't exist. She's a murderer. Obviously I didn't know her as well as I thought I did. Can we put this to a rest now?"

"I guess," answered Rhonda with a sigh as she held Net closer to her. Both of them could no longer keep their eyes open as they fell asleep holding each other in their arms.

***

Despite Net's objections, Tatiana reported for her next shift at the Joker's Wild. She again felt the cold shoulder being given to her by Biff and Lisa from the moment she arrived. The place had its normal raucous crowd with a few young men seated among the regulars. They were very intoxicated when they arrived and they certainly weren't any sober as the evening passed along. Hoping to find anyone to dance with, they continuously focused on the jukebox in the back corner of the bar. They played more music in this one night, then the entire previous month.

Almost eerily, there was a sudden hush in the crowd noise as well as a pause in the songs being played, when the doors of the establishment flew open and in walked two ladies arm in arm. They sat at the bar and drew the attention of everyone in the place.

"Hello, ladies. What can I get you?" offered Biff.

They both ordered martinis and asked, "How late does this place stay open?"

"As late as the customers are here," answered Biff. "If you need anything else, my name is Biff."

"Glad to meet you Biff. My name is Darlene and this is my friend Brenda. We're looking for a good time and this looks like it might be the place." Darlene had blonde hair and blue eyes and looked to be about thirty years old. Her hair was pinned back and held in place by a flower just above her right ear. She wore a dress which showed every curve of her body with as much cleavage to keep men interested.

Brenda seemed to be the shy one although you would never know by her attire. She also had blonde hair cut nicely across the top of her bare shoulders which led to a halter top providing just as much to look at as Darlene. Her skintight leather pants hugged her buttocks tightly which was a wonderful attraction for these young men.

The two ladies had hardly started their cocktails when they were approached by two of the men. "Would you two ladies care to dance?" one of them asked.

Darlene and Brenda swung around on their bar stools to take a good look at these young men who were probably in their early twenties. There really wasn't a dance floor at Joker's Wild, but one could find enough room between tables if you really wanted to.

"Sure thing, honey," responded Darlene. "Are you boys even old enough to be in here?"

The two men were insulted by her comment. "We're older than you think we are. I'm twenty-eight and my friend here is thirty."

The ladies knew they were lying about their age but they thought what the hell. "Are you going to talk or are we going to dance?" asked Brenda.

Darlene looked at Brenda in shock. So much for her reputation as being shy. Brenda took one of the young men onto the floor and pulled him as close as she possibly could. His arms was around her waist but she clasped the cheeks of his ass in both of her hands and began to dance. Darlene giggled at the site and it wasn't long before there was a line of suitors waiting for their turn to dance with one of the two ladies. This was good for business as drink orders began to flourish while the ladies put on a show. All eyes were on the entertainment that they provided as no one even noticed that the music from the jukebox had concluded. Lisa rushed over with a handful of quarters to start the music up again because it meant better tips for her and Biff the more this went on.

To the dismay of the patrons, Darlene and Brenda decided they needed a break and returned to their chairs at the bar. They sipped their drinks at a very slow pace and each wiped their forehead of perspiration from their dancing.

"Your drinks are on the house tonight ladies," offered Biff. He recognized the benefits of keeping them around. "Any night you want to come in here, it will be on the house."

"Oh my. Thanks, that's very kind of you," answered Brenda.

"Are you ready for another go around," Darlene asked.

The two ladies were back up dancing with themselves to the music playing and it wasn't long before they were separated by the males in the bar wanting a dance with these two wild fillies.

The night continued until the wee hours of the morning but finally Darlene and Brenda seemed to outlast all of the other patrons. They never finished their initial drink as the men in the bar kept them busy all night. As the crowd began to depart, Biff called for last drink. Tatiana was off duty and returned quickly to her hotel where Net was waiting.

***

"How did tonight go?" he asked her.

"Good. Biff and Lisa were very busy tonight. Had a good crowd so there wasn't much interaction with them tonight other than drink orders. There were two women who came in stealing the show. They got everyone up and dancing and kept the place rocking all night."

"You didn't happen to talk with them did you? Did you catch their names?"

"There was no time for any of that. They danced the night away with every boy or man in the place. Sometimes even women."

"Were their names Darlene and Brenda?" Net smirked.

"Yes, that may be right." Tatiana looked puzzled. "I think you may be right."

Net laughed out loud almost waking up Rhonda. "I told you I would have you protected, didn't I? Both of them are NOPD." He laughed again trying to control his volume.

CHAPTER 24

Help me Rhonda, Help, Help me Rhonda

Ernest Washington sat back in his office chair calling Nets' cell phone. "Hello J.C., this is Ernest. Do you have a few minutes to talk about the Park case?"

"Sure, just let me close my office door. I don't want anyone eavesdropping." Net motioned Rhonda to come into the conference room and to close the door behind her.

"Okay Ernest, Rhonda is here with me. What can I help you with?"

"I've taken the liberty of hiring a local criminal defense firm, Mathews and Schmitt to assist with the case. One of the partners is a female attorney named Maureen Schmitt. I've asked to be my second chair. I needed someplace local to question witnesses and I figured it wouldn't hurt to have a female on the team. They have been most cooperative in lending me a paralegal to assist in document and witness preparation. I need to talk to several people before we send out trial subpoenas. I was hoping you could help me get some of them to cooperate. The first and foremost on the list is Rodney's wife, Charlotte. I know Rodney doesn't want her called at trial, but I still need to hear from her. It is also necessary that I speak with her doctor and her caregiver."

"I'm sure I can arrange for that. Who else do you need?"

"The two security guards who found the mayor, as well as the coroner who performed the autopsy. I really don't have any suspects in the mayor's murder, so I'm not sure if any of them will be helpful. Now as far as the Lampino murder is concerned, my list is a lot longer. His list of enemies is longer than his list of friends. Again, the coroner's office, the owner and bartender from Joker's Wild, several of the street women he saw on a regular basis and probably some of the local theatre people. If we're lucky we may even find a connection with the Lampino murder and the other murders in the quarter.

"As far as evidence goes, McQueen has the gun and knife with Rodney's prints. Both were found amongst Rodney's possessions. It's going to be an uphill battle disputing this evidence. Unfortunately, we have a short window before the trial starts, so we need to start yesterday. If you can begin rounding up the Jokers people, I'll arrange for Josh Hancock and Charlotte to come in for a chat."

"I'll start on that immediately." Net wasted no time and quickly called the Park household.

"Hello, is this Mildred? This is Agent Net. If you would be so kind to arrange for Ms. Charlotte to meet with Mr. Rodney's defense counsel as soon as possible."

"Ms. Charlotte certainly isn't a suspect, is she?" Mildred asked in a worried tone.

"No Mildred. Not at this time. We just need everyone who has any knowledge of the family to talk with us. Sometimes people know things that they don't realize."

"I will certainly do my part to help Mr. Rodney in any way I can," offered Mildred.

"Mildred, I will pick you and Charlotte up first thing tomorrow morning and bring you two to meet with Mr. Ernest Washington. He's a good man and will do his best to help clear the charges against Mr. Rodney."

This was the easy part for Net. He knew there would be no trouble in getting Mildred to bring Charlotte. The bigger problem was making sure Charlotte arrived with a clear head.

Shortly after Mildred had the chance to discuss this with Charlotte, she informed Net, "Ms. Charlotte asked for a few days to rearrange her schedule."

She agreed to meet on Thursday morning and Net immediately assigned a detail to watch the Park home Wednesday night to be sure Charlotte did not gallivant into the quarter on one of her escapades. Net took it upon himself to travel to the coroner's office to talk with Josh Hancock himself.

***

Charlotte walked into the law offices of Mathews and Schmitt, followed closely by Mildred. "My name is Charlotte Park and I have a 10:00 a.m. appointment with Mr. Ernest Washington."

The receptionist motioned Charlotte to the third-floor conference room, which was being used by Ernest Washington for trial preparation. There had been a long line of witnesses coming and going over the last few days, but Ernest was saving Charlotte for last.

"Good morning Mrs. Park. I'm so glad you have consented to meet with me. Can I get you a cup of coffee, or maybe a soda?"

"No thank you. I just want to answer whatever fucking questions you have and get the hell home. I have a meeting this afternoon with the New Orleans Friends of the Arts. We are planning a benefit for the local theatre group and museum. Rodney assured me I would not have to testify and that you would prove his innocence."

"I'm doing my best, but the evidence all points to Rodney. My first question is do you know of anyone that would want to kill your father?"

"You mean other than me?" Charlotte chuckled. "I'm assuming that anything I say to you is confidential?"

"Well, a wife can't be forced to testify against her husband, but Rodney is my client."

"I hated my father, but he made sure he supported me financially. Rodney only got his job because he married me and my father threw this in my face every chance he got. He hated Rodney and called him the 'fucking country bumpkin from Keister.' I'm part of New Orleans society and I'm expected to toe the line. He protected me from my own mistakes, some of which were not what I wanted. This caused a lot of resentment. I'm glad he's dead, but I didn't kill him and as much as I care for Rodney, he didn't have the balls to stand up to my dad."

"Charlotte, you are aware that the knife used to kill Lampino was in Rodney's car and the gun used to kill the mayor, your father, was found in Rodney's jacket in your bedroom. Do you have any idea how this could have happened?"

"Why are you asking me? Do you think I killed either of them?"

"Well let's face it, both of you had motive to kill Lampino and your father."

"What the hell are you talking about?"

"Rodney told me about your affair with Lampino and that sometimes you disappear during the evening and don't return until morning."

"That's no one's fucking business but mine. I believe this conversation has ended. I will contact my personal attorney. Any further questions can go through him."

"I'm sorry if I upset you Mrs. Park. Can I have a quick word with Mildred before you leave? Mildred, I just have one or two questions. Can you give me a list of people who would have access to the Park home?"

"Well, as Miss Charlotte told you, she is involved with several organizations that meet at the house. We also have staff who take care of the garden, the pool and grocery delivery. On a daily basis I'd say at least three or more people are in and out of the house."

"If you could send me a list of the service companies you use as soon as possible or anything you might recall that would be helpful. Thank you for bringing Mrs. Park in. You can take her home now."

***

Net arrived at the coroner's office and found Josh Hancock seated in his office watching what appeared to be a pornography video on his computer screen. He tried to hide it but he was too late in closing the program. Net decided to ignore what he had seen and sat down for a conversation with the doctor. "How's it going, Josh?"

"Oh, you know. We'll always have a job. People continue to die. That's a given." Hancock was an odd individual. It wasn't often that you would find a politician, as the coroner is, wearing a man-bun on a regular basis. Being around dead corpses all day would make one's personality seem rather peculiar. "Hey, you want a scotch?" he asked as he poured himself a drink.

"No thanks. I'm on duty. You hang around Joker's Wild from time to time don't you?" asked Net. "Also the Le Bon Theatre too, right?"

"I do. Is there a problem?" Hancock immediately turned defensive.

"Not at all. Some of these victims you autopsied, had connections to Joker's and the theatre as well. I was wondering if you were friends with any of them and may know someone that had a grudge with them."

"I guess what you really want to know is where was I during these murders?"

"Well, if you want to offer that information, that would help me eliminate you from the suspect list."

"So, I am a suspect," Hancock commented.

"Well, I consider anyone who knew these victims as possible suspects. I want to chip away at the list until we have the killer."

"Thought you had the killer already? So you're working with the defense and not the prosecution. That's a little different."

"I'm just after the truth no matter where that takes us. Now, what can you tell me about these victims that you may know?" asked Net.

"I don't really know any of them that well. Yeah, sure I knew them but just casually from seeing them working at the theatre and maybe having a drink at Joker's."

"Didn't you try out for parts in plays at the theatre and was rejected?"

"True but that doesn't make me a murderer. I'll have to go through my schedule and see where I was for each murder. I'll get back to you. Otherwise you have all the coroner's reports on each autopsy we performed. There were plenty of similarities in the way each one was killed except for the mayor."

Net could tell he would never get any more information about Josh Hancock himself. He wanted to talk with Hancock's assistant, Jennifer, but she wasn't available. On his way back to his car, his cell phone began to ring. Before he could say a word, the party calling held the conversation.

Net stopped and stood staring at the ground listening. Not a word was spoken on his part, even after the conclusion of the call. There was a few moments of reflection before he reached his car. Again his phone rang.

"I'll meet you at police headquarters," relayed Rhonda. "Are you okay?"

"Yea. I'll be there in a few minutes."

***

Rhonda and Net arrived just about the same time and were immediately greeted by Colin Kennedy and Police Chief Lauren Johnson. "This is a historic day for NOPD to capture such a high profile criminal on the FBI's most wanted list.

"Where is she?" demanded Net.

"Are you sure you want to do this? Let me go in first and see how it goes," suggested Rhonda.

"Probably not a bad idea," Johnson advised. She grabbed Net by the arm prohibiting him from advancing. "As a matter of fact I must insist on it." It wasn't a secret that the police chief did not like Rodney Park and with the mayor gone, she wouldn't be upset to see him convicted. Net was an ally of Rodney and felt he wasn't working in the best interest of the investigation.

"I'm going to step aside for now considering the circumstances, but let me be very clear," Net moved directly face to face with Johnson, "you will not tell me what to do or how I will investigate these murders." Net, with a stern look, stepped back as Rhonda took his arm and stood between them.

Kennedy led Rhonda down the hall into the conference room in the rear of headquarters.

"Well, funny we meet this way," Rhonda remarked seeing Susan Griffin seated with arms and legs handcuffed to the table in front of her. "What should I call you? Stella? Susan? Sabrina? Or is it something else now?"

245

Susan nervously smirked at Rhonda's comment. "What should I call you, Beth?"

"I had no idea who you were when we met at the theatre but now I know. J.C. told me everything."

"You sure he told all? Where is he anyway? I thought he'd be in here in a second if he knew I was here. Maybe you all haven't told him?"

"Oh, he knows you're here. He doesn't want to see you," added Rhonda.

"I don't believe that. That guy was madly in love with me and I him. The feelings we had just don't go away. I'm sure he cares for you but let's face it, you're his rebound girl."

Rhonda tried to hold it together but Susan was very good at selling her story. "I'll be back." Rhonda began taking deep breaths trying to control her emotions as she felt she was about to cross over the table and pound away on Susan.

"She's good," Rhonda stated to Net and Kennedy. "She thinks you still love her."

"Don't let her get to you. She knows this kind of talk will bother you and cause friction in our relationship. I've told you how I feel. I think it's time for me to go in there and let her know what she's in for. I'll remind you. She is a murderer. She's going to jail for the rest of her life."

As Net entered the room Susan just sat there and stared. Neither said a word at first but she had a rather cocky smile on her face.

"I knew you'd come. You can't stay away," she smirked.

"Don't flatter yourself. At one time I would say you would be correct but not anymore. You're a killer and you are going away for the rest of your life."

"But baby, you know why I did it. You know I'm not a bad person. I've never stopped loving you. We have a special connection. More than you know."

"Don't call me that!" exclaimed Net. "You have no right." Despite his denial Net couldn't help but remember the passion and love he once shared with this woman. The room became silent as neither of the two knew what to say.

Rhonda watched and listened carefully to the proceedings from the other side of the one-way window. She was confident that Net wouldn't fall prey to Susan's suggestions. Nevertheless, there was the thought in the back of her mind that Susan was J.C.'s first real love.

After contemplating his next questions, Net began to interrogate Susan as to any connection she might have with the murders in New Orleans. She was too involved with the theatre and Joker's Wild not to be connected in some way. By proving her involvement, he may be able to help his friend Rodney. "Chris Nelson, how do you know him?" Net questioned.

"Nelson? He is an asshole. I've tried to work with him on numerous occasions but he always turned me away or gave me a menial backstage job. What's his problem?"

Susan either didn't know Nelson was dead or she was playing her part very well.

"What about Zack White?"

"What about him? I know who he is but I've never been involved with him."

"Do the names Buck Lawrence, Jimmy Schwartz, Bernard Lampino, Sal Siegel, or Steve Colombo mean anything to you?" Net continued.

"What is this, J.C.? In case you can't get me on the Keister murders you are going to pin me with others. You know you don't want that." She reached her handcuffed hands out as far as she could to touch Net's hand which he didn't immediately move.

Rhonda sighed heavily at the notion of Net's lack of avoidance. Kennedy and Tatiana, standing by her side observed her reaction and attempted to console her. "You know how he feels," comforted Tatiana but Rhonda could watch no more and walked away.

"Don't you have our old friend Pants in custody for these murders?" questioned Susan.

"The police have arrested Rodney but I don't believe, I know, he didn't commit the murders."

"I really liked Pants, err Rodney, as you now call him. I know he liked me. I really hope you can prove his innocence. I really do."

"What are you doing here in New Orleans?" Net asked as he attempted to regain his focus.

"Just some business issues," Susan offered. "I have some investment relationships here so I came here and liked it. I decided to stay a while. I like to participate in local activities so that's why I was trying to work in a small theatre but also keep a low profile."

"What kind of business deals are you referring to?" asked Net.

"Just investment contacts. Nothing more. Nothing less. I'm not a bad person J.C. You know that. Those men who died in Keister deserved to die."

"Maybe, but you don't have the right or authority to take those lives. Let the authorities take care of them." Net realized that he wasn't going to get any straight answers from Susan. He stepped outside the room and told

248

Colin Kennedy to take her down to booking. There was no sign of Rhonda or Tatiana.

***

Tatiana reported for her shift at Joker's Wild later that day and as usual, Biff and Lisa were behind the bar. The place was already crowded so it didn't take Tatiana long to be very busy. For the third night in a row, Darlene and Brenda were in attendance. As usual, they made a grand entrance so that everyone knew they had arrived. Brenda immediately entertained everyone with her version of twerking next to her barstool. Patrons formed a circle around her and cheered her on. As undercover police officers one would think they would want to keep a low profile but not these two. They relished the attention. Maybe they felt by their performance no one would ever imagine that they would be NOPD.

With everyone drinking and having a great time, the noise was at a fever pitch until suddenly the door swung open and T.J. entered with a lady on each arm. There was a sudden hush and dispersal of the crowd surrounding Brenda and Darlene. On his left arm he escorted a very attractive black lady, heavily decorated with jewelry and a revealing red dress covered by a leather jacket. On his right side, there was a pretty blonde, white lady wearing a more business-like attire. T.J., however, was the one who really stood out. He appeared very much like the pimp he was, decked out in an all-purple leisure suit with a matching floppy hat. He even had that walk, where he took long strides with his legs while bending his knees with each step. He released the arms of the two ladies attached to his side and instructed them to find a table to his liking while he conducted some business.

T.J. bellied up to the bar next to where Darlene and Brenda were now quietly seated. "So, you're the two ladies I've been hearing about. Tabares

Jaimez, at your service." He took Darlene's hand into his and kissed the top of her hand. He did the same with Brenda. "I'm a well-known entrepreneur, you might say, and I'm wondering if I can be of service to you two ladies."

"Exactly what service are you offering us?" asked Darlene.

"I'm offering you an incredible opportunity to make as much money as you could ever imagine."

"How do you know that we need the money?" asked Brenda.

"Let's face it lady, you wouldn't be here in Joker's Wild if you weren't looking for something," he suggested.

"Okay. Okay," Darlene agreed. "But what can you do for us?"

"I can make all your dreams come true. I can introduce you to the right people. My clientele are some of the top businesspeople and politicians in this city. I can make it happen."

"Exactly what do we have to do?" Brenda asked.

"I make the introduction and whatever deal you make from there is up to you," T.J. stated. He was very careful not to divulge what he really wanted.

"Listen, umm, was it T.J.?" stated Brenda. "Do you have a card where we can think about it and get back to you?"

T.J. handed both ladies a bright pink business card with his information on it and wished them well as he joined the ladies he came with. It wasn't long before he decided to leave, however, as he grew tired of all the attention his ladies were getting from the patrons in the bar. He had to inform several young men that these two were his and were not available. They were good showpieces though, as he made several new contacts who wanted to make purchases, so to speak.

Darlene and Brenda were suddenly quiet with the departure of T.J. and his entourage. Conversely the crowd in Joker's became smaller as the entertainment provided by the two ladies ceased. Tatiana took advantage of this time to take a break from the normally fast-paced barroom. She stepped outside a rear door to make a phone call in private. Despite the back alley being deserted, the noise emanating from Bourbon St. was still powerful. Pushing the phone as close to her ear as possible, she held her left hand against her other ear hoping to drown out the Bourbon St. sound. With her back turned, she failed to recognize someone in very dark clothes and mask approach her from behind.

CHAPTER 25

Undercover Angels

The dark stranger moved slowly in Tatiana's direction. She seemed a little frustrated as whoever she was calling was not available. Just as this person reached her she turned and received a blow across her face with the blunt handle of a pistol. The intruder quickly turned the weapon and pointed its barrel against her head, warning her to be quiet.

"Better say your prayers. This will be the last breath you take. We don't want Feds spying on us," whispered the stranger.

It was that precise moment that Darlene and Brenda came through the rear door with guns drawn. "NOPD!" screamed Darlene. "Put your weapon down! I said, drop your weapon!"

The perpetrator didn't move an inch. Brenda worked her way around to the side of this person to get a better view of his intentions. "You heard her. Last warning. Put your gun down or we will put you down."

Brenda had worked her way into a position where she couldn't miss the shot and the stranger recognized he had no option but to drop the gun. He fell to his knees, clasping his hands together over his head as Darlene moved in handcuffing his arms behind him. Once she had him secure, Brenda ripped the mask from his face.

The three ladies stood there surprised that this offender was no one they recognized. "Who are you?" yelled Darlene as she pressed her hand against his throat.

"My name is Hank. I wasn't gonna do nothing. Someone just paid me to scare her. Look my gun isn't even loaded."

Tatiana picked up his gun and confirmed that it had no bullets. She didn't care for guns so she quickly handed it to Darlene. Her weapon was the keyboard she sat behind day in and day out.

"You got a last name Hank?" asked Brenda.

"Yes."

"Well, what the fuck is it?" demanded Brenda.

Hank was reluctant to answer but knew he had no choice. "It's Sullivan. Hank Sullivan."

"You got a record Mr. Sullivan?" inquired Darlene.

"Just some minor juvenile stuff."

"Tell us why you did this," Brenda asked.

"A friend asked me to do this. He paid me $500."

"Who's your friend? Give us a name!" Brenda insisted. "How old are you? Are you even old enough to be in any French Quarter bar? At least legally?"

"I'm twenty-one," Hank answered as a matter of fact. "Look, this is the truth. My friend and I were hired by this guy to do this and he knew I needed the dough so he got me to do it. He's going to be pissed at me for fucking this up."

"We need a name, Hank." Darlene was beginning to get annoyed with his delay tactics.

"Okay. My friend's name is Diego. Diego Dominguez. Most people call him One-Eye because his wife caught him in bed with another woman and in an effort to keep him from looking at any other women, she poked his left eye out. He managed to stop her before she got the other one."

Darlene shook her head and looked at Brenda. "I know One-Eye. He's a troubled young man. Surprised he's not behind bars right now. Look Hank, even though you claim you weren't going to hurt anyone, we've got to bring you in. Pointing a weapon at anyone, even an unloaded one is a crime. This may be the hardest $500 you ever earned. Who's the guy who hired you?"

While Brenda and Darlene questioned Hank, Tatiana had messaged Net to let him know what had transpired. It didn't take him long to arrive.

"You're done here now. Should have ended this after your first attack. Darlene and Brenda, can you take this scum bag down to police headquarters? I'm going to escort Tatiana back to the hotel and I'll meet you there in about an hour."

"Sure thing. Come on Hank. We have a lot more questions coming your way."

"Can I at least make a phone call? I've seen enough police shows to know I have a right to make a call, in private."

Brenda and Darlene handcuffed Hank and put him in a waiting police car.

***

When they arrived at headquarters they showed Hank into an interrogation room and remove his handcuffs.

"Would you like a cup of coffee or soda? We are going to wait until Agent Net arrives before we begin our questioning. If you'd like to use the telephone, the one on the desk is available."

"Diego, this is Hank, man I really fucked up. I tried to scare that FBI broad like you asked, but two police bitches caught me. Man I'm scared, they took me down to police headquarters. I don't know what to do, but I ain't doing no fucking time for you and $500."

"You at police headquarters now? What phone are you using?"

"The phone in this little room."

"You stupid fucking moron! You called my number from the police phone. Holy shit! If they don't fry your ass, I will. Don't say a fucking word and don't mention my name or number."

"Too late for that. They forced it out of me. You better tell your boss to send an attorney to help me."

"Sit tight and I'll call the boss."

***

"Boss, this is Diego. We're in deep shit and its going down fast. I subcontracted to my boy Hank to scare the FBI bitch and he got picked up. He's at police headquarters now and spilling his guts. I'm getting out of the city now and I think you better do the same."

Diego hung up the phone and threw his belongings into a duffle bag. He headed out the door and started running towards the bus station, believing it would be the hardest route to trace. As he crossed Poydras Street he heard the screeching of tires and barely saw the truck before he flew into the air and landed on the neutral ground. As he lay bleeding he caught a glimpse of the writing on the door of the truck, as he took his final breath, "New Orleans Coroner."

Police arrived on the scene as Josh Hancock was futilely trying to administer CPR to Diego.

"He ran out in front of my truck. There was no way I could stop in time. He worked part time in my office. I don't know why he was in such a hurry."

By the time the ambulance arrived, Diego Dominguez was pronounced dead at the scene.

"Dr. Hancock, it's obvious that this was an accident, but Chief Johnson is going to want you to pass by headquarters and give a statement."

"No problem officer. I had just left the coroner's office on my way to a meeting, but I can pass by police headquarters in about an hour."

"That will be fine. I'll tell them to expect you."

***

Net and Rhonda arrived at police headquarters and began questioning Hank Sullivan about his involvement in attacking Tatiana. He stuck to his story that a friend gave him $500 to scare her, but claimed he only knew the friend as Diego Dominguez. It was obvious to both of them that he was lying. Brenda had traced the call Hank made on the phone in the interrogation room and passed a note to Net with her findings. Net showed the note to Rhonda.

"Okay Hank, it's time to cut the bullshit. We know you placed a call from the interrogation room to the coroner's office. Who were you calling and why?"

"Man, I'm not going down for this shit. Diego offered me $500. I've run a few jobs for him in the past. Mostly drug related. I don't even own a gun and never was arrested for anything other than drunk in public for fighting. You can run my records man, I'm clean."

"What ties does Diego have to the coroner's office?"

"No fucking clue. I didn't know that was the coroner's number. I usually meet up with him at Joker's. Diego had a deal with the bartender and owner to push his drugs on customers at Jokers. I just got this phone number yesterday when Diego gave me the gun to use and the details of the job."

Darlene entered the room and asked Net to step outside for a minute.

"I'm afraid Diego just met an untimely death. He was just killed on Poydras Street by a truck driven by none other than Josh Hancock. Early indication is that it was nothing more than a tragic accident. The officer at the scene arranged for Dr. Hancock to come in for a statement. He should be here any minute."

Dr. Josh Hancock arrived a very short time later. He seemed shaken by the accident that took place earlier. Net finished with his interrogation of Hank Sullivan and sent him with officers to be booked for assault with a deadly weapon.

"Dr. Hancock, thanks for coming in and I'm sorry for what you had to endure this evening. Can you tell me what happened?" questioned Net.

"I don't really know. Diego just ran out in front of my vehicle and I struck him crossing the street. Never saw him. I had no chance to stop. I tried to perform CPR at the scene but he was already gone. Just a tragic event. Something I won't forget anytime soon."

"Did you know Diego Dominquez?"

"Yes. Sadly, he was an employee of the coroner's office. He cleaned up around the facility and when we needed something moved, like a body, he'd help out," Hancock offered.

"How long did he work for you?" Net continued.

"I'd say about six months."

"Did he have any family or anybody close to him?" asked Net.

"That I couldn't say. Really didn't know him on a personal basis."

"Were you aware that he was running drugs through Joker's Wild?" Net shared.

"Are you kidding me? From the coroner's office? I had no idea!" exclaimed Hancock.

"So you're telling me you had nothing to do with or was aware that this was going on from your office?"

"Absolutely not! I'd never be involved in anything like that. I resent that you would think I would. We run background checks before any hire, so I'm sure he was clean or we would not have hired him."

"Nobody said you had anything to do with this, Hancock. I've got to ask. Do you know a Hank Sullivan?"

"No, who is he?" Hancock now seemed to be on the defensive.

"Well, Diego hired him to put a fright into our undercover agent at Joker's Wild. He told Sullivan that his boss wanted this done."

"I may have been his boss at work but not on these behind the scenes shit," demanded Hancock.

"Wait here a few minutes. I'll be right back," Net stated as he walked out of the room. He met Rhonda on the other side of the one-way glass who had been watching Net's questioning. "I think we need to look into this guy. Something just doesn't feel right."

"What do you suggest?" asked Rhonda.

"First we look for someone new to go into Joker's Wild and see if they are able to buy drugs. Let's check into Hancock's background, who he associates with and if there is any relationship with him and the victims."

"I'll get Tatiana on that right away," offered Rhonda as she passed Net on her way out of the conference room.

FBI Agent Caden Caruso was standing nearby waiting to talk with Net. "Agent, two U.S. Marshalls just arrived to take custody of Susan Griffin. Paperwork looks in order but just wanted to be sure you were notified before she left."

"I've got nothing more to say to her," answered Net. "Just make sure they know she's a slippery little bitch and they need to watch her closely."

"Got it," affirmed Caruso as he departed to release Susan into the Marshalls custody.

The front desk clerk had already started the process of releasing the prisoner into the officer's care. NOPD officers were present to make the exchange so Caruso made sure that he warned them per Net's request. He thanked them for their attention and returned to his desk afterward.

The two Marshalls were both tall and lanky with a close-cropped haircut. Their appearance was more military rather than law enforcement in style. Both were uniformed officers which was unusual for federal law officers. Once the paperwork was completed, they wasted no time in removing Susan to their vehicle. Without a word, they hurriedly drove away while NOPD officers looked on.

Less than 20 minutes went by before two men in dark suits appeared at NOPD headquarters, asking for Agent J.C. Net.

"Agent Net, I'm U.S. Marshall Lawson and this is Marshall Davies. We're here to take Susan Griffin into custody."

Nets face dropped. "You've got to be fucking kidding me? Two Marshalls from your office just left with her 15 minutes ago! Quick, Tatiana, bring the video surveillance tape from outside our building up on your computer."

Tatiana opened her computer screen and witnessed the two Russian men from Joker's Wild ushering Susan Griffin into a black SUV. As the car passed by they could see Susan in the back seat laughing. Net ordered Caruso into the office.

"We need to put out an all-points bulletin on the black SUV in this video. They were headed west from here. I want this bitch found. She is not going to get away again. If you have to use a helicopter or Air Force One, I want her found!"

***

The SUV crossed the Bonne Carré Spillway and into a wooded area. Susan spoke to the driver in fluent Russian.

"We need to turn around and go back into the quarter. I need to pick up my son."

"*Nyet.* Our orders were to get you away from NOPD, not to bring your son. We have a car waiting for you at a location in LaPlace. Your Father was a great operative for Mother Russia and our country was indebted to him. What you do after we drop you off is your business." Each Russian kissed Susan on the cheek and wished her safe passage. "You know where to find us if we are needed."

The car pulled into a driveway of a home that had been abandoned since the last hurricane. One of the men exited the vehicle and pulled the car cover off a white minivan. They handed the keys to Susan."*Udachi.*" As soon as Susan exited the car the SUV took off, headed towards Baton Rouge. Susan got into the minivan and headed back to New Orleans.

Her son was again under the supervision of her neighbor Mrs. Van. The first thing Susan did was enter her apartment and secure her belongings which weren't very much. She had moved so many times over the past couple of years she didn't have the opportunity to accumulate very many possessions. She took what she could and loaded everything into the back of the minivan.

Mrs. Van didn't often miss anything happening in her neighborhood. She saw Susan packing the back of the vehicle and came to the door. "My dear, where are you going?" she shouted to Susan.

"I've got a job opportunity out of state but I have to leave now. I'm coming to get my boy but I need to get that car seat I gave to you a while ago."

"Do you have to leave in such a hurry? I want to spend a little more time with this baby. I've become very fond of him."

"Look I don't have time to fuck around with you. Give me my baby and my seat and we will be gone!"

"Oh my!" Mrs. Van was quite rattled by the excessive intimidation of Susan's voice. She brought Susan's little boy into her doorway as Susan abruptly snatched the boy from her arms placing him in the seat of the car.

Without a thank you or even another word, Susan sped away in her vehicle as Mrs. Van looked on, bewildered by the event.

***

Despite the extensive search conducted by not only NOPD but also the police departments of all the surrounding parishes, there had been no sign of the black SUV that had taken Susan Griffin from police custody.

Time passed and all law enforcement except for J.C. Net had given up on the idea of finding the elusive Susan Griffin. Even Net had turned some of his attention back to any connection involving the Joker's Wild and the coroner's office.

Net sat in his temporary office he had been assigned in the New Orleans office of the FBI, when a female clerical assistant informed him that he had a gentleman visitor in the reception area. When she couldn't tell him who the visitor was, he sighed and said he wasn't taking any visitors at this time. Before she had the chance to move away, he recanted his statement. "Go ahead, let's have him. If it's a reporter, I'm not here."

The young lady escorted the man all the way to Net's office. "That's no gentleman!" screamed Net as the man stood before him in the doorway. "Christie, this is the Honorable Senator Greg Slidell. Greg, how in the hell are you?" Net embraced his old friend and invited him to sit down. "Senator, can we get you anything? Coffee? Water? Anything?"

"No thanks, J.C. I can't stay long but I'm hoping you and Rhonda can have dinner with the Mrs. and me, maybe tonight?" asked the senator.

"I'm sure that can be arranged but why are you here? I know you don't pay personal visits very often."

"You're right, J.C. I don't and this isn't really one of them either. It's really good to see you old buddy." Net and Greg were college roommates but their friendship had begun in kindergarten. Even though they were the same age, Greg's hair had turned prematurely gray along with a matching slight beard. He had married his wife Michelle about ten years ago after Net had introduced them when he and Michelle worked together with the Louisiana State Police. They didn't have any children but that was more of a choice they had made when Slidell decided to get into politics. They did not want to raise any children in the cloak and dagger world of U.S. politics.

"So what brings you here?" inquired Net.

"I got a phone call from Police Chief Lauren Johnson. She's concerned that you are too close to Rodney Park and can't seem to accept the fact that your friend is guilty of murder."

"Oh, I see." Net thought for a moment so he could carefully choose his words. "Well, Greg, I know this man. I just don't think he is capable of what he is being accused. While there is evidence pointing to Rodney, there are others that also have motives. Isn't the idea that we want the correct resolution? I'm not interfering with the case against Rodney. I'm just looking at possible alternatives to make sure we have the right outcome."

"You know I'm 100% supportive of you. That's all I wanted to hear. I had to appease the chief by coming here. You do what you do best. That's all I have to say. Now you gather up that lovely fiancé of yours and meet us for dinner." The Senator departed shaking hands with everyone in the office hoping they were all registered voters in his district.

CHAPTER 26
The Trial Begins

Ernest Washington was the first to arrive in the courtroom and sat quietly behind the defense table awaiting the jury pool to arrive. Papers were spread across the table in sequential order of the defense points he wanted to cover during the trial. Slowly media members who were chosen to attend the proceedings began to filter in. Because of this high profile case, the judge decided to limit the number of the media. Families and close friends of the accused and of victims were also limited. Subpoenaed witnesses were sequestered in a private room across the hall.

Patrick McQueen arrived with all the fanfare of a champion wrestler. The only thing missing was music when he and his entourage of four entered the courtroom. All eyes were on him as he exaggerated every motion of taking his seat at the prosecuting attorney's table. He glanced towards the media, then offered a confident smile towards Ernest. McQueen pulled out his jury form and waited his turn to *voir dire* the potential jurors. Ernest motioned to Maureen Schmitt to take notes during the jury questioning as she took her place beside him.

Longtime bailiff Bruce William entered the room and commanded all present to rise in honor of the judge. Judge Jim Welch entered and took his seat at the bench.

"By the look on some of your faces, I'm sure you are surprised to see me," offered Judge Welch. "Judge Kathy Jeffers has been called to the White House for a possible appointment to a federal court. I have been assigned to this case."

Ernest seemed to be the most surprised by this circumstance as his process in selecting a jury may have to change. He whispered something to Maureen who then quietly stepped out of the courtroom carrying a folder.

The prospective jurors entered the room and filed into the jurors box one by one. The prospects were equally divided between men and women, black and white, and young and old. Defense attorneys and prosecutors would have equal time questioning each juror to determine if they were acceptable.

Judge Welch gave his opening statement. "Ladies and gentlemen, you have been summoned here today to participate in a murder trial. If found guilty, the defendant, Rodney Park may possibly be sentenced to death. He is accused of the murder of Mayor Clyde Hebert and Bernard Lampino. My first question to all of you is to raise your hand if you personally know the defendant, Rodney Park, the victim, Mayor Hebert, Bernard Lampino, or either of the attorneys trying this case, Ernest Washington or Patrick McQueen."

Several hands were raised in the jury pool. One by one, over 20 jurors were excused because of dealings with the police chief, Lampino or the mayor. Three of the potential jurors were excused because they were represented either by Patrick McQueen's old law firm or Maureen Schmitt's firm. Once all the challenges were heard a jury of twelve were seated, with two alternate jurors.

Judge Welch addresses the jurors. "I have a question that I'm directing to all y'all. What are your feelings about the death penalty?"

One elderly man raised his hand. "I'm from down on the bayou and we believe in an eye for an eye. If Park killed his father-in-law, he should fry."

Ernest Washington asked to approach the bench. "Your Honor, we request that this juror be excused for cause. It's obvious that he already has judged my client."

Judge Welch agreed and dismissed this juror after thanking him for his time. This same procedure played out on both sides for several hours, until each side ran out of challenges.

"Ladies and gentlemen, we have selected a jury. In a potential death penalty case we are basically going to have two trials. The first will be to unanimously decide if the defendant is guilty and the second trial will be to decide if his guilt warrants death or life in prison. Since it is getting late in the day, we ask that you return to this courtroom by 8:00 a.m. tomorrow, at which time I administer the oath to y'all and we will begin the trial. Do not discuss this case with anyone, including the attorneys in this case, their staff, the witnesses or each other. When the trial is completed you will then be given the opportunity to discuss the evidence with fellow jurors.

"Please avoid watching or reading anything about this case, or posting or reading anything on social media. Any violation of these orders could find you in contempt of court. I will decide by tomorrow if we need to sequester y'all. Just in case, please bring with you a small suitcase with enough clothes and personal items for three days. Thank you again for participating in your civic duty and I will see each of y'all selected in the morning."

***

Net remained in the FBI office reviewing over and over again, all the evidence collected in not only the murders of Mayor Hebert and Bernard Lampino but also others that he thought may be connected. The one lead he intended to follow up on was any possible connection that the coroner's office may have to any of these murders. He asked Caden Caruso to meet him in his office and Caruso arrived right on time.

"You wanted to see me, Agent Net."

"Yes, come in Caden. How do you feel about doing some undercover work at Joker's Wild?"

That brought a wide smile to Caruso's face. "That's why I joined the FBI, sir. Tell me what the objective is and I'll do my best."

"I want you to go to Joker's Wild as a customer, have a couple of drinks and observe if drugs are being sold. Pay close attention to Biff Holder and a bartender by the name of Lisa. We think they may be the people pushing the drugs. We want to find out first, if they are dealing drugs, and second who their supplier might be. This could go all the way to the top of the coroner's office. Buy the drugs and report back to me."

***

Caruso followed Net's instructions and found a seat at the bar. He ordered a beer and Lisa was serving drinks at this time. There was no immediate sign of Biff but it was early and Caruso knew that quality of evidence was more important than time. He said quietly enjoying his beer and trying to make casual conversation with Lisa. Without any help, she didn't linger in front of Caruso very long and he didn't want to make her suspicious by being pushy.

"Say haven't you been in here before?" Lisa abruptly asked taking Caruso by surprise.

"I guess I probably have," he responded which was probably the safest response. "I'm always looking for a place I feel comfortable and I can get whatever I need."

"Well, this is the place." Lisa smiled as she walked off to serve another customer.

It was about thirty minutes later that Biff Holder appeared through the rear door. He walked behind the bar drying his hands on a towel hanging from the handle of a cooler. Lisa walked over by him and whispered something in his ear as both of them glimpsed in Caruso's direction. Wiping the bar with a rag, Biff slowly strolled over to the area of the bar where Caruso was seated.

"Want another one, man?" he asked Caruso.

The agent raised his bottle to see how much beer remained in his bottle. "No, I'm good for now." This is the guy that Caruso really wanted to talk with but he didn't want to be too aggressive. He wasn't sure what Lisa had told him so he thought it best to remain uninterested. Caruso sat a little while longer and waited for some of the excessive crowd to leave. "Hey, I'll have that other beer now," he yelled across the bar to Biff.

"Coming up." Biff slid the beer from a short range landing it in front of Caruso. He still didn't travel to that end of the bar.

It was getting late and Caruso didn't want to lose this opportunity to find out if they were dealing drugs from this bar. "Hey, Biff. Did I hear your name correctly?"

"Yeah, that's it. What's it to you?"

"Well I hear that you are someone that's good to know. Ya know, somebody that can set me up," Caruso stated.

"Set you up with what?" Biff seemed annoyed at the suggestion. "I ain't no pimp, man. You can make your own deal. I ain't involved in anything like that. They are all over the French Quarter. Take your pick."

"No. No. I hear you can hook me up with something a little stronger than this booze."

"Again, what the fuck, man. I don't know who told you this but they are wrong. It's time for you to fucking leave." Biff removed the remainder of Caruso's beer from in front of him and showed him the door.

Caruso made his way slowly to the door having failed at his assignment. He began walking down Bourbon Street when he was grabbed from behind and pushed into a side alley. "What the shit are you doing?" yelled Caruso recognizing Biff.

"Who told you about me?" asked an anxious Biff Holder.

"Some guy named Hank." Caruso thought he would continue to play it out. "Look I don't really know this guy but I met him in another bar and he told me where I could score."

"You don't fucking ask me in front of other customers at my bar that kind of question. You want us both to get busted?" demanded Biff.

"So, are you saying you are the guy?" asked Caruso.

"Could be. What are you looking for?"

"I need a bag for myself but I'm looking to score a big supply for my employers."

"What kind of supply?" asked Biff.

"Big. Talking a couple of million," Caruso added wanting to see what interest he would attract.

"That kind of buy, my boss would want to do his due diligence," Biff offered.

"Wouldn't have it any other way. I'll let my employers know and you set it up on your end and give me a call when it's ready." Caruso handed Biff a business card the FBI used for undercover work.

"Your name if Fred Fenchurch? And this is your number? My boss will check you out thoroughly before we meet. You better be legit."

"Not a problem." Caruso was confident of what they would find about Fred Fenchurch. Backgrounds on names used for these purposes are previously set up to match connections to, in this case, the drug community.

"I'll be in touch," Biff concluded as he returned to the Joker's Wild.

***

The next morning found the front steps of the courthouse consumed with media, both locally and nationally. If you were one of the lucky reporters to be allowed in the courtroom you were already seated waiting for the trial to begin. The opening remarks by both the prosecution and defense was non-eventful but consumed most of the morning. Both claimed they would prove guilt in the prosecution's case or innocence in the defense's case. The prosecution would present their case first and called their first witness, one Wendy Zander.

"Objection, your Honor!" Ernest Washington rose and shouted. "This witness is not on the prosecution's witness list and the defense has no idea who this is or has had time to prepare for such witness."

"Your Honor, this witness just became known to us and her availability was limited," Patrick McQueen stated. "We would have no objection to give the defense time to investigate this witness' testimony should they feel the need."

"Judge, this is a ploy by the prosecution to catch us unprepared for this witness," countered Washington.

"Gentlemen, approach the bench."

The two attorneys stood in front of the judge while he held his hand over the microphone. "Mr. Washington, let's see where this will lead us and if you need time, I will be more than happy to give it to you. Mr. McQueen, don't think you will get away with this again in my courtroom."

"Thank you, your Honor."

"Bailiff, please swear in Miss Zander."

Bruce William was the bailiff in Judge Welch's court. He was a large muscular man with a moustache that was often talked about in the courtroom. Whiskers had grown over his upper lip so much so that his lip could not be seen. The sides of his moustache grew past his chin with a heavy emphasis on the thickness of hair at each end. He talked with a deep southern drawl which made him sound like a radio host rather than a bailiff in a courtroom.

Rodney Park held his head in his hands as Wendy Zander took the stand to testify. He leaned over and whispered into Ernest Washington's ear. Ernest said nothing in return but the look on his face showed he was suddenly uncomfortable.

"Good morning Miss Zander. Can you tell us about your relationship with the defendant and how long did it last?" questioned Patrick McQueen.

"I was in love with him. I guess you could say I was his mistress," Zander answered seemingly unhappy.

"Your Honor, objection!" Washington exclaimed. "What does this have to do with the charges against my client?"

"We hope this will show the character of the defendant," answered McQueen.

"Proceed, Mr. McQueen," ordered Judge Welch.

"About six months," answered Wendy.

"Where did you meet?"

"The mayor hired me and gave me a job at police headquarters. Mr. Park saw me and started making passes at me almost immediately. I felt my job would be in jeopardy if I didn't oblige."

Washington was watching the expressions on the faces of the jurors and from appearances they were believing her. Zander was a very attractive young blonde with a vibrant personality. No doubt the jurors would understand any man being attracted to her.

"Were you still seeing him at the time of his arrest?" asked McQueen.

"No sir," she answered bitterly. "He used me and when he was through, I was discarded probably for his next fling."

"Objection!" Again Washington was not happy. "The witness is making the assumption that he had affairs after her. Unless she has firsthand knowledge, she can't come to that conclusion."

"The jury will disregard the witness' last statement," ordered the Judge. "Please confine your answers to your firsthand experience."

"Yes, judge. I would like to say, he told me he loved me and that he would leave his wife. He hated his father-in-law and he despised her for an affair she had."

"Do you mean the affair she had with Bernard Lampino?" asked McQueen.

"Objection, your Honor!" Washington's frustration was beginning to show.

"I'll withdraw the question, your Honor," answered McQueen knowing full well that the jury heard his point. "I have no further questions of this witness."

"Since this witness was unknown to the defense, I will adjourn court for the remainder of the day. We'll pick up with your cross examination tomorrow Mr. Washington."

Ernest hurriedly gather his papers to rush from the courtroom. He waited by the elevator but as the doors opened he was face to face with J.C. Net. "How did it go today?" asked J.C.

"McQueen called an unexpected witness today that we weren't prepared for. I've asked the bailiffs to arrange for me to meet with Rodney in the first-floor conference room to find out more about this Wendy Zander. I'm on my way now. Why don't you join us?"

Rodney was already seated in the room cuffed to the table. "That woman lied about everything!" he exclaimed.

"So you didn't have an affair with her?" asked Washington.

"Well, that was true but not to the extent she claimed. I did flirt with her, but not before she came on to me. I had just found out that Charlotte had slept with that Lampino creep and I guess I was vulnerable to her charms. No excuses but it was only once and I confessed it to Charlotte after it happened. Never happened again and she later left the department."

"Did you give her any idea that you would leave your wife for her?" asked Net.

"Absolutely not. We never even discussed it again after that one time."

"Well, McQueen placed a possible motive for killing Lampino with that testimony," suggested Washington. "If I cross-examine her, I need to be sure I don't compound that motive in the jurors' minds."

Bailiffs Bruce William and his brother, Bobby, came to collect Rodney and return him to the lockup. Bobby didn't rock the same facial hair that Bruce did but he did sport a man-bun on top of his head. He had that same southern drawl of his brother which the ladies seem to really like. "Time to go, Deputy Chief Park," requested Bobby. They still treated Rodney with respect because he was well liked among law enforcement officers.

Caden Caruso awaited Net outside of the conference room. "I need to speak to you, agent," he asked.

"Come in here," suggested Net. "How did things go?"

"Bottom line is I told Biff Holder, I had a big buyer of his product and he was to get with his boss and set something up. Now we wait for them to contact me."

"Good job Caruso. Let me know when it's a go." Upon Caruso's departure, Net immediately went to his cell phone. "Tatty, I need you to find out whatever you can, and by any means necessary, about a Wendy Zander. I need whatever you can find by this afternoon."

"By the way, Boss, Rhonda wanted me to tell you she wasn't feeling very well and she decided to go back to the hotel for a little while," Tatiana stated.

"What was wrong?"

"Nothing serious. Upset stomach or something. I will get right on the Wendy issue, but in the meantime, I did a background check on Josh Hancock. Did you know that Hancock was married, but his wife disappeared about two years ago? She just dropped off the face of the earth and was never heard from again. I found no record of his divorcing her. He also had a prior drug arrest in college, which almost kept him out of medical school. You'll never guess who had his record expunged, Mayor Clyde Hebert. Before he ran for mayor he served as district attorney for three years. It was also the mayor that backed Hancock when he ran for coroner.

"I couldn't find any direct evidence of quid pro quo, but it does make Hancock and the mayor unlikely bedfellows. I tried to do a check on all of Hancock's employees, but could find nothing on Jennifer Davison. It was as if she never existed. I finally tried to get the FBI office in Washington to investigate her and I was told in no uncertain terms to back off!"

"That's interesting. I have Caden Caruso setting up a drug deal, so hopefully we'll catch a few big fish. We're meeting with Rodney and Ernest Washington this afternoon and will be cross examining Wendy first thing in the morning. Oh, I have to go. I have a call coming in. Hello, J.C. Net here."

"Net, this is Agent Caruso. The meeting has been set up for 11:00 tonight in a parking lot by the riverfront. Can you arrange for backup in the area?"

CHAPTER 27
Angel in Disguise

J.C. Net and Ernest Washington sat in the conference room of the courthouse anxiously awaiting that important phone call from Tatiana Sokolov. It took longer than they had hoped but when it finally came through, Tatiana had as much information as they needed to discredit Wendy Zander.

"What you got?" asked Net as he put the call on speaker phone.

"Well, Miss Goody Two-shoes is not the poor little innocent person she tries to portray. She has a record including prostitution, theft and carrying a concealed weapon while on probation. What's interesting is she was in jail at the time District Attorney Clyde Hebert began his campaign for mayor. Interestingly she was released from prison and went directly to work for Hebert as an assistant on his campaign committee and later at NOPD. She was a paid employee making six figures. I spoke to a couple of people who were associated with his campaign back then who believed she was his mistress. With his wife away in a hospital, Zander was often seen wearing her wardrobe and jewelry."

"Will they testify to that?" asked Ernest.

"They are hesitant but with the mayor dead, I think they could be convinced. Wendy was not very popular amongst them."

"Just to play devil's advocate, wouldn't the district attorney be aware of all of this?" questioned Net.

"I was about to tell you that," explained Tatiana. "Miss Zander changed her name a while back. Her birth name was Abigail Pratt. But her stage name, or street name if you will, was Pixie Dust. You may not want to know how I know this."

"What do you mean?" asked Washington.

"Let's just say Tatiana knows her way around the computer world. Sometimes it's best not to ask," confided Net.

***

The dark SUV pulled into the lot near the river around 10:30 p.m. Caruso wanted to make sure he arrived first to case the area and make sure he wasn't being set up. The area was in total darkness, except for the lights from an occasional barge passing down the river. He parked the SUV facing the gravel road in case he needed to make a quick exit. About a hundred yards away, Caruso saw an old car appearing to be broken down and abandoned which he hoped contained his back up officers.

Around 10:50 p.m. a large dark SUV pulled into the lot and stopped around a hundred feet from Caruso's car. Caruso flashed his headlights twice and the other car sent the same signal. The door to the SUV opened and both Caruso and Biff Holder exited simultaneously. The rear door opened in Holder's vehicle and a man and woman exited the car and started walking towards Caruso. When they got within 10 feet of each other Caruso recognized Josh Hancock and Jennifer Davison.

"Mother fucker," yelled Hancock. "I know that prick, he's FBI. I thought you checked him out before we set this up?"

Josh Hancock pulled a gun from his waistband and was using Biff as a shield when he suddenly felt a cold steel gun barrel pointed to his head.

"Federal Agent, drop the gun," shouted Jennifer Davison.

Josh dropped the gun from his hand and Caruso pulled out his gun and walked toward Biff Holder and Josh Hancock. Two more agents who were watching from the abandoned vehicle were now at the scene accompanied by their trained police dog, Gabby. Gabby was a veteran police K9 for the past 7 years who had accumulated several police awards for heroism. One agent yelled at Jennifer Davison to drop her gun.

Jennifer Davison dropped her gun after making sure that Caruso had his weapon trained on Holder and Hancock.

"I'm reaching into my pocket for my credentials. My name is Jennifer Davison and I'm an agent with the Federal Drug Enforcement Agency. I've been working undercover in the coroner's office for the past year." Davison held a medical degree from Harvard which was a desirable profession for undercover work with the DEA. She was an expert on various lethal drugs that were trafficked through various cartels around the country. She had become a major asset to the agency.

Police cars from both directions converged on the scene blinding the area with their flashing lights. Josh Hancock and Biff Holder were quickly placed in handcuffs and driven away in police custody. Upon inspection of the vehicle Hancock arrived in, hidden under the floor where a spare tire is normally stored was over one million dollars' worth of cocaine.

Caruso shook hands with Jennifer Davison and thanked her for saving his ass.

"I've been undercover in the coroner's office since last summer, watching Josh Hancock. We had information from an informant that he was dealing cocaine and Fentanyl from his office. When he told us he had a buyer tonight, we expected it to be someone from Lampino's crew that he would be meeting. When you got out of the car I knew there would be trouble."

"Just glad it was you. I need to report back to J.C. Net. I'm sure he'll want to speak with you later."

"Tell Net, Jennifer said hello and I'm willing to meet with him at any time."

"Agent Net? This is Caruso. We just busted Josh Hancock and Biff Holder for selling drugs. Apparently, DEA has had an undercover agent watching Hancock in the coroner's office. Believe it or not, it was Dr. Jennifer Davison, the assistant coroner. Did you know her? The way that she said to tell you hello made me think you were friends."

"Good work Caruso. I only met Davison once or twice at the coroner's office. I'm finishing up with Ernest Washington now and will be heading downtown to interview Hancock and Holder."

Net arranged for Rhonda to meet him at NOPD lockup to assist in the interview. They decided to start with Biff Holder and save the big fish for last.

***

"You fucking bitch," said Holder. "I should have known you were a cop from seeing you both at the theatre and snooping around Jokers."

"Shut your mouth Holder, or I'll shut it for you," threatened Net. "You realize you'll be going away for a long time. Dealing drugs is a federal offense that will get you twenty or more years in Pollock. The fact that Lampino, who owned Jokers was murdered, several prostitutes who frequented Jokers and the director from Le Bon Theatre where you acted were all killed, points the finger at you for more than just a drug charge. If you have any brains left in your head that you haven't destroyed with cocaine, you better start talking fast."

Rhonda looked at Net then faced Holder. "Who was your supplier? Where did the Fentanyl come from? We also need to know your whereabouts during each murder. If you cooperate with us it will be easier on you."

"Look, I don't know nothing about the murders. I'm just a small-time dealer. Josh Hancock approached me over a year ago and asked if I wanted to make some easy cash. He'd supply the cocaine and pills and I got thirty percent of whatever I could sell them for. I don't know who his supplier was, but I'm sure Lampino had his fingers in it. If you give me the dates of the murders I'll prove I wasn't involved. I'm not going to rot in prison for a few hundred bucks a week."

Hancock was next. Net and Rhonda walked into the cell where Hancock was being held. "I got nothing to say to either one of you. I want my lawyer. That's all I'm saying."

"Probably a smart move," Net replied. "Although, we don't really need you to talk. We've got you on federal drug charges which is going to put you away for a long time. I also think you are a murderer. New Orleans has had a number of deaths from drugs laced with Fentanyl. If we tie any of those deaths to your product, then that's murder."

"We also think you are involved in the murders of Bernard Lampino and Mayor Clyde Hebert and maybe others as well," Rhonda interjected. "Do you have an alibi when they were killed?"

Hancock remained silent for several moments. "You guys are just grasping at straws."

"So you don't have any alibis?" questioned Net.

"Go fuck yourself. I'm not saying another word."

CHAPTER 28
Hush Hush Sweet Charlotte

"Good morning ladies and gentlemen. I take it you slept well and followed my orders not to discuss the case or watch anything regarding this matter," Judge Welch greeted the jurors. "Please raise your hand if any of did not follow my instructions."

No one in the jury box raised their hand.

"At this point we will be continuing with Mr. Washington's cross examination of Ms. Wendy Zander. Bailiff, please escort Ms. Zander into the courtroom. Ms. Zander, I remind you that you are still under oath and are expected to testify to the whole truth. Mr. Washington, you may begin."

"Ms. Zander, you testified yesterday that you had an affair with my client, Rodney Park."

"Yes, we dated about six months."

"And during that time you were employed by the NOPD?"

"Yes."

"What capacity did you work at NOPD, what was your job?"

"I worked in the record room. My job was to tag and file evidence."

"Since you were in the record room and my client was the deputy chief of police, how did you come to meet him? Weren't you in separate buildings?"

"Yes, but I would go to the main building to have lunch and that is where I met Rodney, uh, Mr. Park."

"Did you introduce yourself to him?"

"Yes, I had seen his picture on the news and I thought he was cute. I wanted to meet him."

"Okay, now when you introduced yourself, did you tell him your name was Wendy Zander, or Abigail Pratt, or perhaps by your street name, Pixie Dust? Isn't it true you changed your name because of past criminal infractions?"

The jury let out a gasp, and Wendy started to squirm in her seat.

Patrick McQueen jumped to his feet. "Your Honor, I don't see the relevance of this line of questioning."

Wendy stood up from the witness chair. "You told me they wouldn't find out about my past. You promised me I just had to tell them about me and Rodney and you would see that I would get a ticket to Miami."

The judge pounded his gavel. "Ms. Zander, or Pratt, or Dust, whoever you are, please sit down. Mr. McQueen your motion is denied. Mr. Washington you may continue with your questions."

"Ms. Zander, how well did you know the deceased, Clyde Hebert?"

"I refuse to answer that question."

"Your Honor?"

"Ms. Zander, you will answer the questions from Mr. Washington, or be held in contempt of court."

"Yes, I knew him. I worked on his campaign."

"Isn't it true that you were having an affair with Mayor Hebert?"

McQueen jumped up. "Your Honor, Mr. Washington is badgering the witness."

"Denied. Mr. Washington and Mr. McQueen approach the bench. I'm not going to tolerate this bickering back and forth in my courtroom. What is your point of this line of questioning, Mr. Washington?"

"Judge, the prosecution opened this line of questioning of her personal life. I'm trying to show there is more to her background that is being offered by the prosecution. The jury should be able to hear the entire story."

"Very well," the judge agreed. "Mr. McQueen, I'm very disturbed over the accusation that you coached this witness to only tell half the story and even more disturbing is offering her something of monetary value for her testimony. If you encourage her in this manner the Louisiana Bar Association will be very interested in delving further into your trial methods."

"No your Honor. I told her to tell the truth. We were not aware of this other life she apparently lived." McQueen turned slightly and glanced towards the table where his second chair was seated. He returned to his seat obviously upset with his staff.

"I will have to take you at your word, Mr. McQueen. Ms. Zander, you will answer the defense's questions until you are notified not to," instructed the judge.

"Now, repeating my question, were you having an affair with the mayor?" asked Washington again.

"Yeah, I fucked the bastard. The old man was horny as could be with his wife away. But he used me until I was no use to him any longer."

"Ms. Zander, please refrain from that language in this courtroom," ordered the judge.

Upon that revelation, almost every media member rushed from the courtroom to break this story as soon as possible.

Judge Welch looked around the emptied room. "Well, now maybe we can have some order in here."

"Your Honor, I have no further questions for this lady....err person," Washington stated.

"You may step down Ms. Zander. Mr. McQueen, please call your next witness."

Judge Welsh faced the jury. "Ladies and gentlemen of the jury, I'd like to remind you as you hear each witness testify that it is up to you to decide the validity of their testimony. Mr. McQueen, please continue."

"Prosecution calls Agent Rhonda Bordelon." Bailiff Bobby William swore her in. "Agent Bordelon, can you tell me what this is?" McQueen showed her a clear plastic bag containing a knife.

"Yes, it was determined this was the knife that was used to kill Bernard Lampino."

"And who determined this?" asked McQueen.

"Forensics." Rhonda wasn't happy testifying for the prosecution but she had no other choice.

"And where was this knife found?"

"Under the front seat of Rodney Park's car."

"And who found it?" asked McQueen. By now he had to feel like he was pulling teeth trying to get each answer from Rhonda.

"I did."

"So you, yourself found this bloodied knife that has been found to have killed Mr. Lampino. No further questions, Your Honor."

"Your Honor, asked and answered," Washington cited.

"Continue on, Gentlemen." Judge Welch seemed annoyed.

"Nothing further, your Honor but I reserve the right to recall this witness at a later time," McQueen stated.

"I don't have any questions currently for this witness," countered Washington.

***

Charlotte had decided not to attend the trial on this day. Instead, she and Mildred sat in the kitchen having a cup of coffee. "I hope the trial is going well," she wondered.

"Miss Charlotte, are you sure you don't want to be there today?" asked Mildred. "You know Mr. Ernest said it was important for you to be there to show your support for Mr. Rodney."

"I know Mildred. I feel so good today, I just want to enjoy the day without being in that depressing courtroom." Charlotte continued to slowly sip the hot coffee when her phone suddenly rang.

"Hey Charlotte, this is Rhonda. Ernest Washington didn't see you in court today and wanted me to check on you. Is everything okay?"

"Yes, everything is great and I feel better than ever. The weather is great and it just feels good to be alive. Hold on one second. Okay Mildred go ahead and enjoy. Sorry Rhonda, Mildred was just informing me that she was going to take a bath. She's been kind enough to stay with me until Rodney gets home."

"Charlotte, I've got to stop at the drug store and then I'd like to stop by to see you. Is that okay?"

"Sure. Why not?" Charlotte thought for a moment. "Hey, listen. I get all my prescriptions filled at this little local drug store around the corner. They have my prescription ready. The pharmacist is a longtime friend of the family. Would you mind picking it up for me? I'll call them and let them know you are coming. Ask for Mr. Wright, the pharmacist. I'm sure they have whatever you need as well."

"No problem. I'll be over in a little while."

***

Rhonda left directly after her conversation and arrived at the drug store in due course. She found the items that she needed and then approached the drug counter. "I was told to ask for Mr. Wright, the pharmacist. I'm here to pick up a prescription for Mrs. Park."

"Oh, yes ma'am. I have it right here," announced the clerk.

Before she placed the prescription bottle into the bag, Rhonda was able to glimpse at the pills. "Are those for Mrs. Park?"

"Yes, ma'am. These are the ones she takes daily. Do you still need to talk with the pharmacist?"

"No, I guess not. I've got everything I need."

"Let me put all that in a bigger bag for you," offered the clerk. As she packed the bag, the clerk smiled and winked. "Good luck, ma'am."

Rhonda went directly to the Park's home. Charlotte greeted her at the door with a rare smile. "Come on in. Mildred and I just had a nice cup of coffee would you like one? Oh, hand that prescription bag to Mildred."

Mildred had just walked up after taking her bath. "I'll take care of that," offered Mildred. "And I'll put a fresh pot of coffee on as well."

"Please have a seat, Rhonda. Make yourself comfortable."

"Charlotte, you really look good but I know Ernest is concerned about you not being in the courtroom today. It's really important for you to show you support for your husband."

"And I do support him. I love him. I will be there after today. I've been feeling really good. I've slept well at night and no memory lapses. You

288

know I've gone out at night and the next day I don't remember a thing." Charlotte made that announcement as though it was a secret.

Mildred interrupted the conversation when she brought in a tray with the fresh coffee. "I'll come back and join you after I wash the cups in the sink we used earlier."

"Nonsense. Join us now," Charlotte demanded. "The cups will still be there later for you to take care of."

***

J.C. Net decided to take another run at Hank Sullivan and this time, had him brought to his office. "This is something I want you to see." He placed several photos spread out across his desk in front of Sullivan.

"What's all of that?" asked Sullivan.

"You should recognize your friend Diego Dominguez. This is what was left of him after he was run down in the street by Josh Hancock. Hancock had no respect for Dominguez. He needed him out of the way. You were probably next. He was making sure there were no witnesses to his crimes. This picture is Dominguez's family. He leaves a wife and three young children behind. Do you have a family, Hank?"

Sullivan stared at the pictures for a few moments. "I do. I have a baby boy."

"How do you think your family would feel if this was you in this picture?" Net slammed the picture of Dominguez in front of Sullivan once again.

"What do you want from me?"

"I want you to tell us the details of Hancock's drug operation at the coroner's office. I need you to help us put this trash away for good. I'll tell the district attorney you cooperated and maybe he will consider a deal." Sullivan reluctantly nodded his head in agreement.

"Have Colin Kennedy step in here," Net requested over the phone. "Detective, escort Josh Hancock to booking and charge him with the murder of Diego Dominguez and drug trafficking."

As Sullivan was removed from Net's office, Ernest Washington entered. "So far things aren't going our way in court. Please tell me you have something for me."

"Not yet. We just charged Hancock and I'm having Tatiana check his whereabouts at the time of each murder. Once we have that, we may have something to talk about. My gut tells me Hancock wasn't involved in the murders."

"What are you thinking?" asked Washington.

"I just don't want to believe it, but there are some things that point to Charlotte," Net admitted.

"Well, give me what you got and let's get her on the stand."

Net's phone began to ring. "Will you excuse me, Ernest? I need to take this call. Hey, babe, what's going on?"

"I need to talk with you," Rhonda declared.

"Where are you?" Net asked.

"I'm visiting Charlotte. I just picked up her pills from the drug store and we need to talk."

"I'm worried about Charlotte. Let's get a DNA sample from her while you are there so we can compare to DNA found at the murder scenes," requested Net.

Charlotte and Mildred went upstairs, as Rhonda prepared to leave. As soon as they were out of sight, Rhonda swiftly entered the kitchen, picked up some items and then out the front door.

***

The courtroom was once again packed with media, victims' families and friends awaiting the afternoon session to begin.

"Ladies and gentlemen of the jury," Judge Welch began. "Since it's Friday afternoon and I have some matters to discuss with the attorneys in this case, I'm going to dismiss you early today. I remind you that you are not to watch or read any news reports pertaining to this case. I will question each one of you on Monday morning. You are reminded that if there is a violation of these rules you will be held in contempt of court, which could mean jail time and a fine. This is a high profile case and I do not want a mistrial. Bailiff, please escort the jurors from the room."

The jurors were dismissed from the courtroom. "Mr. McQueen and Mr. Washington. Please approach the bench. We have an issue with one of the prosecutor's witnesses, Joshua Hancock. I have been informed that he has been arrested on possible drug charges. How do you want to proceed? I can have him appear in court, or if Mr. Washington agrees, we can just file the coroner's report into the record. The problem with my last suggestion is that Mr. Washington will not have the opportunity to cross examine the witness."

"Your Honor, I'd like the opportunity to discuss this with my client, Mr. Park. Can I let you know on Monday morning how we'd like to proceed?"

"I have no problem waiting for Mr. Washington's decision on Monday," McQueen offered. "We have other witnesses we can call before Dr. Hancock."

"I'm glad to see y'all working together in this matter. Trial will resume at 9:00 a.m. on Monday. Please be in the courtroom by 8:00 a.m. with a mutually agreed decision. Have a good weekend gentlemen."

CHAPTER 29
All in the Family

Judge Welch entered the court room before the jury had been seated.

"Mr. McQueen and Mr. Washington. I assume you have discussed the Joshua Hancock matter amongst yourselves. What decision have you made regarding his testimony?"

"Your Honor, the defense will stipulate the cause of death of the mayor was by gunshot and the cause of death of Bernard Lampino was a knife to the neck. As a result, we are willing to accept the introduction of the coroner's report into evidence."

"Thank you Mr. Washington and we may proceed. Bailiff, will you please escort the jury into the room? Good morning ladies and gentlemen. I hope you had a restful weekend and followed my orders to not discuss the trial or watch any media reports. Mr. McQueen, please call your next witness."

"Your Honor, the prosecution calls Detective Colin Kennedy to the stand."

Kennedy was sworn in and testified that he was the officer who found the gun hidden in Rodney Park's jacket inside his bedroom closet. He also confirmed that the caliber of the gun was one used to kill the mayor.

"Mr. Washington, do you wish to cross examine this witness?" asked Judge Welch.

"I do, your Honor. Detective Kennedy, would you say that Deputy Chief Rodney Park is a good police officer?"

McQueen leaped from his chair. "Your Honor, this is calling for a conclusion from this witness. It's an opinion. Not to mention a leading question."

"I'll allow it. Detective Kennedy should be in a position to offer his opinion on this subject. You may answer the question."

"I think he is a great policeman and individual."

"One more question, detective. As such a great police officer, in your opinion, why would anyone with his experience leave evidence, a knife and a gun, where he knows police would find them?"

"Your Honor?" McQueen raised his objection again.

"I don't have any more questions judge." Washington had already made his point.

Next witness was NOPD Forensics expert Karen Cooper. She testified for the prosecution. "Ms. Cooper, can you tell us, was this the gun used to kill the mayor?" asked McQueen.

"Yes, it was. We tested the bullets taken from the mayor's body and found that they were shot from this very gun that was found in the defendant's closet. Also the fingerprints of the defendant were clearly on the handle of the gun."

McQueen next held up a plastic evidence bag containing a knife. "Ms. Cooper, this knife was previously identified by Agent Rhonda Bordelon as the knife found under the seat of Rodney Park's vehicle. What can you tell us about this knife?"

"Once again the knife had Mr. Park's fingerprints on it and the blade matched the cut across the throat of Bernard Lampino."

"Thank you. No further questions."

"Mr. Washington, do you have any questions for this witness?" asked the Judge. Ernest sat in his chair staring at his notes. "Mr. Washington, I'll ask again. Do you have any questions for this witness?"

Again he didn't immediately answer but then stood. "Yes, I do have one question. Ms. Cooper, was it determined which direction the cut was made?"

"Yes, the perpetrator was standing behind the victim and the cut was from left to right."

"So that would indicate a right-handed killer. Is that correct? It would be natural motion for a right-handed person standing behind someone to cut from left to right, correct?"

"Yes, that would normally be the case."

"Thank you. No other questions." Washington was returning to his seat when he turned. "I do have one more question, your Honor."

"Make up your mind Mr. Washington," the judge demanded.

"Ms. Cooper, were you the first person to examine this knife?"

"No, I wasn't. Apparently the state lab saw it first."

"Nothing further. Rodney would you pour me a glass of water?" requested Washington returning to his seat.

Rodney raised the pitcher of water on the desk with his left hand and poured the water into the glass before him. He handed the glass to Washington using his left hand.

McQueen rose from his chair. "Your Honor, please!" he begged the judge. "Mr. Washington is putting on a theatrical performance."

"Mr. Washington, if you pull something like that again I will not only hold you in contempt but I will report you to the Louisiana State Bar. The jury will disregard Mr. Washington's stunt. Please proceed Mr. McQueen."

"Ms. Cooper what were the findings of the state lab?"

"The same as mine."

"And was proper procedure followed in transferring this knife into the lab's custody?"

"Yes, it was," she concluded.

"Your Honor, the prosecution rests," McQueen announced.

"With that in mind, I think this is a good time to call it a day. We'll pick things back up tomorrow at 9 a.m. Court is adjourned." Welch slammed the gavel on the courtroom desk.

With all the evidence pointing to his client, Ernest Washington knew he needed a miracle to turn his case around. He hoped J.C. Net had discovered something, anything that would provide him with information he could use in his arguments.

***

"Tell me you have something," he requested of Net as he entered the agent's office.

"I wish I could, man. I'm still trying to tie Josh Hancock to all these victims."

Just as he offered the bad news to Washington, Tatiana walked into their meeting with news of her own. "I checked out crime and street cameras around the city and at the time of the murders of Lampino and Mayor Hebert, I found Hancock's car elsewhere in the city when the crimes were committed."

"Did you actually see him in the car?" asked Net.

"Unfortunately, yes. He could clearly be seen in several of the videos," Tatiana responded.

"So we are back to square one," announced a dejected Washington.

"Not necessarily," said a voice behind them entering the room." Rhonda joined the group and had some fresh information. "Tat, please take these and have DNA run on them as quickly as possible. I put in a call to Emily Livingston in Baton Rouge. She's agreed to stay all night if necessary and have the DNA run. Can you drive this up to her tonight? You'll need to wait for the results and drive them back as soon as possible. I'm hoping Ernest can get the judge to allow for a brief continuance until we get the results. I'm having a car prepared for you now. Please meet me downstairs in twenty minutes. I'll need you to sign for the evidence to preserve the chain of custody. When you arrive at the lab, you are to not let the evidence out of your sight."

She handed Tatiana two plastic evidence bags. Turning to Ernest, she said, "We need to be sure Charlotte is in the courtroom tomorrow. Make sure Mildred knows to have her there."

***

Tatiana signed for the evidence and loaded up her car to drive to the crime lab in Baton Rouge. It took almost two hours to drive there with the afternoon traffic. When she arrived, Emily Livingston was waiting for her since the office was closed.

"You must be the Tatiana Sokolov I've heard so much about. I have arranged for Barbara Crews, a forensic specialist to stay with us and perform the test."

Emily took the bag from Tatiana and they both entered the lab.

After five hours of investigation, Barbara Crews handed the bags back to Tatiana, together with her written report. Tatiana had both Emily

Livingston and Barbara Crews sign the chain of custody paper and put everything neatly into her car to drive back to New Orleans.

Tatiana called Rhonda to let her know she was leaving Baton Rouge and would meet them at FBI headquarters with the results. Driving down I-10 Tatiana noticed bright lights in a car behind her getting closer. She sped up and changed to the right hand lane, hoping the car will pass. It was getting close to 11:00 p.m., so the highway was almost deserted. The car was dark in color. It stayed a safe distance behind Tatiana for a while. Suddenly the car was directly behind her, striking the FBI car from behind and jolting Tatiana forward. Making a move around the FBI vehicle, the car swerved in front of Tatiana's car, causing it to drive off the highway and into a tree. The car continued leaving Tatiana slumped over the steering wheel of a smoking car.

***

The morning quickly arrived and Ernest Washington was again the first person in the courtroom. His papers were scattered in front of him, yet he sat there staring at the clock as though he was waiting for something to happen. The media slowly arrived as did Charlotte, Mildred, and Rhonda. Rhonda would leave shortly to wait in the witness room as she was scheduled to testify for the defense. Dr. Jeff Howser, Charlotte's personal physician also arrived and was escorted by Washington to the witness room.

Judge Welch entered the courtroom and asked the bailiff to seat the jury. Slowly each one entered the jury box, with all appearing to be weary of the length of the trial. "Let's get started. Mr. Washington, please call your first witness."

"The defense calls Agent Rhonda Bordelon."

The bailiff secured Rhonda from the witness room and she took the stand. "Agent Bordelon, please remember you are still under oath to tell the truth," reminded the judge.

"Agent Bordelon, you were requested by the defendant's spouse to pick up her medicine at the local pharmacy, were you not?" asked Washington.

"Yes, I was."

"Are these the pills you secured?" Washington handed her a bottle of pills for her identification.

"Yes, these are the green pills," responded Rhonda.

"I'd like to enter these pills as exhibit A for the defense. No further questions at this time but I reserve the right to recall this witness."

"Your Honor, I have no questions of this witness but I do not see the relevance of this information in this case," McQueen argued.

"Your Honor, if you give me a little leeway, I will make it very clear shortly."

"I'll cut you a little slack but get to it Mr. Washington."

"Defense now calls Jack Wright."

"Bailiff, please swear in Mr. Wright."

"Mr. Wright, please advise us of your profession," requested Washington.

"I'm a pharmacist."

"Are you the pharmacist who fills prescriptions for Mrs. Charlotte Park?"

"Yes, sir."

"Can you look at our exhibit A, these pills and advise if this is the prescription for Mrs. Park.

Wright took the bottle in his hands and opened it to look inside. "Yes, these are her pills."

"Your Honor?" McQueen jumped up to plead with the judge to stop this unnecessary questioning.

"Just a little more time your Honor. I promise," Washington begged. "I don't have any more questions for Mr. Wright."

Before the judge could rule, there was a stirring among the media in the courtroom as Agent J.C. Net, Detective Colin Kennedy, and FBI Agent Caden Caruso, along with two uniformed police officers entered the courtroom. An injured Tatiana Sokolov slowly limped in behind them. Her face was bruised and scratched and her arm was in a sling.

"To what do we owe this visit, Agent Net?" asked the judge.

"I'm very sorry for the interruption judge," announced Net. "We are here at the request of the defense."

"Okay, please take a seat and I don't want any more disruptions in this case," demanded Judge Welch. "Please proceed, Mr. Washington."

"Your Honor, may I have one minute?" asked Washington. Without waiting for the judge's response, Net walked up to Washington and handed him some papers. They both looked them over as Net pointed to several items he wanted Ernest to observe.

"Mr. Washington, please proceed." The judge seemed to be getting annoyed.

"Defense calls Dr. Jeff Howser. Dr. Howser, please tell us about your relationship with Charlotte Park."

"I'm her personal physician."

"Can you identify the pills I show you which are defense exhibit A?"

"Yes. That is the antipsychotic mood-stabilizing medication I prescribe for Charlotte."

"Can you tell us what would happen if she did not take her pills as prescribed?"

"She may become delusional. She could have uncontrollable manic episodes."

"Now Doctor Howser, during one of these episodes could she engage in sexual promiscuity without any recollection?"

"There is that possibility. Especially if she would mix her medication with alcohol or other drugs."

"One final question, Doctor. I show you these white pills and ask if you can identify them."

"Not in evidence, your honor!" objected McQueen.

"I ask you to enter these as Exhibit B," requested Washington.

"No objection," stated a frustrated McQueen.

"Doctor?"

Dr. Howser looked over the pills for a few moments. "This is nothing more than acetaminophen."

"Thank you doctor. No further questions."

"I have no questions, your honor, but I still don't understand where the defense is taking this."

"Your Honor, I'd like to call Charlotte Park to the stand."

Rodney pulled Washington by the arm and yanked him down into his chair. There was a moment of heated debate between the two but Washington managed to convince him this was best for his defense.

Charlotte slowly made her way to the witness stand and was sworn in. She seemed very nervous by the entire spectacle of this trial. She found it difficult to look directly at Rodney. She trembled at the mere mention of her name by Ernest Washington.

"Good morning, Mrs. Park." Ernest sensed her uneasiness as he stood in front of her. "Mrs. Park, I show before you two bottles of pills and I ask you to pick the ones you take on a daily basis."

"These." Charlotte pointed to the alternate bottle of white pills that was entered as Exhibit B.

"So these are the pills you take and not these?" Washington repeated.

"Your Honor, asked and answered," demanded McQueen.

"Let's move on," commanded the judge.

"Mrs. Park, while on these pills, which you identified as the ones you took daily, did you encounter any of these episodes that Dr. Howser described?"

"I guess I did. So they say. I really resent this line of questioning, Mr. Washington."

"I'm sorry you think so but I'm just trying to establish a sequence of events. Mrs. Park, isn't it true this bipolar condition was discovered when you were a teenager and isn't it true that you had many sexual encounters during those years including one with Nathaniel Lawrence otherwise known as Buck. Isn't it true that he impregnated you and your father sent you away to have the baby?"

"Yes! Yes!" she screamed.

Rodney jumped from his chair. "Stop! Stop this! I don't want you to ask her anymore."

"Your Honor, may I have a quick word with my client?" Washington whispered in Rodney's ear which seemed to calm him somewhat. "Mrs. Park, I'm sorry to bring up old memories but what happened to that baby?"

"I don't know. It was taken from me before I even knew the gender. I suppose someone adopted it."

"Defense now calls Mildred Monroe," Mildred didn't immediately respond to her name being called until the judge demanded her acknowledgement. She stepped slowly into the witness stand and was sworn in.

"Judge, I don't understand why I'm being called to testify. I don't know anything about this case and I don't want to speak badly about Mr. Rodney or Ms. Charlotte."

"You must answer whatever questions the attorneys have for you," lectured Judge Welch.

"Miss Monroe, what is your relationship with the Parks'?" asked Washington.

"I'm Ms. Charlotte's nurse. I take care of her."

"So you provide her with her medicine each day?"

"I guess you can say that."

"Do you or don't you?"

"Yeah, I do."

"You've heard Dr. Howser and Jack Wright testify as to the pills Charlotte Park should be taking so I will asked you which pills did you provide to her?"

"Those." She pointed to Exhibit A.

"Actually, Charlotte testified that these white pills are the ones that she took every day. Can you explain that?" asked Washington. "Judge, please instruct the witness to answer."

"No idea why she would say that. I gave her the green pills."

"Okay, moving on. Do you recognize the coffee cups in these two bags?"

Mildred looked closely at the contents of the bags. "Yeah, it looks like the same pattern that belongs to Ms. Charlotte's dinnerware."

"That's correct. They were taken by Agent Rhonda Bordelon who will testify to this. She took them after you and Mrs. Park drank coffee from them. Do you see that lady in the back of the room? That's Barbara Crews who's a forensics expert. She is here to testify that she ran DNA tests on these cups and guess what she found? What she found is that you and

Charlotte Park are related. As a matter of fact it proves that you are the daughter of Charlotte Park."

Charlotte stood in the audience with her hand covering her mouth. "Oh my God! All this time you were right there with me."

"Shut up bitch!" Mildred yelled. "You never looked for me. Your fucking father took me and sold me to the highest bidder. I lived with dozens of foster families, each one worse than the previous one. I loved putting bullets into that fucker."

Judge Welch hammered his gavel on his bench attempting to calm Mildred but to no avail.

"And we also compared your DNA with that on file for Buck Lawrence. He was your father."

"He got what he deserved. It was a pleasure slicing his dick off. Lampino, yeah, he arranged for me to be sold to a couple who made a living off me performing sexual acts for their friends."

"Your Honor, the defense rests."

"Mr. McQueen do you have any comments?" asked Judge Welch.

"Yes judge. I'm going to ask Agent Net and company to take this lady into custody and we will drop the charges with our apologies to Deputy Chief Park."

Abruptly, every reporter inside the courtroom rushed to the door in order to report their story first. Chaos was incurred as members of law enforcement tried to move forward while the media stood in their way. Charlotte attempted to reach her daughter but was held back by the bailiff. In all the confusion, Mildred used this opportunity to remove the pistol from the bailiff's holster and quickly reaching Charlotte, placed the barrel of the gun to her head.

"I'll kill this bitch. Back up and drop your guns," she screamed at the law officers. She fired the gun once hitting the back shoulder of a reporter who fell into the crowd trying to escape the room.

Using the confusion in this room, Net was able to exit the back door and work his way through the judge's chambers to a door behind the judge's bench. Waiting for the right opportunity, Net had his gun poised to fire at the back of Mildred's head. The media had finally cleared the room and agents and police officers pleaded with Mildred to drop her gun.

"This is not going to end well for you," Colin Kennedy stated.

"Mildred, please," Charlotte begged. "I didn't know. Why didn't you tell me who you were? We could have worked it out."

"Too late bitch. I'm not going to jail. We will die together right here."

Net slowly worked his way to the witness stand on his hands and knees waiting to get a clean shot. He suddenly chose this moment of distraction to leap towards Mildred, striking both ladies to the ground. Net secured his hold on Mildred as he pulled her arms behind her back with handcuffs. Rodney hopped over the defense table to rescue Charlotte from the struggle.

Rodney hugged Charlotte and helped her to her feet. She struggled to get near to Mildred, with tears in her eyes. "I'm sorry for all the pain my father caused. I never wanted to leave you. I will be here for you if you need me."

Mildred turned toward Charlotte and spat in her face, telling the police, "Get me the fuck away from her."

EPILOGUE
Until We Meet Again

The sun rose from the East just as on any other day. To the delight of the city of New Orleans, a serial killer and drug dealer had been taken off the streets. However, the biggest loser in this whole debacle was Charlotte Park. She had lost a child, not once, but twice in her lifetime. She had also lost her father, although some might argue if that really was a loss, and almost her husband. It had been several days since the conclusion of the trial.

J.C. Net, Rhonda Bordelon, and Tatiana Sokolov remained in the city to take a few days before their return to Boston. They wanted to spend some time with the Parks and help guide them through what has been an exhausting period of time. The night before they were to leave, they had plans for all to meet for dinner.

J.C., Rhonda, and Tatiana had arrived early and sat at the bar enjoying a drink. Net ordered his usual beer, Tatiana had an Elit vodka, neat, while Rhonda was drinking a club soda. Net had received an earlier text that the Parks were running a little late but they had a surprise.

Net raised his glass to Tatiana. "To the best damn friend and employee of the FBI. We couldn't do what we do without your expertise and you went even beyond that with this case. You put your life on the line several times and you were certainly a hero."

Tatiana couldn't hold a straight face because she knew they were staring at her broken arm, scrapes, and bruises, not to mention the black eyes on her face. All three burst into laughter at the same time.

"Does Charlotte know that we had her tailed?" asked Rhonda.

"No, and I think we should not mention it. That would not solve anything but embarrassment for her," answered Net.

"Did not know that myself?" Tatiana mentioned. "You all kept that quiet."

"Yep. I didn't want anyone to know we were watching her," Net explained. I wanted to be sure before we pursued that angle. Nothing came out of it. Seemed like the nights we watched her house she never left and when she did, she went to a bar and then home."

Rodney, Charlotte, and another lady walked up about the same time. "Well this is a jovial crowd. Fill us in on the joke. We need that," Rodney suggested. No one immediately spoke up. "Okay, maybe later. I'd like all of you to meet Reba Hebert, Charlotte's mother.

Charlotte stood there tearfully as the others looked at them, astonished. "We went to the hospital to visit Reba with Dr. Howser and he found her to be of sound mind. Turns out Clyde was paying the staff and doctors to falsify papers in order to keep her there. We have notified state authorities who will begin an investigation."

They all hesitated for a moment but Rhonda took the initiative to stand and give Reba a big hug. Net and Tatiana followed suit and said they were so happy to see her. "And how are you feeling Charlotte?"

"Now that I'm back on my real medication, I'm feeling great. No alcohol or drugs. Just following my doctor's orders."

Rodney put his arms around Charlotte. "This is like a new honeymoon for us and even sweeter now that we have Reba back in our lives."

As they approached the maître d' for their table, Ernest Washington joined the celebration. "I couldn't leave without spending some more time with my good friends. However, let's not wait for a murder to occur before we have a reunion."

"Rumor has it that Patrick McQueen was going to make a run for governor," Net mentioned as they reached their table. "He had the mayor's support. Gotta believe he may be looking for another line of work now."

"You may very well be right. He won't have my support. Charlotte and I have a lot to discuss as to whether we stay in New Orleans or not. Just curious, Mildred was charged with other murders. What was her motive for those killings?" Rodney asked.

"I think Tatiana has earned the right to tell the whole story," Net suggested.

"You really want me to do it? Okay, I'd love to tell this story," Tatiana said laughing but the laughter also brought along the realization of who she was with. "Charlotte, are you sure about this? Some of this might be difficult for you to hear."

"No, I'm fine," Charlotte responded. "I need to face my behavior and get it behind me. I want to move forward with a renewed life with my husband." She took Rodney's arm in hers and smiled, placing her head on his shoulder.

"Okay, well, let's talk about Josh Hancock first," Tatiana began. "The city will be looking for a new coroner. He has been charged under a federal drug indictment, as well as the murder of Diego Dominguez. During interrogation he also admitted to the murder of Chris Nelson. Evidently Nelson discovered his drug operation going on at Joker's Wild and wanted a piece for himself. I mention this because he did his best to try and copy the type of knife used in the other murders by Mildred. Being the coroner, he knew the exact knife to use. Speaking of which, the police are still putting evidence together but here's what we know. Are you sure you are up for this Charlotte?"

"Yes, I need to hear what she has done. I don't condone her actions but I want her to get the help she needs."

"Okay. Charlotte, it seems when you went on your nightly escapades, Mildred followed you. She dressed like you, wore one of your wigs, and even your jewelry, and after you departed, she entered, posing as you and killed the person you had just been with. It seems at first she was trying to frame you for the murders. For whatever reason, maybe she will eventually tell us, she changed and focused on Rodney being the killer. Maybe she wanted you to suffer by taking him away from you. Anyway, she discovered her father was Buck Lawrence and your father, Clyde Hebert were involved with her being placed in foster care at birth. Jimmy Schwartz was the attorney who had handled the paperwork in the foster care system and Bernard Lampino used his mafia connections to place Mildred in foster care without any government intervention.

"Lorena Gonzalez, despite being a prostitute, everyone seemed to like her. She worked at the Le Bon Theatre for quite some time. We believe that Lorena witnessed Mildred dressed as Charlotte and may have been able to identify her. She met the same demise as the others.

"Sal Siegel, aka Honey Moon, police are still looking into that one but Mildred has admitted to killing him. There were others that she has admitted to killing but we are still trying to determine the motive. While in foster care, Mildred was a victim of sex trafficking for her foster parents' benefit and she has admitted to having a grudge against men looking for prostitutes. Searching her home, authorities found a box containing a paralytic drug she used in some of the murders.

"Sidney O'Conner was one who met his demise under that influence. She admitted that the drug was used on her and she stole them from her foster parents' residence when she escaped their control. She hasn't admitted to the stabbing of Josh Hancock but we believe she slept with him posing as Charlotte and she couldn't take the chance he knew who she was."

"My poor daughter," Charlotte cried. "My father. He was just a horrible man. I'm not making excuses but Buck Lawrence raped me and my father covered it up. He would not let me talk about it."

"Clyde Hebert was the devil himself. Look at the destruction the man has caused," reflected Rodney. "Who knows what would have happened if that baby had lived with her mother in a happy home."

Reba Hebert was quiet this whole time but she too was a victim of the mayor. "Gang, aren't we here to celebrate? I know I am. I'm so happy to be back in my daughter's life," she exclaimed hugging Charlotte close to her. Let's have another toast! To Rodney and Charlotte, may they live a life of fulfillment and happiness." All raised their cocktails to the toast except Charlotte, and Rhonda hoisted a club soda.

"What's with the club soda?" Net asked Rhonda.

"Whatever do you mean?" Rhonda shyly answered.

"Oh my God!" Tatiana screamed.

"What? What is it?" stated a very anxious Net.

Rhonda reached down into her purse. "Remember I told you I had to pick up some supplies at the drug store besides Charlotte's medication?"

"Yeah. Okay."

"This is what I was after." Rhonda placed the item on the table.

"A thermometer?"

"No, you dumbass! She's pregnant!" screamed Tatiana.

Rhonda took out a tiny pair of baby shoes from her purse and handed them to J.C. He was so surprised that he just sat there dumbfounded for a few moments. When it finally registered in his brain he jumped up to hug and kiss Rhonda but Tatiana had already jumped ahead of him.

"Are you happy?" Rhonda asked J.C.

"I couldn't be any happier. I guess you know what this means don't you?" he asked.

"Yes. You have to marry me. By the way, I have more exciting news." Net wondered what could possibly be exciting after hearing he was to become a father. "We have two other additions to our family. Merry and Sugar."

Net needed no further explanation nor did he want one. He felt it better to leave things alone.

The celebrating went on for hours and then moved to the Park's home to continue.

***

A minivan was travelling on a dark desolate road in the back country of Mississippi not far from Jackson. There were no highway lights and very little traffic in either direction. The pavement was slick from an earlier shower but the minivan continued to travel at a high rate of speed. There was a small motel up ahead on the right side as the vehicle pulled into their parking lot. A lady retreated from the van into the motel lobby with a young boy.

"Pretty nasty out there tonight ma'am," announced the clerk.

"I need a room and something to eat," Susan Griffin demanded.

"Kitchen's about to close but I'll see what they can rustle up for you. How long will you be staying with us?"

"I don't know," Susan replied.

www.ingramcontent.com/pod-product-compliance
Lightning Source LLC
Chambersburg PA
CBHW020337180626
46812CB00001B/241